"Is he our daddy?"

Little Timmy looked at the man sleeping on the sofa bed. "I can't tell," he answered his twin sister. "His face is under the blanket."

Timmy and Tammy advanced toward the bed. Their warm breath and hovering figures woke Michael, and he opened one eye and peered out at them from under the covers.

"Whose daddy are you?" Timmy asked him.

"Nobody's," Michael replied grumpily.

The children looked disappointed. "We thought you were ours."

He'd heard as much, he thought, sitting up, and it shocked him down to his toenails. But not as much as the sight of the twins standing in front of him—cherub-faced blondes with twinkling hazel eyes.

These kids could pass for his! If he had any kids, which he certainly did not, he quickly reminded himself.

Still, it was impossible not to wonder....

ABOUT THE AUTHOR

Leandra Logan simply loves to write! She made her debut with young-adult romances and has written twelve books in the past eight years. Nominated for many awards, she won the *Romantic Times* Reviewers' Choice Award for Best Harlequin Temptation novel in 1992. This is her first American Romance title. In her free time, Leandra speaks on the craft of writing at local schools in Minnesota, where she lives with her husband and two children. When asked what other interests she had, she was, for the first time, at a loss for words!

Books by Leandra Logan

HARLEQUIN TEMPTATION
420—THE CUPID CONNECTION
462—DILLON AFTER DARK
493—THE LAST HONEST MAN
533—THE MISSING HEIR
572—JOYRIDE
591—HER FAVORITE HUSBAND

Leandra Logan
SECRET AGENT DAD

Harlequin Books

TORONTO • NEW YORK • LONDON
AMSTERDAM • PARIS • SYDNEY • HAMBURG
STOCKHOLM • ATHENS • TOKYO • MILAN
MADRID • WARSAW • BUDAPEST • AUCKLAND

For
Debra Matteucci
and Barbara Bretton,
delightful divas of distinction

ISBN 0-373-16559-5

SECRET AGENT DAD

PART ONE

Prologue

Six Years Ago

The young couple strolling along the strip of beach behind Cancún's luxurious hotels could have easily been mistaken for average tourists. Michael Hawkes and Valerie Warner, their lean, hard bodies on display in skimpy swimsuits and their tanned skin glossed with oil, blended well with the crowd of sun worshipers, scattered about the swath of powdery white sand.

Like many other visitors to the resort strip, they'd just chartered a boat for a cruise on the emerald Caribbean waters. But unlike the others, a recreational tour was the last thing on their minds. They were on assignment.

Based in Washington, D.C., they were intelligence agents from the prestigious Cornerstone Group, a privately owned and funded corporation that specialized in undercover operations. A larger-than-life task force that charged larger-than-life fees. But people in big trouble usually had big money, so apart from some pro bono work, the fees and services were usually in perfect balance.

To Michael Hawkes, this mission was just another case so typical of those that routinely fell into their hands. Different faces, different places, but a variation of the same old game.

He and his team were on commission to rescue kidnapped actress Prudence Manders. He knew next to nothing about television stars, but apparently the seventeen-year-old was the reigning princess of the American sitcom. She'd been snatched from a Cancún nightclub several nights earlier by an unknown assailant while partying with her latest lover. A three-million-dollar ransom demand had been delivered to her parents in Los Angeles, who in turn had involved the producers of her hit show, "Stepfamily Robinson." They made the decision to hire Cornerstone to locate and retrieve the girl.

Michael and his crew had taken over, eventually tracking Prudence to the nearby island of Zapata. Some lavish bribery and exploration of poverty-stricken paradise isle had led them into the jungle to a primitive hut inhabited by a young raven-haired waif and two Mexican males.

Odds were that it was Prudence. But Hawkes had sent two of his agents back this morning to make certain. If the ID checked out, they'd be rescuing the actress tonight.

It would've been a routine job from start to finish to the thirty-two-year-old, world-weary team leader—if Valerie Warner hadn't suddenly given in to his advances and fulfilled his longtime dream of possessing her inside out.

Michael's blood raced with renewed desire as he gazed down at the tantalizing redhead gliding along the sand beside him in a black tank suit cut high on the hip. The mirrored aviator glasses resting on his angled jawline concealed the clearest of blue eyes, burning every bit as brilliant as the hot tropical sky above.

Valerie had been teaching psychology at a small Maryland college when Cornerstone's chief controller recruited her as a consultant on human behavior. Alexander had presented her to Michael as an energetic educator with a streak of daring, an honors graduate with a genius IQ and an impressive sense of people.

After a period of basic training for fieldwork, Michael gave her the opportunity to round off his illustrious team. Along with Kim Krenz and Neal Henderson, they'd completed numerous missions together in the past year, working to blend their personalities for the common good.

It was Hawkes's policy to avoid intimacy with his colleagues. And he usually had no problem adhering to it. But Valerie was so different from the women he normally encountered in his dark line of work. Her unique blend of daring and compassion had proven irresistible. Making her the exception to the rule had seemed a natural progression.

Though his personal background hadn't included a middle-class high school, he imagined that being with her was like dating a bubbly cheerleader, who was up to a little making out in the back seat and occasionally pulling pranks on authority figures. Naughty and nice.

Hawkes still marveled that Alexander had managed to recognize and appreciate Valerie's diverse talents in the first place, that he had shopped for and found a psychologist who could not only perform operative tasks but could empathize with people on a sensitive level. Most agents could not.

Alexander generally specialized in a more mercenary sort of recruitment. He was a pro at honing youths into tough renegade agents willing to stop at nothing to get the job done.

Michael knew firsthand because he was Alexander's most prized pupil.

But as seasoned and hard as Michael's shell had grown over the years, it wasn't thick enough to protect him from what was to be his first crush. Valerie Warner had somehow reached the only tiny emotional corner remaining inside him—and left him yearning for a taste of her sweetness.

This Prudence Manders rescue mission proved to be his lucky charm. The warm breezes and shimmering moonlight had tipped Valerie over the edge of temptation. Her body had responded to his like a taut instrument. She wasn't a virgin at twenty-five, but she was new to many pleasures, and so eager to learn.

Desire surged through him as they walked along. In step. In unison. The beach was teeming with scantily clad women, skipping in and out of the frothy tide, laid out on the sand for inspection, admiration. But all he could see was a banner of red. Valerie's mane of soft hair whipping in the hot, wild wind.

He would have her one more time in their hotel room before they rescued the young actress from the island. Before they catapulted out of paradise, back to reality and their Washington, D.C., home base for a briefing on their next assignment.

"I hope the girl's all right," Valerie said suddenly, causing Michael to lurch out of his sensual reverie and back to the business at hand.

"I know you do." He drew a tolerant smile, squeezing her smooth shoulder. Valerie had the softest heart on the team—in the whole damn corporation. But it was that capacity to feel that made her especially effective in her psychologist's role. Her instincts often proved invaluable, a welcome edge that he himself was incapable of providing. "She's a reach away now," he said. "And it's my feeling that any kid who has the guts to keep an entire production company on edge also has the grit to put a mess like this behind her."

Valerie released a sigh of agreement. From all private accounts, Prudence Manders had to be a corker for sure. Though considered a dimpled, dark-haired darling to her legions of fans, the prototype of a sweet big sister, she'd matured into teenage prima donna, prone to tantrums and outrageous behavior. Inner circles had panicked at the news of her kidnapping, but no one had cared in a compassionate way. The production executives had promised to handle everything for the Manderses, because the couple had washed their hands of their uncontrollable daughter some time earlier.

It all boiled down to assets. The show was still a gold mine after seven years on the air, and Prudence was the show, the all-American sweetheart everyone adored and faithfully tuned in to see.

Apparently keeping Prudence's on-screen persona squeaky-clean had been tough enough without this catastrophic turn. If the kidnapping reached the papers even after the rescue, so would Prudence's whirlwind Mexican vacation with her costar, Chet Winston. Unfortunately Chet was her on-screen daddy.

The executives didn't even mind paying out—for the rescue and for the ransom. They just wanted Prudence safely back in the States and the entire fiasco kept out of the press.

Valerie knew that Michael prided himself on never doing anything halfway. It was his intention to recover the girl without giving up the money. It was a simple matter of timing. Invading prematurely and unexpectedly, snatching her back even before the drop sight was arranged.

Tonight was the night. One last team meeting would finalize the plan.

"Look, Michael, they're all waiting for us in the bar," Valerie noted a short time later, as they came upon the back of their hotel, the Oleaje.

Michael scanned the row of round tables topped with bright umbrellas lining the deck overlooking the beach, his coarse dark hair blowing slightly in the stiff breeze. "Where, baby?"

"Yellow-and-white umbrella, second from the end," Valerie specified, dusting traces of sand from her slender oiled arm. "Neal and Kim are dressed for the beach—" she smiled "—and Alexander is dressed for Mardi Gras."

He squared his solid bare shoulders with determination. "Let's get busy."

He might as well have said, "Let's get it over with."

Valerie knew well that he was anxious to get this last checklist over with so they could return to their room. She inhaled sharply as Michael's huge palm pressed into the small of her bare back, guiding her with purpose across the sand to the wooden staircase leading up to the hotel complex. She knew he'd linger on the stairs as he had so many times during the past few days, so he could watch her from behind, graze his arm against her with every step.

She quivered slightly just thinking about it.

She trembled openly when he did it.

Things were so fanciful in this tropical atmosphere, so different from the conservatism of Washington, D.C., and the drabness of so many of their missions. As they wended their way through the cheery, relaxed crowd, she perused the revelers with renewed wonderment. Nylon patches and straps passed for swimwear. Romantic trysts were flaunted on the beach and in the nightclubs. Cancún was the ultimate amusement center for adults, an uninhibited paradise where sea sirens sang to lovers, urging them to explore.

Valerie was guilty of succumbing to its lure.

For the first time in her life she'd recklessly followed her desires, reaffirming what her heart already knew.

She had let Michael seduce her because she had fallen in love with him. After months of verbal foreplay, she'd mustered the courage to surrender, to luxuriate in his lovemaking.

Valerie was convinced that Michael was everything she'd ever wanted in a man. If only he could let go completely, face his emotional needs. His job and his stark background had left him secretive, suspicious and scared of commitment. But she felt sure she could change that. Given the chance. Given further encouragement.

After all, it was her job at Cornerstone to evaluate people, to predict their moves with precision. It was much like playing chess on a grand, life-size scale. Not only did she have the skills to perform to Alexander's standards, but she had the guts to stand by her deductions, see a mission through. And it would take all her courage and determination to go the long haul with Michael Hawkes.

Michael was in dire need of nurturing. She would have to reaffirm over and over again that it was right between them. Especially in the beginning. She would have to bring him round with doses of love and loyalty. He understood these concepts on some levels, but it was unlikely that he'd ever dug deep enough to find them in himself. As a child, he hadn't been shown how, and as an adult, he'd chosen not to learn.

Until now.

No man could make the passionate love he had this past week and not want it to last forever. She would assure him that their relationship could endure, could grow, could become more satisfying with time. It would be his cue to succumb, just a little bit. To admit that he too wanted something satisfying. But of course this all would have to wait until after the mission. It was time to get down to business again. Iron out the last details of tonight's rescue.

The threesome at the table greeted them with deliberate holiday spirit as Michael pulled out a chair for her. Their cover at the hotel was simple and believable. Alexander was the sixtyish father figure treating his "sons" and their "wives" to a vacation. He was playing his role with relish, donning wild shirts and Bermuda shorts, and a variety of straw hats. Neal and Kim were playing the other happy couple. Though in their case, there was no real feeling involved. They slept in the same hotel room, but in separate beds. Valerie was surprised that Neal never made a play for the statuesque blonde with the husky voice and sharp wit. But like his teammate Michael, it was petite russet-haired Valerie that Neal really went for.

It was well-known that Neal and Michael had been rivals for years. It was an understandable conflict, considering how alike the men were. Both were workaholic overachievers who trotted the globe, leaping from one mission to another with insatiable interest and ambition. Both viewed all situations as temporary, frequently renting things rather than owning them. They even shared some physical characteristics: dark hair, impressive height, handsome features. Neal's hair was more curly than coarse, however, and he was a bit huskier than the pantherlike Michael, but all things considered the two men were almost cast from the same mold.

Almost.

In Valerie's mind Michael Hawkes stood out prominently as the man for her. Only the ancient chemical reaction between a man and woman could explain her choice. After all, it was Neal who had shown her a courting kind of interest during the past few months. Who had sent her flowers and candy, as a sincere suitor would. Michael was far too preoccupied with his work to go through such romantic motions. But she loved him just the same. Had loved him for quite some time. Their physical consummation had only enhanced the sentiments already in her heart.

Alexander ordered a round of dark Mexican beer while small talk was exchanged. It wasn't until the waiter delivered the drinks that they got down to business.

"So, is the boat taken care of?" Alexander asked Michael, his gaze direct under the brim of his straw hat.

Michael pushed his sunglasses up the bridge of his nose and nodded in affirmation. "Fastest cruiser available. Once we hit the water with the Manders girl, nothing will be able to catch us."

"If anybody cares," Kim retorted with a toss of her fair head. It was her opinion that Prudence Manders herself had staged the kidnapping for publicity.

"C'mon, Kim, she's being held against her will," Neal hastened to argue. "We spent some very uncomfortable hours before dawn this morning watching her through a telescope."

"I know, Neal, but I'm not convinced," Kim argued lightly, as though they were wagering on a horse race.

"Take any pictures?" Michael took a long draw of beer, watching Neal intently.

Neal scowled at his own reflection in Michael's mirrored glasses. "No. It wasn't my place."

"It was agreed no photographs would be taken on this mission," Alexander broke in, in support of Neal. "The television producers are after complete secrecy and you can't blame them."

"Damn stupid," Michael argued. "We could have studied the layout of the place in great detail with some good photographs."

"But we viewed the site firsthand," Valerie pointed out, patting Michael's arm.

"Once!" Michael complained. "A quick look yesterday from a distance, playing the bewildered tourists who'd wandered off the beaten path. And there were Kim and Neal back there today—with cameras around their necks!"

"The cameras added to our bird-watching cover," Kim argued in quick defense, tugging at her orange beach jacket. "They didn't even have film."

"And Alexander does have the final word when he's along, Hawkes," Neal put in snidely.

Alexander's eyes hardened. "Michael already knows that, don't you, Michael? I am the controller. Of the whole dang shebang."

Michael made a frustrated noise. He liked to be in command without interference. And he normally was. Alexander didn't usually accompany them on missions. To garner his personal attention, it had to mean a lot to him financially or personally. He respected him like a father, and sometimes was infuriated with him like one, too.

"If we had the photos, even unofficially," he sought to explain again, "we could—"

Alexander cut him off with a raised hand. "Admittedly the pictures would be especially useful in these rushed conditions, but breaching the client's trust that way could tarnish Cornerstone's reputation for discretion. It's unfortunate that it took us several days to locate the girl, but at least we managed to do so."

Neal's tanned features sharpened with avarice as his gaze flicked over Valerie. "I suggested we start with the most primitive areas, but oh, no, we had to check out the tourist traps first. Provide a little R and R for Val and loverboy."

"Why you—" Michael curled his fingers in to fists, preparing to lunge across the table. Fortunately common sense overrode his temper and he sank back into his seat. He spared Valerie a quick sidelong glance. She was openly horrified.

But wasn't this mainly her fault? For a brief intense moment, Michael silently blamed Valerie for the conflict. For distracting him. For disappointing Neal. But ultimately he blamed himself for the passions running so high in all them this time around. He'd seduced Valerie for his own selfish reasons and it was affecting their timing. Their ability to keep in sync with one another was normally their greatest asset as a foursome. Obviously the lines of communication were now distorted and dangerously electric. It would teach him to practice more caution in the future.

"It was my idea to check the cozy spots first," Kim reminded Neal. "I figured that if this was nothing more than a stunt, Prudence would be holed up in some comfortable hotel."

Alexander nodded. "We weren't sure that Prudence was really at risk until we pinpointed her location on the island."

"Yeah, yeah," Neal fumed quietly to Michael. "You'd be angry too, if you'd spent your early morning hours buried chest deep in bug-ridden vegetation, watching a crummy shack through a telescope, waiting for a glimpse of that spoiled teenager."

Michael inwardly conceded that Neal had a point. He and Valerie had spent those same hours together here in Cancún. But there had been many missions when he'd been the one curled up in some ungodly position in some dank place doing the surveillance work.

"It was your turn for the crummy detail and you know it, Neal."

Neal's jaw tightened. "Yeah, maybe. It's just…different this time."

Michael was torn between anger and sympathy for his cohort. Now that Valerie had chosen Michael, it was all too clear just how much Neal wanted to be the one. But there was nothing that could change how the week had unfolded.

"So what did you find out, Neal?" Valerie asked, slicing through the tense silence that suddenly shrouded the table.

Neal cleared his throat, his tone clipped as he shifted to business. "There is a third Mexican in the house that we didn't spot yesterday. A woman."

"We're convinced that she and the two males belong on the island," Kim broke in, "judging by their dress, mannerisms, ease with the jungle. It would be a smart move on the part of the real culprit to put Prudence with the natives. They work cheap and they'd be damn near impossible to track down afterward."

Michael's expression grew keen as he sifted through the facts presented. "You managed to get a clear look at the Manders girl, then? It's her for certain?"

Kim shrugged. "Neal was at the lens when she came into view. I was reapplying bug spray."

"It was Manders, all right," Neal confirmed. "She appeared groggy. Needed help walking. Definitely doped up in my opinion."

"All signs that she is in grave danger," Alexander declared, wiping beer foam from his chin. "No telling what they've given her, or what they've deprived her of."

Valerie's lovely face reflected her concern. "We have to get her out of there without any slipups."

Alexander's eyes flinted over his glass. "We will. Unless we have an attitude problem among some of the team players...." He looked from face to face, his expression shadowed and stern beneath his hat. "If anybody can't play with the team, I don't want them out on the island. This could get tricky."

"We'll manage," Michael promptly assured, flashing Neal a tight, almost apologetic smile. They'd been through so much together over the past decade. The day that he could no longer trust Neal would be a doomed one indeed.

Neal responded with an inscrutable look, which Michael found difficult to read. Surely Neal wouldn't allow his jealousy over Valerie to throw him off-balance professionally. They were both career agents who together had dared the grim reaper many times over.

Alexander drained his glass and rose to his feet, unofficially closing the meeting. "Until tonight, then."

VALERIE AND MICHAEL ended up back in their room. They made love with fevered urgency, their skin sunbaked warm and moist with oil. Eventually they showered, shared a large bottle of mineral water and climbed back into bed, intent on a long rest before the night's mission.

Valerie set the alarm on the clock radio, then sank down against Michael's length. "Michael?"

"Huh?"

"We have to talk."

Michael's stubbled angular face crinkled, as if hoping to ward off the inevitable. "Why is it that women like to discuss every pickin' move?"

"About Neal—"

"Neal will be all right."

"About us, then." Valerie raised up on one elbow to hover over his muscular form, dark and sexy against the white sheets. Her hair tumbled forward, grazing the surface of his chest. He groaned in pleasure over the wispy tickling sensation.

"I know what you're going to say, sweet thing," he claimed thickly, fingering her reddish locks.

"You do?'

Valerie couldn't resist resting her cheek on his breastbone. Closing her eyes, she took a breath, reveling in his scent, counting the beats of his heart. Nestling against Michael left her in a tantalizing jumble emotionally. Never had she felt so safe and so in jeopardy all at the same time. But it did make a fair amount of sense. Michael was indeed the bad boy. But one with promise. With just the right direction, he'd be totally hers.

"You're the most delectable lady I've ever encountered," he said huskily.

"Thank you, sir."

"We'll do this again sometime soon. I promise you that."

Valerie's body stiffened. "What do you mean, Michael?" Her query was barely a whisper. She slowly lifted her face over his, her emerald eyes liquid green fire. "Exactly what are you saying?"

Michael's eyes widened under her scrutiny. "That's what you wanted to hear, isn't it?" he blurted out, anxious to understand her distress. "You can't expect me to give you up completely, just because Neal doesn't like it!"

She gaped at him in astonishment. "I don't believe this!" she eventually managed to sputter.

"I don't want to hear that we've done wrong," he warned, grazing her cheek with a roughened finger. He did it all the time, just to watch her shiver with need. Despite her mental outrage, her body responded instantly to his touch with a visible quiver. "I've been on the fence about our fling, but I've concluded that we have every right to indulge ourselves."

"Michael—"

"I know how you feel about fulfilling obligations," he cut in with earnest eyes. "I share your decision. Nobody's more devoted to the work of the Cornerstone Group than I am. After all, Alexander took me in when I was only sixteen. Being an intelligence agent is my identity. I'm sure you'd agree that the four of us can go on as a team. Neal will survive. He's got the smooth moves women absolutely adore."

"Don't underestimate your own charm, darling." She bit her lip to quell the cry of pain creeping up her throat. He'd been on an entirely different wavelength the entire time! He considered their union nothing but a lark, a diversion.

Valerie felt like pouncing on him, pummeling his chest to dislodge his buried emotions. But she would only be hurting herself. She was the fragile one, the vulnerable one.

And she was the one who had made the mistake.

He hadn't changed his position at all, not in the twelve months she'd been in his tutorial hands.

She'd misread him. Seen what she wanted to see.

But he had helped, dammit! He'd made her feel special. Way too special.

What kind of a man sent out all those promising signals without one promise in his heart?

She knew better than to expose her frailties. Weakness was something Michael couldn't tolerate—in himself or in others. A blowup could leave her bumped from this mission. And she most definitely wanted to be there for Prudence. The team could save her body, but Valerie would be the one to save her mind. Typical of agents, Michael and the others would view her as little more than a commodity—an attitude that Valerie herself should've examined more closely before giving herself to one so completely.

In his arrogance, Michael didn't even deserve to know she cared, she decided. With a sudden surge of pride she realized that she'd rather die than let him know she was dying inside over him.

"Perhaps we can pick this up during our next hiatus," he was suggesting now, much to her fury and despair. "Go off by ourselves. Maybe to Amsterdam. You've never been there, have you?"

"No," she replied with forced lightness, melting back onto her own pillow.

Michael tucked his arms under his head, staring up at the ceiling. "The western half of the old city is something to see. Dam Square. The royal palace. I know you share my thirst for the new and unexplored."

"Always." Valerie twisted under the sheet, turning her face toward the white plastered wall, blinking back the stinting tears.

He yawned audibly. "Until later, sweet."

In your dreams, you insensitive robot.

A master at summoning sleep, Michael drifted off easily. Valerie listened to the rhythm of his breathing for a stretch of the afternoon, analyzing how and what had happened to leave her so devastated. Perhaps this letdown was just what she deserved. Valerie Warner, hotshot agent, always second-guessing others. She'd been such an achiever all her young life, so sure of herself. Her beauty and brains had made her life goals fairly easy to attain. Perhaps it was inevitable that she'd finally have her soul ripped out of her body by a man she'd have done anything for.

A tougher woman could rebound. Stick with the team as though nothing had happened. Accept that Amsterdam offer when the time came and make the most of it. Michael would fulfill the carnal promise. As a lover he held nothing in reserve.

But it wasn't enough, dammit! Not when she'd never settled for anything less than the best. Did she want to go back to the way things were before this supercharged week? More to the point *could* she go back? Was she tough enough?

Valerie thought long and hard about that as the silent tears poured down her cheeks.

When she did finally close her heavy lids, it was with the stark knowledge that she couldn't possibly pull it off. A clean break from Michael and his team was the only way she could survive this romantic disaster. Alexander would have to reassign her, find her another niche in the Cornerstone Group. If he refused, she'd be through with the agency as well.

She'd been a silly fool to believe Michael could ever fall for her.

THE OPERATION WAS SET into motion near midnight. The team made the crossing to the island in the rented cruiser without incident. Alexander and Kim stayed aboard the boat at a secluded marina while Valerie, Michael and Neal set out for the hut on foot.

As predicted, the captors proved to be natives who didn't seem to speak a word of English. The appearance of the trio, carrying automatic weapons, wearing dark clothing and night-vision goggles, sent them scattering into the dark jungle. The only uncertainty was whether they'd gone for reinforcements to reclaim their valuable hostage.

Valerie swiftly examined the girl curled up on the dirty cot and declared her too doped up to walk.

Without hesitation, Hawkes tossed the woozy Prudence over his massive shoulder like a sack of flour. With Neal in the lead, they swiftly tromped back through the jungle paths toward the beach.

As he glided through the dense vegetation, Hawkes amused himself with thoughts of Valerie, comparing her to the skinny, waiflike starlet on his back. Valerie had the good sense to keep fit and filled in. She was curvaceous, yet lusciously lean.

She was woman incarnate.

The first to ever completely intrigue and bedazzle him.

Damn her for being so downright irresistible!

They reboarded the craft with their precious cargo without a hitch. In Michael's mind, all was well as they drifted away from the dock and back out to sea.

But the feeling didn't last long. As Michael piloted the powerful craft through the rough Caribbean waters with his passengers all stowed below, Neal came topside to give him the news about Valerie's intention to leave the team.

Michael, his hands gripped around the boat's steering wheel, tore his gaze from the windshield to confront his partner, his face sheeted in disbelief. "She wouldn't quit us! You got it wrong!"

"She's telling Alexander right now!" Neal insisted, his voice thin on the wind.

Galvanic anger rocketed through him as he absorbed the news. "It doesn't make any sense!"

Neal's arm gripped the sleeve of Michael's black Windbreaker. "What did you do to her?"

"Nothing!" The treacherous swells of water slapping at the boat forced Michael to pay closer attention to navigation, but even with his eyes riveted on the Cancún peninsula, he continued to shout. "It's because of you! Making such a damn stink about everything!"

"I don't think so!" Neal hollered back. He stomped off then, leaving Michael alone, at war with the sea and his own private demons.

A local Cornerstone contact named Manuel Castillo was waiting for them back on Cancún's shores with a sedan large enough to accommodate them all. Within moments they were on the road, headed for a deserted landing strip outside the city.

Prudence's groans and murmurings were the only noises in the speeding vehicle. At some point during the choppy ride back from the island, the actress had been jolted out of her drug-induced sleep. She was disoriented and frightened and jumpy.

Anxious for answers concerning Valerie's abrupt defection, Michael took in all of his fellow passengers with a swift perusal. Alexander and Kim were up front with Manuel, concentrating on the road. Neal had a sulky eye out the back window.

And Valerie was deliberately shutting him out. She was totally immersed in her caregiving role, holding Prudence against her, assuring her over and over again that she was safe and on her way back to the United States. Michael couldn't get close mentally or physical, and it made him boil in bewilderment and betrayal.

He eventually twisted on the seat, joining Neal in his silent back-window vigil. There was always a pair of headlights or the flash of chrome behind them on the narrow, treacherous roads, giving just cause for alertness.

They reached the rendezvous site forty-five minutes later. One of Cornerstone's own utility helicopters was ready and waiting on the deserted field, looming in the moonlit shadows. Neal blinked his headlights to signal the pilot. The return signal was the catch of the gas-turbine engine, the spinning of the rotors.

As Neal and Kim helped Prudence aboard the chopper, Michael seized the opportunity to detain Valerie, trapping her between his body and the car.

"What's this about you quitting Cornerstone?" he hissed in anger, snagging her arm for good measure.

Valerie's heart hammered in her chest. There was no way to escape without telling him. She'd turned it over and over in her mind before her announcement to Alexander. The only way out was right past him.

"I'm not quitting the corporation, Hawkes," she blurted out in a holler above the noise. "I'm quitting you. Only you."

She tried to wrench free then, her red hair whipping wildly. But the decision to break belonged to the strongest. One jerk from Michael brought her flush against his chest.

"So this is the way you treat your team?" he thundered down at her. "Do you know how much I've invested in you?"

Valerie's fingernails skimmed the slippery surface of his nylon jacket. Just what did he believe he'd given her? The fury over his insensitivity had been simmering in her system for hours now, leaving her literally vibrating with voltage. She clenched her fists and her teeth, torn between her wish to be free and her desire to be trapped in his arms forever.

Michael released a growl of rage over her lack of response. "I've been your tutor. Your mentor. Is this how you repay me?"

"The team, the precious team! That's all that matters to you!" she incredulously shouted back over the engine's roar. "Even now. Even after..."

Sudden enlightenment crossed his features, bringing on a wave of fresh fury. "You can't give up everything just because we were lovers. Grow up, Val!"

"There's more to life than this work. This team." She attempted to reason with him.

He shook his head in slow disbelief. "Not for me. I thought you knew that."

She waved her hands helplessly. "But you seemed so responsive—so in sync with me."

"Sexually, yes. But sex and sentiment don't even belong in the same breath."

"You don't know the first thing about sentiment, Hawkes."

His face hardened. "It makes a man weak. Vulnerable. A target."

The chopper's rotors were slicing hard and fast now, blowing the vegetation at their feet flat against the ground, tugging hard at their clothing and hair. They stood staring at each other for a long, intense moment. Then it was time to go. Everyone was waiting for them. In a last-ditch effort, she frantically searched his beautiful blue eyes for a glimmer of compassion or desperation, a sign that he could want her for his one and only woman.

Ultimately she came up empty.

"It's all over for us, Michael," she exclaimed with forceful finality.

"No! This is all wrong!" He cupped her shoulders through her black jacket, drilling his eyes into hers to make his last words count. "You should be thanking me, Val. For sparing you from a dead-end relationship."

That's when she slapped him. Hard across the face.

"Thank you, bastard," she cried out brokenly, the last of her control shattering with the smack. "Thank you very much!"

He appeared momentarily stunned, numbly releasing her as he massaged his burning cheek and his delicate ego.

Valerie knew she was ultimately outmatched, so she wasted no time in darting for the open door of the helicopter. She'd obviously been treading a thin line with her stance against this lethal man, but she needed to cut him off with some dignity. She owed it to herself.

There was more to life than being an agent. He was the bigger loser here.

But even so, Valerie felt as though she'd hit rock bottom as she crawled into the cockpit.

Michael didn't follow as expected. He remained rooted in place near the sedan, like a wounded warrior with his spine and jaw stone rigid. Alexander leaned out to hail him aboard, but Michael waved them on their way. The controller, already openly disenchanted with his surrogate son's behavior, conceded to his wishes and secured the door.

The craft lined, swiftly swooping forward and up into the blackened sky.

Hawkes was struck dumb for a long moment. How could things have been so right, only to turn so wrong?

The small, wiry driver flashed him a sympathetic smile when he finally eased back into the front seat of the sedan. "Back to the hotel, Hawkes?"

The thought of those bed sheets heavy with her scent sent a jolt of pain through his system. "No, *amigo*," he muttered on a huge sigh. "I don't want to sleep. Take me anyplace else. Any dive will do."

Manuel's eyes gleamed with pleasure. "I know of many places that will do you right. If you want to wash the day away with some local *especial*."

Hawkes's hand nearly strayed to his singed cheek, but his ego checked the move in midair. Raking his coarse brown hair instead he said, "Yeah, yeah, let's wash away today with the worst tequila in town."

"Ah, but it's the best you want, when you feel the worst."

Hawkes shook his head in grim denial. "I've already had the best, and it's cost me way too much."

PART TWO

Chapter One

The Present

Valerie Warner wasn't in the habit of doing her grocery shopping during the workweek. And her five-year-old twins, Timmy and Tammy, were prompt to protest this unexpected Friday-evening excursion to the supermarket. The fair-haired youngsters stomped through the store's sensored glass door ahead of her, their round freckled faces alive with curiosity and disgruntlement.

"What are we doin' here in the dark?" Timmy demanded in squeaky complaint over the relaxing background music.

Tammy spun round on the shiny tile floor, her short pigtails bouncing at her ears. "And where's the free-food ladies, Mama?"

Valerie instinctively drew the children closer to her side. "I'm afraid Saturday is the only sample day."

"Not every day?" Tammy was disappointed. "Don't those ladies live here?"

A glimmer of wry humor touched Valerie's emerald eyes as she gazed down into their sober hazel ones. "No on both counts, I'm afraid."

"Let's just come back tomorrow," Timmy said with inspiration. "We'll see the ladies then."

"We're s'posed to come here on Saturday," Tammy huffed, throwing her small arms in the air. "After cereal and cartoons."

With a fortifying sigh Valerie adjusted the purse hanging from her shoulder and moved up to the row of shopping carts banking the wall. She dislodged one and pushed it forward with a quavering breath. She'd been so distraught during the past few hours, that it hadn't even occurred to her that the twins would protest this untimely trip.

"Let's just make the best of it, okay?" she suggested on a pleading note, herding them along with her free hand. "Pretend it's a game," she added on impulse. "A game to break our routine."

A game indeed. Valerie's fingers curled around the cart's handle as she ventured down the produce aisle. Reaching for lettuce and cabbage, she scanned her fellow shoppers. Most of them were single adults, their moves lackluster as they poked cantaloupes and squeezed tomatoes. Despite the evening hour, they were still dressed for work, suits for the business oriented, sweaters and slacks for the scholars. It had been a rainy day in collegetown, unseasonably chilly for the beginning of June and the last day of school. A night to be curled up at home with a good book.

She knew this particular market to be the latest mecca for Ferndale's singles. And she knew she was at this very moment being perused as possible date bait. It wasn't her scene at all. She shopped here strictly for the bargains. Despite the fact that she had been single for nearly four years, she dated sparingly and cared little about the current pickup spots.

Valerie had better things to do with her time. After a long day of teaching over at the college, she was always anxious to spend quality time with her children. The routine today had been no different.

Until she realized that an intruder had arrived home ahead of her.

Valerie was in the habit of heading straight upstairs to her bedroom to change into comfortable jeans and top to tangle with household duties. But she'd sensed something off kilter this afternoon, the moment she'd stepped through the back door. Things were out of place. Not tossed around, but moved around.

Her heart pumped wildly as she relived the moment of realization all over again in the produce aisle. She'd come to a screeching halt in the center of the kitchen, her gaze darting every which way, taking in the differences. The cookie jar on the counter. The dish towels on the swing-arm rack near the sink. The ruffled curtains on the window overlooking the backyard. Nothing was exactly as she'd left it.

She'd run through a spectrum of emotion in a matter of seconds. Shock. Denial. Followed by grim reality.

Somebody had invaded their private space.

Touched their personal belongings.

It wasn't your run-of-the-mill break-in either. The incursion was to have gone undetected. Absolutely nothing seemed to be missing. In fact, she had found something—a small gold pin.

The twins had tried to enter a couple of beats behind her. Before the babbling pair knew what was happening to them, Valerie had them back on the road, still dressed in their kindergarten outfits and yellow rain slickers and wondering why. Valerie shared their disgruntlement. This was supposed to be the rousing start of their three-month break. They were supposed to be in grubby clothes by now, eating junk food, as she had promised.

In an effort to make amends, she'd treated the twins to dinner at a hamburger joint near the Ferndale campus. They didn't understand, of course, but they were appeased. While they worked on hot fudge sundaes Valerie had put in a call to Alexander. Her fingers were shaking as she punched in the Cornerstone Group's public telephone number in Washington, D.C., then Alexander's private four-digit extension. As it rang on the other end, she prayed that her ex-boss was still at the same desk after nearly six years.

He was there. As calm and cool as always. As willing to help as always. And he treated her with an unexpected reminiscent respect, as though she were still an operative from his organization and not the frantic single parent she'd become. He wanted to schedule an immediate meet, someplace convenient for her. She wanted someplace familiar, as to not upset her children.

The local supermarket seemed an ideal choice.

Valerie had gotten no feel for a possible tail, but she went through a series of subtle maneuvers to shake away all doubt. By the time she'd pulled her silver van into the shopping center parking lot, she felt reasonably secure. She'd moved on with strengthening confidence, unbuckling the kids, hustling them into the market. It was imperative that she learn to trust her intuitive signals all over again. Once upon a time…she did, when she'd been one of Cornerstone's top agents.

Damn! It was so hard to accept that someone was bothering her now. She'd felt so safe in her cozy college town of Ferndale, Maryland. Where she'd grown up herself. Where she was raising her own children.

Maybe it was nothing.

For the time being, she would have to act on the assumption that it was a big something.

Despite her quaking insides, she was beginning to slip back into her operative skin with a measure of success. And she was already fighting back, summoning help. If she could just keep her knees from knocking together under the hem of her dress.

She wheeled through the store, automatically tossing weekly staples into the cart, all the while keeping a sharp eye out for Alexander. What would she do if he hadn't shown up?

But Alexander hadn't let her down. He was waiting in the magazine section.

She'd never been so happy to see anyone in her entire life.

Waves of relief poured through her as she pushed her cart down the aisle toward him. A smile tugged at her full mouth as she watched him thumb through a newsmagazine. As always, he was relishing the challenge to blend in with the scenery. Her last mission leapt to mind. The Prudence Manders rescue in Cancún. He'd so thoroughly enjoyed portraying a jolly high-rolling tourist. Tonight he was playing the bewildered scholarly type so common in Ferndale, dressed in a maroon cardigan and twill trousers, both a size too large for his wiry frame. His gray hair was deliberately tousled and his expression one of bogus bemusement.

He turned as she approached with her clattering cart and chattering blond bookends. Closing the magazine, he regarded her over the half lenses perched on the tip of his bony nose.

"Alexander!" she greeted in a hush of relief.

His lined face lit up with pleasure as he took in her appearance. "Don't you know that only spies are supposed to wear tan trench coats?"

"It's the latest fashion trend for harried teachers as well," she returned on a wry whisper.

"Yes, you are the respected Professor Warner now. Or is it Henderson?"

"It's always been Warner," Valerie said, swift to clarify. "I never did take Neal's name."

"You always did have an individual sense of identity," he said with a faint smile. "And insatiable energy. I was happy to hear you went on to school. The respected educator...." He ran an appreciative eye over her sleek, sophisticated look. Her red mane, once loose and long, was now tamed at chin level. Her clothing had subtle recognizable designer lines. The image was understated chic. "How did you manage to accomplish so much?"

"My parents made it possible," she candidly admitted. "They value education very highly. Both teach at the college."

"Ah, yes, I remember now."

"Well, along with my little sister Stephanie, they helped out with the child care and the housework. It certainly changed my whole life for the better."

"Just never figured you to settle back in your own hometown," he admitted with a shrug. "After seeing so much of the world through Cornerstone."

"You just hate losing an operative, don't you?" Valerie smiled, recognizing the sore-loser look in his eyes.

"Hate losing a good operative like you," he clarified. "Especially over a lover's tiff."

Valerie stiffened at the mention of Michael. Their bitter parting was the last thing she wanted to think about right now. "I like my life just as it is," she assured him fervently. "My roots looked pretty darn good after all that travel. And being a parent was my lifelong dream. The kind of new beginning I'd always counted on."

"Nothing stays the same," he philosophized with a wistful sigh, setting his magazine back on the shelf. "And I must admit, your life as Professor Mom seems to suit you."

As if on cue, Tammy and Timmy peeked out from behind the folds of her flowing coat. As svelte as Valerie was, they'd never really been out of sight. But Alexander did have the good grace to express surprise as they scanned his face for shock value.

"Hello, Mr. Alexander," Tammy peeped, her face impish.

'Hello, Tammy. And Timmy." He turned to the boy on the button side of Valerie's coat. "You certainly look like your sister, don't you?"

Timmy's nose wrinkled. "She looks like me."

"We look like each other," Tammy explained patiently.

"Yes, indeed." Alexander leaned forward to study the pair.

Timmy returned his look with keen interest. "How do you know our mama?"

"We're old friends," he explained with a faint smile. "I know your father as well."

The pair of cherub faces instantly lit up.

"You see our daddy, mister?"

"For real?"

Alexander lifted his gaze back to Valerie, offering her an apologetic smile. "Sorry."

Valerie's expression grew stony for a moment, but she swiftly recovered. "It's all right. I am a true believer in honesty."

"Your only failing as an agent," he uttered wistfully under his breath. Clearing his throat, he again addressed the children. They were waiting for his response with keen anticipation, identical sets of eyes trained on his mouth. "I am your father's boss, so I do see him on occasion. But Neal travels all over the world to do his work."

"We never see him," Tammy confided softly.

Timmy nodded soberly. "He sends us stuff instead."

"Fancy dolls we can't even play with!" Tammy huffed.

"I'm sure he loves you both very much," Alexander said.

"Why don't you take a look at those crayons and coloring books," Valerie intervened, gesturing to the reading shelf devoted to children's supplies.

Alexander watched them scramble by, then drew Valerie into quiet conversation.

"It's a shame your marriage to Neal didn't work out. Especially after producing such beautiful children."

"Yes," Valerie conceded simply. She and Neal had wed on impulse shortly after the Prudence Manders rescue. Everything had moved along so swiftly—the wedding, the pregnancy, the birth of the twins. They'd both been swept up by their desire and determination to make it work and hadn't stopped to think about the long-term outlook.

But eventually their differences caught up with them. They were forced to face the fact that their goals weren't streamlined as a young family's should be. They were actually moving in opposite directions by the time the babies were a year old.

A full-time mother at that point, Valerie had settled down completely and wanted to continue her education, return to teaching psychology at Ferndale College, where her parents were still driving forces in the art-history department.

Neal was bored with the daily commute to Cornerstone's headquarters in Washington, D.C. Tired of the local routine assignments. Their stately colonial home was a prison to him. He yearned for the perilous missions of days gone by, the freedom of world travel and the thrill of unpredictability. In short, he wanted his old life back.

When the time came to decide whether to merge or break, they were forced to face the reasons why they'd married in the first place.

Valerie appreciated Neal's honesty, even though it was delivered with a harsh edge. He had convinced himself that his infatuation with Valerie was real love, strong enough to sustain a lifelong commitment. And he'd fooled both of them into believing that unlike his rival Michael Hawkes, he was prepared to settle down.

Valerie, on the other hand, had been in serious denial over her feelings for Michael. A hard retrospective look had brought fresh insight. She'd been on the rebound from Michael when she'd sailed into Neal's waiting arms.

She'd been as tattered as a rose in a hailstorm. Michael had been her first serious love. And he had led her on shamelessly during the months she'd served on his team with Neal and Kim, stringing her along with verbal foreplay and games of seduction.

When she'd finally surrendered herself to him in Cancún, the romantic tropics had tipped her over the edge. She'd tumbled into his arms with abandon, with a forever dream on her mind.

To her it had seemed like a natural progression. A relationship in full bloom.

To Michael, it had been a means to an end. A score, pure and simple.

In retrospect, Michael's methods were only too clear. He'd wanted to bed her from Day One. He'd just taken his sweet time about it. Savoring, hovering, waiting for the day when she was ripe with need, heavy with heat.

When he had in fact finally taken her, she was literally trembling to the touch.

He was an animal with a keen predator's instincts. A dangerous man who made her feel like a dangerous woman. In and out of the sheets.

Michael. It rankled Valerie to the core to know that her marriage to Neal and their subsequent divorce ultimately centered around that heartless rover. He'd been like a lingering spirit between them. A shadow they could not shake.

How disappointing that Neal Henderson had proven to be Michael Hawkes's prototype. The wanderer. The loner. Neither of them knew how to commit and didn't want to know how.

Valerie had eventually worked Neal out of her system for good.

She'd not been so lucky with Michael. He still lived inside her as though she'd seen him yesterday, scaling the thin line drawn between love and loathing. Valerie could not think of him without jolting with emotion. Jumbled emotion which she, even in her professional capacity, couldn't bear to dissect.

"You look more angry than frightened."

Valerie snapped out of her reverie at the sound of Alexander's voice, eyeing her ex-boss with a measure of uncertainty and hidden embarrassment.

"That is a good thing, Valerie," he hastened to assure her.

"Yes," she agreed breathlessly. "This has been a shock. But the training, the mind-set, it's all coming back. You taught me well."

"You never were the type to cave in to fear. I imagine you can be one fierce professor and mother," he gently teased.

"This just doesn't make any sense," Valerie lamented softly. "Why would anyone toss my house?"

"Someone was either looking for something, or leaving something behind."

"I know you're thinking of bugs left behind, but there was something else more obvious." Valerie dug into the side pocket of her shoulder bag and withdrew a small gold stickpin. "Mean anything to you?"

Alexander held it at arm's length, studying it through his reading glasses. "No, can't say that it does...."

"I found it on the floor of my kitchen, wedged halfway under the stove. It could be nothing. Dropped by a neighborhood kid, perhaps. But under the circumstances..."

"Yes, I'll take it along." He slipped it into his pocket as Tammy scooted up with a large box of crayons.

"There's six and four in here!" she squealed in delight.

"Sixty-four," Valerie corrected.

"Let's buy six and four crayons," Timmy suggested excitedly. "I'll have six and Tammy'll have four."

Valerie's mouth quirked at the corners. "All right. Now pick out a coloring book each."

"So, you've thought this through and have no inklings at all?" Alexander brought them back to their discussion.

She raised her hands in a helpless gesture. "I have nothing worth stealing and say nothing worth monitoring."

He drew a perplexed frown. "We'll just have to sort this out, won't we?"

"I hope you don't mind my calling you in...."

His bushy gray brow lifted in surprise. "You'll always be part of the Cornerstone family. A distant relative these days, but connected just the same. And Neal is still an active agent," he pointed out. "Despite your divorce, he's still the father of your children. So you see, we're still all intertwined in various ways."

She smiled over at her blond cherubs. Neal had called their union regrettable in the end. But she was too embarrassed to admit it to Alexander, who treated her ex-husband like a son.

"I'm sure he cares for the children in his own way," Alexander remarked. "But he isn't cut out to be a family man. I don't recruit that kind."

Valerie detected a chiding note in his tone, the message that she should have known better than to expect one of his male operatives to settle down. He was right of course. Alexander wasn't in the habit of inviting husband material into the Cornerstone fold. He sought out the predator-personality type. Michael and Neal were his best. Ruthless, intelligent, ambitious. And he liked to get them young, mold them in his own image. Neal had been a hotshot right out of college. Michael much younger than that.

"Neal never did like to fail at anything," Alexander went on to offer in consolation and explanation. "I'm sure he grew frustrated when he didn't excel in marriage and fatherhood. But he's always spoken highly of you."

That was shocking news. Neal had grown so cold and negative, rarely communicating with her.

"You want to send him home to deal with this, don't you?" Valerie suddenly realized in alarm.

He nodded.

"Forget it! He won't want to come, and I don't want him to."

Alexander sighed in disappointment. "It just seems like the easiest way. Your house was once his house, too. The children recognize him as their father."

"The hell they do!" Suddenly she gave up the pretense. "A stranger would get on better. At least the children's hopes wouldn't be dashed when he disappeared again."

Alexander's pale eyes flickered in surprise.

Valerie raised a warning finger. "And don't you dare even consider Michael Hawkes for this, either."

"Now you're insulting my intelligence. The personal chemistry between you is too explosive. It would be like sending in an arsonist to put out a forest fire."

A rosy glow infused her skin as she sputtered for a comeback. He'd been lying in wait to spring that one on her. "It isn't that at all, Alexander," she finally blurted out. "I simply cannot trust him to guard us. To care enough to—"

"He would get the job done and you know it," he inserted quietly. "But he is a most unsuitable choice because he loses his razor-edged reason where you are concerned."

"I recall exactly the opposite," Valerie returned coolly, visions of their last confrontation vivid in her mind.

Alexander shrugged under his roomy sweater. "You somehow managed to short-circuit his system during your last mission in Cancún. The very mention of you changes him in a way that even I—who raised him as my own—cannot fully comprehend. Why, after all this time, he still can't find closure in your parting."

"Parting slap you mean."

"Indeed." Something indiscernible crossed his lined features. Amusement? Fascination? It was gone before Valerie could pinpoint it. "The man has been shot, punched, kicked and nearly run over more times than he can count. But it's the sting of your palm on his face that still pains him the most."

"Good."

"He doesn't mention it, except after a few brandies, of course."

"Of course," she echoed. "Rough-and-tumble agent that he is."

Alexander stared at her tight-lipped expression for a few thoughtful moments. "You want Kim, I imagine."

"Is she available?" Valerie wondered on a pleading note.

"I had something else for her," he admitted.

"Which was why you hoped I'd settle for Neal."

"You remember all my tricks." He smiled briefly. "But I will shift things around immediately." He glanced to his watch. "It's seven o'clock now. I really prefer you don't reenter your house without an operative on hand."

"I wouldn't dream of it," she concurred. "Not with the twins in tow. And there is my sister, Stephanie, to consider as well. She's staying with me through July, while our parents are touring Europe."

"Where is she?"

"At a friend's house. I'm going to pick her up now."

"How old is she?"

"Fifteen."

"Is she the levelheaded type?"

"At fifteen? Oh, Alexander, drama is the name of the game for girls that age!"

He visibly cringed. "She'll be your wild card, then."

Valerie nodded in agreement. "The twins always obey me without too much of a fuss. But Stephanie will take this hard, demand an explanation for any new precautionary measures."

"Be as vague as possible, until we know what's up," he advised.

"I can't believe this is happening to me." She gazed upon the children, approaching with coloring books in hand. "Maybe it's just some of my students having some fun. Today was the last day of the spring semester. Everyone, including myself, is grateful to have the summer off. Lots of parties on campus. A fair amount of pranking, too.''

"Experience tells me it's delayed Cornerstone business,'' he stated with practicality. "Regardless of the source, we will clean it up for you. Just consider it a retirement benefit.''

Their eyes locked in a moment of mutual understanding. No one ever retired completely from the Cornerstone Group. Especially the operatives in the field, who couldn't help but leave some loose ends with the closure of each case. The more cases closed, the higher the risks.

Having an unknown quantity invade her private life suddenly drove home the lifetime link she had to the perilous world of espionage.

For the first time ever, Valerie fully understood the haunted look in Michael Hawkes's face. Where most had some happy memories with family stored away for reference, he had only cases, with loose, lingering strings attached to each and every one of them.

"Drop in on a relative or friend,'' he suggested, giving her hand a parting squeeze. "Don't return home until sometime after ten-thirty. By then, Kim will have checked things out.''

He said goodbye to the children, then turned on his heel to continue down the aisle toward the exit.

"Oh, Alexander,'' Valerie called out. She moved up behind him, rummaging through her purse. "Here's a spare house key for Kim.''

Alexander stared down at the key as though it were a foreign object. "Is that really necessary?'' he chided gently.

He considered her place a cracker box. And it undoubtedly was, by Cornerstone's standards. But she lived in a sleepy residential area where space was respected. "I prefer she use it.'' Valerie pressed it into his palm. "The idea of anyone entering my home without a key bothers me a great deal.''

His face wrinkled in perplexity. Alexander existed in a world where the ends always justified the means; where every locked door was an irritant rather than a deterrent.

"It's my way of keeping some degree of normalcy in my home," she explained, her captivating green eyes flaring. "Look, I don't expect you to fully understand the rituals involved in my present life-style. Please, just humor me and give her the key."

"Very well." Alexander sauntered away, a warm bewildered feeling infusing him. He couldn't begin to understand her homebody reasoning, but she still had a provocative way about her. The ability to take in a man without allowing him to reason why.

Enchanting. Valerie was still as enchanting as ever.

And absolutely the last thing Michael Hawkes needed in his life right now, Alexander reaffirmed with resolve. At thirty-eight, Hawkes was in his prime, a Cornerstones agent *extraordinaire*, with years of experience in the field, his body at its peak. Alexander couldn't let him stumble over this woman again. She'd almost managed to pull his heart out of its dormant cage the last time, nearly transformed him from hot-blooded male to warm-blooded human.

But what if he saw her, saw the setup with the children? The controller cringed at the possible consequences. He'd move heaven and earth before he'd allow that wolf into her nest.

Hawkes had never been informed enough to want those things, and it would spoil him as an agent if he ever learned to want them.

Chapter Two

"What are you doing here, Hawkes?" Alexander demanded, as the operative's familiar shadow crossed his office doorway. "It's after eight and the shop's closed."

Michael's jawline tightened in suspicion. It was true that the Cornerstone staff had thinned down considerably, but the store was really never closed. And it wasn't unusual for him to camp out between assignments in his own office located on the floor below. Though he called his Washington, D.C., apartment home, it was at the Cornerstone building downtown that he spent most of his off-hours. His fellow operatives were his only companions—aside from the women who paraded through his life at a brisk high-heeled clip. Unfortunately most of them were looking for a future, for security. Things he couldn't provide in his line of work. He preferred the other women, the ones looking for a good time. But even they eventually wanted to climb inside his head. It was always the beginning of the end.

"Michael," Alexander pressed. "You didn't mention any plans of checking in tonight."

Since when did it matter? Since when wasn't he welcome in Alexander's space and confidence?

Michael's shoulders squared. Something was very peculiar here. Alexander's sharp, skittish attitude toward him was astonishingly uncharacteristic. As was the presence of

Kim Krenz, seated on the opposite side of Alexander's desk, her face flushed to the roots of her blond hair. He, Kim and Neal had returned on a commercial flight out of London just a few hours earlier, where they'd been commissioned to steal back some priceless paintings conned away from a renowned gallery. The mission had gone off without a hitch. The embarrassed gallery owners had paid the Cornerstone fee for quick, discreet service. Everybody was happy with the outcome.

Especially Alexander.

He'd been so happy, in fact, that he'd greeted them at National Airport this afternoon with the Cornerstone limousine. He had wanted to thank them in person for their efforts and had insisted upon dropping them off at their respective D.C. apartments.

He was a totally different man tonight. Gruff and guarded.

Had he missed something? Michael mentally replayed the conversation in the limo. Neal planned to attend a political fund-raiser. Kim was keen on a hot shower and a fresh outfit, griping because Alexander had given her back-to-back assignments. She was supposed to be on her way to Dallas tonight to play courier for some custom jeweler.

Instead she was in the lamp-lit sanctum of Alexander's plush office suite, conversing with the chief controller in hushed distress. Still dressed in the same outfit she'd worn on the plane this afternoon, it was obvious that she'd been called in urgently and unexpectedly.

"Is there something you want, Michael?" Kim asked impatiently.

He realized they'd fallen silent at the sight of him.

They were waiting for his next move with cool expectation. So he moved inside.

Their reception was growing chillier by the second, but it didn't matter. Because of his powerful presence, Hawkes automatically owned every room he entered. He hovered over them with his hands on his lean hips. Dressed in black denim and leather, his whipcord-lean figure was a menacing shadow in the pale light.

"If something has broken open, I'd like to know about it." His voice was low and modulated, pleasant in a pandering way.

"There's nothing for you," Alexander denied, peeling off his specs. He tossed them on a folder and tipped back in his comfy spring-loaded chair. "We're just chatting."

Like hell. Michael gazed down at the silver-haired man, his curiosity building with his temper. Alexander had greeted them at the airport in a gray cashmere suit. Now he was dressed like a dotty, old professor.

A slow smile spread across Michael's mouth as he eyed the boss's desk. Alexander was shrewd, but like everyone else he was a creature of habit. Whenever an unwelcome visitor disturbed Alexander in his walnut-paneled nest, he dropped his reading glasses on whatever he deemed most confidential.

"I thought you'd be on your way to Texas by now, Kim," he remarked, stepping closer to her chair to place his hand on her shoulder. She immediately fidgeted under his touch. He couldn't resist pressing his fingers into the cotton fabric of her jacket, feeling her entire body stiffen.

"I sent Neal instead," Alexander briskly cut in.

"I just wasn't up to it," Kim explained, wrenching free of his grasp with the toss of her blond head.

"It's not like you two to lie," Michael said in mocking reproach.

Alexander's features remained neutral under Michael's accusatory scowl. "Perhaps this is just none of your business."

"It's not like you to blow me off, either," Michael commented conversationally. A stir of air, a slash of shadow and he held the telltale file in his hands. By the time Alexander had rescued his flying wire glasses, Michael had opened the folder and was scanning its contents near the glow of the desk lamp.

Valerie Warner's personnel file.

The pages blurred under his furious gaze.

"Why?"

"Michael—"

"Why, dammit!" Michael's eyes blazed blue fire as he slapped it back down, nearly demolishing the lamp in the process.

Even Alexander, who knew exactly how Michael ticked, was nonplussed by his explosive reaction.

"This doesn't concern you—"

"It does if she thinks she's coming back to work," he growled. "That's it, isn't it? She's bored to tears with the kiddies and the classroom and she's dropping back into espionage." Michael nodded with self-satisfied fervor. "Bails out on our team to marry Neal. Disrupts a perfectly balanced foursome. Now, years later, she wants back in." With a strangled sound he prowled round the room, pausing at the window to stare out at the city lights of Dupont Circle.

Kim shot Alexander a panicky look.

"You've got us there," Alexander confessed, his gray eyes glaring at Kim's in an effort to keep her quiet. "I thought we could just let her down without you ever finding out. That's why I held Kim back on the Dallas assignment. Figured it might come easier from another woman. She can make our Professor Mom understand better than we fellows could."

Michael ran a hand through his thick brown hair. "Yeah, I see your point. But you should've been up-front with me, Alexander. I expect it of you always."

"Well, I just thought you might still have a bit of a sore spot over her." Alexander leaned back, lacing his fingers over his middle.

"That's ridiculous!" he thundered. "Our entanglements are history. Even Neal and I managed to mend our fences. Had our old rapport back since I don't know when."

Since Neal divorced Valerie. Another silent transmission between Kim and her boss. The pair had behaved like schoolboys, fighting over her as though she were the campus queen.

To Alexander's relief, the men had begun to recapture their old camaraderie the moment Neal left Valerie to return to active field duty. Neal had admitted that marrying Valerie had been a mistake—which was exactly what Michael wanted to hear. A mistake Neal obviously didn't want to repeat, Alexander found out tonight. Alexander had to explain Valerie's plight to Neal when he passed along Kim's Dallas assignment. Neal's voice had choked a bit when he eventually responded. He agreed that he'd be better off going to Texas, leaving the protection of his ex-wife and children in the hands of Kim.

Michael's fierce display here in the office was proving to be far deeper than a little huskiness around the edges. Even Alexander, who had trained Hawkes from adolescence to be the consummate soldier for hire, was taken aback by the force of his response. Valerie's effect on Michael was even deeper than he feared.

Alexander felt a sinking sensation in the pit of his stomach over the idea of being disloyal to his surrogate son. He didn't lie to him very often.

"So, what's the game plan?" Michael leaned over, piercing Alexander's cocoon of thought. "You sending Kim over there to break the news? First thing tomorrow, I hope."

Alexander sighed in resignation. "Well, Michael, that sounds as good as any diversionary tactic we could've come up with."

With his hands planted on the desk top, Michael swiveled to confront Kim at eye level. "Do you think you'll be convincing enough to head off trouble?"

Kim nodded, a good-natured glitter in her tilted brown eyes. "You can believe I'm already working on my shtick."

"Next time, just be straight with me from the get-go, Alexander." With a curt goodbye, Michael strode out of the room.

Alexander rose in pursuit, making the doorway just in time to see Hawkes enter an elevator at the end of the hall.

"If he ever finds out that he's the trouble we've been trying to head off..." Kim whistled under her breath.

"He won't, if we're careful." Alexander shoved his office door into place with a huff of frustration, then stalked back across the carpet and dropped into his chair. "Luckily he didn't sift through these," he said, tapping the files beside his phone. "Every case Valerie worked on is in this stack. We'd have never scammed our way out of it, then."

Kim's wry gaze had followed him from the doorway. Shifting in his seat, he asked her what was on her mind.

"Well, you know, Alexander, this whole scene probably could've been avoided, had you closed that door at the beginning of our meeting."

"Barely a soul around, and he skulks in to eavesdrop," he grumbled. "I still can't believe he returned so promptly."

"He always did have a radar sense concerning Valerie."

"Yes, very astute hindsight on your part," he conceded grandly. "I trust you'll take those keen observation skills over to Valerie's house. Meanwhile, I'll comb through her cases to find any dissatisfied customers. Hopefully, between the two of us, we can clear this up in short order."

"How fortunate that Michael leapt to the wrong conclusion," Kim said, rising to sift through the folders with her boss. "Had he discovered the truth, he might have insisted on playing hero."

"Hard to say. His feelings for her are so unpredictable." He shook his head, placing his glasses back on his nose. "If nothing else, this stunt tonight proves that he'd be incapable of providing her with effective coolheaded protection. So, we'll just let him believe that she wants back in—"

"And that I'm barreling over there to set her straight on her past disloyalties to the company and her naïveté over an imagined open-door policy," Kim finished.

"That vision should give him enough satisfaction to cover ten slaps, easily compensating him for the one he actually did receive at her hand."

"You make Michael sound like a spoiled kid."

He peered over his lenses with a twinkle. "You're being astute again, Kimberly. Now skedaddle across the Maryland border and see if you can't put that poor girl's life back in order."

"I DON'T GET ANY OF THIS, VALERIE!"

Stephanie Warner, seated in the passenger seat of Valerie's van, shot her sister a frantic look of disbelief. Several hours had passed and they were finally headed home. The dozing twins were strapped into the back seat, the sacks of groceries stowed in the compartment behind them. The smell of thawed pizza permeated the interior of the vehicle.

Valerie gripped the wheel as they eased off the thoroughfare and into their neighborhood. "Keep your voice down, Stephy."

"Why would anybody search your house?" Stephanie asked under her breath. "You don't have anything worth stealing—"

"Thanks a heap!" Valerie whispered back, though she'd thought the same thing herself.

"You know what I mean. You've got no real jewelry or serving stuff. Mom has all the family stones and silverware. Face it, you're an unlucky pick. That's probably what the burglar discovered," she rushed on to theorize. "That's why nothing's missing. He took a good look around and left in disappointment. Bitter, bitter disappointment. Never to return."

As Valerie stopped for a red light, she glanced over at her sister to gauge the girl's emotional state. Stephanie's profile was so much like her own. Upturned nose, high, rounded cheekbones, lush red hair. Her chin was held high as well, reflecting Valerie's own spunky spirit. If it hadn't been for the quivering lip, Valerie would've been totally fooled by her little sister's bravado.

"I'm sorry, honey, but I'm afraid this break-in is somehow connected to the Cornerstone Group."

Stephanie flipped back the mane of hair curtaining her shoulder. "How did my things look?"

"I don't know," Valerie replied. "I never got past the kitchen."

There was an uneasy silence between them for several blocks, punctured by an occasional sniffle from Stephanie or a sleepy groan from one of the twins. Valerie wished she could give her sister a more concrete explanation. Steph had been just a child when Valerie was working as an operative. It had seemed glamorous to the girl then. Valerie had been the brave, romantic heroine who sent her gifts from all over the world, just as Neal now did for the twins. Valerie had never spoken of the dangers of the business. She'd hoped she'd never have to.

"Let's just reserve judgment until Kim reports on what she's found."

"So your friend will be waiting for us?"

"Alexander promised."

It seemed that he'd kept that promise. Valerie rolled up their avenue moments later, to find their white two-story colonial openly occupied. There were lots of lights gleaming through every black-shuttered window on the main floor and the shadow of a vehicle in the driveway. She swung onto the concrete apron fronting the garage, her headlights illuminating a car parked off to the side. It was a red sports coupe with personalized license plates which read KIK.

"That's Kimberly Irene Krenz, all right," Valerie deduced, with a measure of relief. She reached up to the sun visor and tapped the garage-door remote. The huge door rose and there was the striking blond operative dressed in navy knit slacks and an oversize top, waiting for them by the service door. She waved them forward with an exigent motion, bringing the door down the moment Valerie cut the engine.

With a cry of pleasure, Valerie bounded out of the van to embrace her pal. Valerie had impressive height for a female, at the five-foot-six mark, but standing a whole half foot taller, Kim had the build and carriage of a statuesque goddess.

They exchanged rushed, excited platitudes, Kim pausing to meet Stephanie and take a look at the snoozing twins.

"Tell us about the house," Stephanie pleaded, wringing her hands. Their three-minute conversation had seemed like a three-hour one to the teenager.

Kim's generous mouth tightened. "I went over the place with a fine-tooth comb. I don't think your intruder got beyond the kitchen-family room area in back."

"So I was right!" Valerie marveled with a measure of pride.

"So nobody got up to our bedrooms." Stephanie sighed with a measure of relief.

Valerie cringed in embarrassment. "Not even the housekeeper."

Kim regarded her in wonder. "Since when have you ever doubted your instincts, or worried about a messy room? Or dressed in classic clothing?" The blonde's husky laugh echoed through the garage as she inspected her old Cornerstone cohort from head to toe. "You certainly have changed, Val. Physically and temperamentally. It's particularly noticeable beside your carbon copy here," she said, gesturing to Stephanie.

So her fifteen-year-old sister now looked more like the old Valerie than Valerie did herself. Valerie shrugged nonchalantly, though the observation was a bit hard to take. Of course she'd changed. Kim was still a single globe-trotting secret agent. She was a mother of two. An educator grounded in routine. She wasn't a coltish kid anymore, and she didn't want to be.

"Shall we go inside where it's more comfortable?" Valerie suggested, tired of the oily smell of the sealed-up garage.

Kim inhaled sharply. "It isn't as comfortable as you may think."

Valerie arched a thin russet brow. "What do you mean?"

"The telephone line is tapped, and the kitchen and family room are wired for sound," Kim reported. "I have the feeling you chased away your intruder when you stepped inside the back door this afternoon."

Stephanie erupted in a squeal, clutching the sleeve of Valerie's trench coat.

"But the house is clear and safe now," the agent went on to guarantee. "There's no reason not to go inside. We just have to watch what we say downstairs."

Valerie nodded. "Let's just get the twins up to bed."

"Can't you just disconnect the bugs or whatever they are?" Stephanie demanded in a huff, as the women moved to ease the dozing children from the van. "I mean this is creepy!"

"It is crucial that we find out who's doing this, and why," Valerie explained. "Tipping off our eavesdropper now would probably drive him back into the shadows."

"Best to get it over with now," Kim agreed, easing Tammy onto her feet in the same way Valerie was handling Timmy. "They remind me of a couple of zombies," she chuckled, catching the little girl under the armpits as she slumped against her. "Miniature zombies in yellow slickers. Could make a good sci-fi flick."

Valerie wrinkled her pert nose in annoyance. "You haven't changed a bit."

Kim blew her pale bangs from her eyes. "Nope."

"Open the door for us, Stephanie," Valerie directed. "And please act as naturally as possible. Those microphones will probably pick up every sound on the main level."

The teenager paused with a hand on the doorknob. "I'll try. But if you think I'm going to use our telephone under these conditions, you're crazy!"

Frazzled and exhausted, Valerie shot her sister a smug look. "So there is a silver lining in even this dark cloud, after all. I'll be receiving some incoming calls for a change."

The women guided the children up the stairs and into their cheery bedroom decorated in bold crayon colors and circus animals. Stephanie moved ahead of them, switching on the clown lamp on the dresser, pulling down the covers on the pair of narrow beds.

"When we do go back downstairs, I think we should behave as though I'm an expected guest," Kim suggested in a hush, easing Tammy onto the bed opposite her brother's.

"All right." Valerie took their little slickers and set them over a chair, pausing to regard her idle sister. "Stephanie, why don't you go back down now and start unloading the groceries from the van?"

"Alone?" she gasped in mortification.

Kim chuckled. "I'll help you, hon. But there's nothing to be afraid of. This place is completely safe and sound now. I activated the security system that your sister apparently had installed but never bothered to use."

Valerie's shoulders stiffened as she peeled off her own coat. "Neal put it in when we bought this place, but we never bothered with it." Under Kim's amazed glare she added, "This is a small college town. The crime rate is extremely low."

"Sure doesn't sound like Neal," Kim objected.

"Neal wasn't really interested in anything that went on around here," Valerie said with a twinge of bitterness. "Bothered with nothing near the end."

Kim flashed her a sympathetic should-have-known-better look, just as Alexander had in the market.

To her surprise, the feeling of being left out of their old world stung a little. They were all still bonded by their mutual job, still immersed in a life-style that she could no longer identify with. Even producing an agent's offspring didn't guarantee a lasting link.

"I don't expect you to understand," she eventually said with a resigned sigh. "But I feel that by walking away from his children, Neal has denied himself some of the greatest pleasures on earth."

"Oh, Valerie..." Kim trailed off helplessly. "I don't know what to say to make it better."

Of course she didn't, Valerie realized. Agents kept relationships simple and unemotional.

"But I can unpack groceries." With wry smile she steered Stephanie out of the room.

Valerie peeled the children down to their underwear before she realized that their pajamas were in the laundry basket in her bedroom. She kicked off her pumps and moved swiftly down the hallway to the master suite with a nylon rustle, tugging the gold pearl earrings off her ears, yearning for her own T-shirt nightie, stuffed beneath her pillow.

To sleep. To dream. To forget.

Boring had become a blissful chosen life-style.

And she deeply resented this strange intrusion.

She would promptly put an end to it, she decided with inner resolve. If she had to draw on the skills of the past to preserve the present, she would do so. Whatever it took.

The master suite was the last doorway on the left. She automatically raised her hand to the wall switch and gave it a flick, fully expecting the overhead fixture to glow to life.

But the room remained hollow and dark. With an impatient hand she clicked the button up and down.

It was a bad sign. One that didn't register until it was too late.

A male's powerful arms were already locking around her chest and her belly, lifting her off her feet. She squirmed and kicked as he dragged her toward the bed, sorry that she'd discarded her shoes only minutes ago.

Her thoughts were a dizzy haze of horror. Somebody had penetrated Kim's wall of security. Made it all the way up here.

But now? Who?

Then, in a flash, she knew. As he tackled her on the mattress, her senses were flooded by his scent, his touch, the sharp contours of his body.

She tried to roll, to wrench free, but he'd poured over her like a second skin, tacking her wrists high above her head, squeezing them together with one huge hand.

Her breaths came in long, hard puffs, as she focused on his features, sharp and shadowed in the sliver of moonlight streaming in the window.

"What's . . . your game, Hawkes?"

Valerie's cool, breathless question left Michael usurped for a brief moment. But the bravado had to be a bluff. She was pinned hard and fast beneath him, and it had to rattle her just a little bit. Didn't it?

Hawkes hadn't expected to be so affected by his own trap. He was here to teach her a lesson. To do the necessary rattling. But the tender tip of her nose was pressed into his stubbled upper lip like a cuddly kitten's and her every breath washed hot against his throat like a lover's sigh.

It felt just too damn good for his own good. The cushy crush of her breasts against his rib cage. The soft, shimmery hem of her dress was bunched up between her hipbones.

An erotic invitation.

But an unintentional one.

The real story was in her eyes. They were open wide, staring into his with stormy liquid-green fury. Every so often she arched and twisted, as though testing his hold.

She was only testing his willpower.

The slither of her stockinged legs against his denim-clad thighs sent bolts of lightning through his system.

He secretly savored the head-to-toe sensations for a brief, delicious moment. A moment so fleeting, that she couldn't possibly be the wiser. This reunion was far afield from its purpose to strike a chord of fear into her. With a lurch of regret, he withdrew in one fluid motion.

"Hey, aren't you forgetting something?"

Her challenge caused him to pause over her in a prone position. "What would that be?"

"My light bulbs," she smartly returned. "You loosened them. You tighten them."

He rose up on the mattress like a huge, sleek animal, making the adjustments to the overhead fixture. Light suddenly flooded the room. He looked down at her disheveled state with a surge of uncomfortable sensations. Passion. Tenderness. Desire.

It was difficult to believe that he was in the same room with her again. That he'd actually lain with her again. Even with clothing and a measure of hostility, it had been a pleasure.

Valerie struggled to her knees on the mattress. She made an attempt to adjust her dress.

His eyes gleamed as they followed the stroking motion of her hands, smoothing the clingy knit fabric over her abdomen. "Too little, too late," he purred.

"As the story goes with you," she lashed out.

He drew a wistful breath. "It seems I'm always a disappointment."

Not always. Their eyes locked for brief telepathic exchange.

"So what's this all about, anyway?" she demanded, anxious to break the electric spell. "Have you finally flipped your lid? Developed some kind of secret-agent syndrome?"

He shook his head in bewilderment. "You cut your hair, Val. Why'd you do that?"

"Is that all you have to say?" she gasped in indignation.

He rubbed his chin in private contemplation. "Almost grabbed the other one. Thought she was you."

That admission openly shook her. "Thank heavens you didn't! That's Stephanie. My sister. And she's only fifteen years old."

"Looks more like you than you do."

Valerie bristled at the disappointed inference regarding her new image. First Kim, now Hawkes. She wasn't Grandma Moses. Not yet. But the irritating rub made it easier to keep her defenses high.

She was going to need them. Michael Hawkes looked better than ever.

He leapt off the bed to the apricot carpeting like a sleek cat, prowling round the pencil-post corners as though attempting to burn off excess energy. He had to be on the far side of thirty now. Silver threaded his hair above the ears. Deeper lines fanned his striking eyes. The look was leaner, more shopworn. But not meaner. If anything he seemed a trifle off-balance. A bit perplexed under his surface disgruntlement.

"So, to what do I owe this pleasure?" she demanded on a saucy note. "You just pop in to play a little bed-bouncy?"

He stopped at the footboard, his mouth twitching. "I could be available for that."

"Those sort of games—teasing games, in general—don't interest me anymore."

"The hell they don't, lady." His eyes gleamed a dangerous indigo. "You know exactly why I'm here!"

Valerie eyed him for a long, speechless moment. He was the last person she would have expected to find in her bedroom. Tonight, in particular.

"Don't give me that innocent stare," he chided with a wag of his finger. "I have it all figured out."

"But—"

"Val, how could you possibly hope to waltz back into your old job?"

Her rosebud mouth sagged open. "Do what?"

"Alexander and Kim were discussing your situation earlier this evening when I walked in on them," he explained with an impatient gesture. "So I know. You contacted Alexander because you want back in. Kim volunteered to set you straight. Though she did say she was coming tomorrow...." he recalled with a measure of irritation.

"So you thought you'd beat her to the punch," Valerie finished with new understanding.

"As a favor to all of us," he promptly affirmed. "To prove you incapable before you foolishly quit your teaching job. It was far too easy to overpower you, Val. I'm disappointed."

The smug Cornerstone cowboy with a fresh notch in his belt. Valerie sought a snappy comeback but came up empty.

Michael Hawkes was the consummate espionage agent, with an impeccable worldwide reputation. Numerous governments and organizations had attempted to recruit him over the years, because of his skills and sense of loyalty. But it was this same loyalty that kept him bonded to Alexander and his organization.

Hawkes was many things to many people.

To Valerie, he was the arrogant bastard who had run like hell from her affection. But given the chance to prove her unfit for field-agent duty, he'd swooped in without a second thought. After six long years of silence.

It scorched her heart like a first-degree burn.

"Hey, we thought we heard a thump—" Kim stopped short just inside the doorway, with Stephanie on her heels.

"Some thump!" Stephanie exclaimed in a squeak.

"It's all right, Steph," Valerie hastily intervened, with hopes of guiding the conversation. "This is Michael Hawkes—"

"The one you were—"

"Yes!" Valerie cut in, a flush rising from the hollow of her throat. "He just stopped by to prove that I was unfit for operative duty."

Kim was prompt on the uptake. "I'm sorry, Valerie," she said with feigned resignation. "I intended to break it to you gently. But there are no open field-agent positions at Cornerstone right now. And, quite frankly, Alexander doesn't think you're up to the challenge, either."

"Oh." Valerie hung her head, tucking her chin-length hair behind her ears. There still was a chance to rid herself of this infuriating man before he learned the truth. He was too thorough to walk away from a plight such as hers. He would hunt and probe and pester his way to the solution.

She couldn't bear to have him around. His touch still caused the same old tingle. A tingle a single working mother couldn't afford to play around with. Just like six years ago yesterday, commitment was still number one on her male wish list. And it was so much more important now, with her pair of darling children so anxiously hunting for a father figure.

She swallowed hard, as though she'd just finished the last bite of humble pie. "Now that you've proven your point, I'd like you to leave."

"What is going on here, Val?" Stephanie asked on a bewildered whine. "You already have a good job—"

"Listen to your little sister," Michael suggested with a mirthless grin.

Stephanie mustered the courage to look Michael straight in the eye. "And how did you get in here? Kim just said our security alarm is supposed to be great."

"The security system is working perfectly," he assured. "Neal and I designed it, so naturally we both know how to crack it."

Stephanie eyed him keenly. "Were you here earlier, messing around?"

"Stephanie!" Valerie gasped in mortification.

"I just got here," he replied. "Cut through the woods behind your house."

Stephanie groaned into her pillow. "This is so creepy."

He eyed Valerie dubiously. "What's the matter with her?"

"Nothing! She's tired. We're all tired." Clenching her fists behind her back, she forced herself to remain calm. "You've accomplished your little mission here, Michael. I won't be troubling Cornerstone again."

"I merely wanted to show you that you're too rusty for fieldwork," he reiterated, as though he'd expected a much harder sell.

"And made a splendid job of it," Valerie conceded.

The peacock in him was tremendously pleased. But his finely tuned intuition was flashing a warning red behind his eyes. Valerie was hiding something from him. As always, a crackling tension energized the air they breathed. And it was bound to be a furious friction, considering their parting circumstances. But there was something else, an unexpected, indiscernible something causing her beautiful body to twitch.

Fear.

The answer threw him off-balance, but it was right on target.

Valerie was scared!

But of what? Of whom?

Certainly not of him! Michael's forehead furrowed as he deliberated. She'd been momentarily unsettled by his pouncing appearance, but she'd fought back with gusto.

Now she was trying to get rid of him.

He had expected her to take the opportunity to tell him off. To assure him that she was up to any job, in or out of Cornerstone. To bawl him out for this stunt. She should be protesting this test of reflex. Instead, she was showing him the door. It just didn't make sense.

Unless the whole job story was a sham....

Maybe she was in some kind of trouble. The retroactive kind that sometimes plagued retired field agents. She could've turned to Alexander for help. And he subsequently could've dispatched Kim.

Michael began to replay the meeting at Cornerstone. Alexander and Kim had been discussing Valerie's plight when he'd walked in on them. Then they'd fed him that story about Valerie's wish to rejoin his team.

Or had it been his story right from the start?

Yes, that was it. He'd told them how things were with Valerie. They'd simply verified his assumptions. It had been an elementary diversionary tactic, and he'd eagerly swallowed it.

But hadn't he always behaved like a chump, where Val was concerned? Apparently even a half-dozen years hadn't diminished the fascination. The mere mention of her name and he'd invented an excuse to charge right over—an insight he wasn't especially comfortable with.

Her obvious discomfort only made the moment worse. She was staring at him now. Expectantly. Uncertainly. Angrily.

He was the last hero she thought she wanted under her roof. And his sixth sense was assuring him she needed one.

Valerie had grown extremely nervous since her sister and Kim had arrived on the scene. It was as though she'd been giving the snappy performance of her life, only to have these

two new bit players walk onstage, unrehearsed and uninformed.

Michael didn't acknowledge emotion as anything more
than a weakness, but he knew that Valerie fueled herself on
it. She was quaking from head to toe now, as she eased off
the bed. The truth was one nudge away.

"Goodbye, Michael," she said in curt farewell.

He snagged her wrist as she attempted to fly past him,
causing her to cry out in alarm.

"Aren't we jumpy?" he purred, drawing her close.

"I'm kind of busy tonight," she haughtily informed him.
"My twins are asleep down the hall, in need of their pajamas. So, if you don't mind..." She tried to shake free of his
grasp, only to feel his fingers curling deeper into the tender
flesh of her inner arms.

"Maybe he's the one who's bothering us!" Stephanie
proclaimed, her eyes round with indignation. "Are you the
one?"

Chapter Three

Valerie's heart slammed against her rib cage as Michael's fingers climbed up the back of her neck, taking a handful of hair. "Don't you dare tell me another lie. What is the girl talking about?"

"None of your damn business, Hawkes. And that is the truth."

"You never intended to return to Cornerstone at all, did you?" His query was a silky statement of fact.

She closed her eyes with a surrendering sigh. "No, never."

"Why are you so anxious to get rid of me? Why, Val?"

Valerie flinched as he tugged gently at her hair, tipping her gaze up to his. *Because you tempted me, took me and then abandoned me, like the others before me. But I wasn't like the others. I loved you and wanted to spend the rest of my life with you.*

"Michael," she croaked, "this is small-time stuff to a man like you—"

"What is going on?"

"Someone broke in here this afternoon," she confessed in a reluctant rush, watching the jumping pulse point at his throat. "I went to Alexander for help and he sent Kim over."

"But Kim was busy," he objected. "Alexander had to reassign Neal to her Dallas mission. Why not settle for Neal? He was available. And you are raising his kids!"

Valerie forced herself to keep eye contact. It was like staring up into the eye of an approaching funnel cloud, facing the thrill of uncertainty and anticipation. His features had sharpened with age, but they were as flawlessly arresting as ever. He didn't understand any of this and he didn't like it. But this was no place for him. This was her quiet, little home, on a quiet, little street. He could make matters so much tougher. He would invade from within, proving himself far more disruptive than her eavesdropper ever could hope to be.

"Please just go away," she cried out in fury.

"Answer me, woman. My key team players are involved. I have a right to know what's going on."

"No, you don't," she snapped back. "I'm not a part of your team anymore—as you so frantically rushed over here to tell me."

"Start talking," he prompted on a quieter note.

"Kim is just the best choice for us."

."But Neal—"

"Neal doesn't want to be here, Michael," she blurted out in embarrassment. "Does that satisfy your curiosity? I knew better than to even suggest it."

Hawkes balked at the explanation. "Naturally, I'm aware of the fact that your marriage didn't work out, but that's because Neal isn't cut out for home and hearth. That was obvious to most of us all along."

Agents make lousy husbands. Michael obviously couldn't wait to set that record straight and absolve himself from any wrongdoing concerning her.

"If he understood the situation, I'm certain he would've stepped forward—"

"You don't know any such thing! You don't know anything about it at all!" Valerie blinked rapidly to quell the hot tears already misting her lashes. "I agree that Neal didn't adjust to the routine of placid married life. But even I don't completely understand everything that went wrong, so how the hell could you?"

"So what did you come up with?" he demanded, with a shifting of his gaze to Kim.

"The kitchen and the family room are bugged," she answered. "Nothing seems to be missing. Seems like the sort of thing we've done many times over ourselves."

Michael's blue eyes slanted back to Valerie. "Figure it's an old enemy?"

"I don't have any new ones," she returned coldly. "I'm a teacher now. A mother."

"Professor Mom."

Alexander's words. But on Michael's tongue they sounded amazingly provocative. Oh, who was she kidding? He couldn't address her without sensual undertones. A simple "Val" from his mouth was a stroke of verbal velvet.

A small inner voice cried out to her in caution. She was toe-to-toe with the most dangerous man she'd ever known. The only man who'd ever made her feel like a dangerous woman. She had to get rid of him. Before she made the same mistake all over again.

"Now that your curiosity is satisfied, and you've judged me unfit for field duty, I don't see any reason for you to stay on."

He managed to smile at the tired, distraught woman eyeing him with her last ounce of spunk. "I am going to help you out of this mess, honey."

"Kim—"

He pressed a finger to her lips. "Kim is going home."

"We already have plans," she objected, throwing up her hands. "She intends to play my houseguest. The old friend who—"

"I will play the houseguest," he cut in calmly, folding his arms over his expansive chest.

She shook her head. "No, it wouldn't be the same."

"What's the difference?" he challenged, cutting a grin that could rival the big, bad wolf's any day.

"You would automatically take over. And I'm looking for an assistant, not a tyrant."

"Call me what you like, but I'm the best," he claimed in an overruling motion.

"Hey, I resent that," Kim protested from the doorway.

"This is a delicate situation," Valerie argued. "I intend to keep my children in the dark about this whole thing. I won't have their world disturbed. I've worked too hard to make it right."

"I will only be of help."

Valerie shook her head in doubt. "If it is an old enemy, he just may know about our unpleasant breakoff. How could we possibly justify a visit from you now?" One look into his amorous eyes told her how. "Oh, no, mister. You are not going to play the role of my renegade lover."

"What a charming idea."

"It's your idea!"

"So it is. But we can make it work. Together. As a team. Like before."

"You don't know the first thing about settling into a daily routine."

His mouth curled in jaded impatience. "I've been everywhere. Done everything."

"Everything else, perhaps."

"I can manage."

"Make my kids believe that you're my loving suitor?" she hooted. "Manage to make someone else in the espionage community believe that you want to spend time with me in a Maryland college town?"

"Anyone who knows us will know we burned pretty hot," he reminded her. He stepped closer, grinning when she instinctively backed away. He kept on coming, crowding her into the tall mahogany dresser near the closet. "Do you hate me so much that you can't even pretend that I'm welcome here?'' he murmured low in her ear.

She slowly inhaled, as his fingers glided over the delicate contours of her face. "Is there anything I can say to make you go away, Hawkes?"

He drew a crooked grin. "Offhand, I'd say no."

"All right, then. Stay. Knock yourself out. Convince 'em the bad boy's found a home. But don't expect much help from me, aside from being nice to you in the kitchen!"

His eyes shone with a lust that belonged more suitably there in the bedroom. "Who'd have ever predicted that you'd one day own a set of pots and pans? Or that you'd be juggling me along with them?"

She squinted meanly. "I have fancied the idea of chasing you with a skillet more than once."

"I bet you catch me every time."

"Hawkes," Kim cut in. "Maybe you should just go home."

His subordinate's voice snapped him back to reality fast. In a sudden chameleon-like switch he was all business.

"You are out of here, Kim," he bit out in direction. "I want you back at Cornerstone right away. I imagine Alexander's already busy digging into Valerie's old cases. You can get on the computer, streamline the search. We'll have to set the stage here first, of course, make this shift of help seem natural. I'll start by cutting back through your yard, Val. I'll get my Firebird and arrive like it's for the first time. I have a standby tote in the trunk. Plenty of clothing to last me."

Valerie knew of the tote. It was standard issue for agents, to be packed full of necessities and kept within reach.

He pinched her chin. "Act like you're expecting me, like you want me. We'll play up the reunion for a while. Kim can then make her excuses and leave. Simple. As easy as falling off a log."

"Can I play, too?" Stephanie asked hopefully.

'No!" Valerie exclaimed. "Now go to bed."

With an extravagant sigh, the girl flounced off down the hall.

Hawkes paused for a private, pensive moment. "Okay. Let's get busy."

Valerie was shaken and simmering as he eased off with that trademark tag line. Just another mission to him, was it? Imagine, Hawkes believing that he could slip into home life with the ease of changing his socks! Well, he was about to learn otherwise. He'd be begging for the field after a few days around her unpredictable, demonstrative brood. And he'd leave with a valuable lesson on what real love and commitment meant to her.

Hopefully, she'd gain something herself. With any luck, the sight of him bumbling around on her turf would be enough to dull the glittering romantic finish that still shone in her memory bank. Watching their worlds collide would be a good dose of reality for the both of them. It would bring bittersweet closure to the union she should've shaken a long, long time ago.

IT WAS THE STRANGEST encounter her kitchen had ever seen.

Valerie replayed the fabricated reunion in her mind sometime after midnight, as she made up the foldaway bed for Hawkes in the small upstairs study. Cornerstone agents gathered round her table, reminiscing about the old days. Drinking cola, pretending it was a fine wine she didn't have. Making it fond, fun and poignant. Michael proved amazingly capable of playing the role of repentant suitor. He mastered intimate murmurings, teasing innuendo and had surely taken in the most cynical eavesdropper.

It was so important that she not be taken in.

His charms had fooled her before, she begrudgingly admitted as she tossed a blanket over the sheeted mattress. Even if he hadn't meant to do it, the signals had deeply affected her. He'd made her fall in love with him.

Damn him for coming back. Damn him for being so sexy, so strong, the same as before, only more.

She bent over and started to edge around the small bed, tucking in the covers as she went. A sudden tweak to her bottom brought her up fast.

"I didn't hear you come in!" she squealed, rubbing the spot.

"You are so rusty it's pathetic," he chided mildly, with the shake of his toothbrush. He moved over to the rolltop desk where he'd left his tote bag, stuffing the brush back in his shaving kit. "Six years away and you're soft."

"You've turned a different color since our little show downstairs. No more microphone, no more sweet suitor."

The complaint was a mistake. She knew it the moment the words popped out of her mouth. Here he stood in his low-riding jockey shorts and she in her cotton nightshirt. And she'd been simpleminded enough to encourage his attentions.

"Tell me what you want." He closed the space between them in two strides, crowding her back against the sofa arm. His bare form overtook her vision and his hands sought possession of her back, pressing her nightie into her spine. A shiver raced her length as he boldly caressed her with large, roving strokes.

It had been a good, long while since a man had gotten this close. And this particular man already had the advantage of knowing exactly where her buttons were.

Before she could even alert her senses, Michael cupped her breasts and teased her nipples to arousal through their cotton-knit barrier. When she parted her lips to release a heady moan, he dipped his mouth to swallow it up. The sound and kiss deepened simultaneously. Michael sliced his tongue into her warm softness, drinking, exploring, reveling in the wet heat.

Her hands stole to the hairy expanse of his chest, tracing the familiar planes of his pectoral muscles.

They clung to each other for several hungry minutes, reacquainting themselves on a sensual level so far away from the issues.

She wanted to forget all pain, to remember only the pleasures their union could bring. And for a little while she did. For a little while she rode with him on a rainbow of tantalizing sensations.

Until they were a heartbeat away from consummation.

Valerie knew that one gentle push would bring them down onto the small foldaway bed. He was waiting for her to make the move.

But Valerie was a firm believer in looking out for tomorrow. Tomorrow—when they would have to get up again; when he would be gone all over again. It would be a repeat of the Cancún affair, a roller-coaster ride of exquisite pleasure, followed by the searing pain down into nothingness.

She'd let it go too far already. With great reluctance, she peeled her mouth from his with a marked break.

He reared back a little, staring at her in disbelief. "Why, baby?"

"What are you trying to do to me, Michael?" she demanded in a weak desperate rush.

He was trying to climb back inside her and find out just why she was such a lingering itch. An unforgettable conquest. But it was all so deeply personal to him, so unsettling, that his natural shields immediately rose into place.

The blank-slate look. Valerie groaned in disappointment as it fell over his features like a mask. But she would not give it up. If he was going to dally around here, he was going to dig inside himself.

Placing a hand on her hip, she took a step back. It was difficult to keep her eyes away from the turgid flesh straining his white knit briefs, but she had to try.

"I...I want to know exactly what you are doing here. And you know what I mean. You came to bawl me out about wanting my agent status reactivated, but you've stayed. Stayed when you didn't have to. Kim could've handled this."

He growled in complaint, rubbing his hands over his eyes. "What a time for a talk!"

"Nothing could please me more than a talk right now."

"Liar."

"Let's just say that a little talk makes the rest feel right."

"Kim is a whiz at the computer keyboard," he offered in basic explanation. "It takes me forever to punch things in."

She hooted in disbelief. "That's your excuse?"

He shrugged. "Well, yeah."

"Well, no!" She marched after him as he retreated. "You're really charged up over this whole thing."

"All right." He sank on the bed, clenching his hands in his lap. "I am steamed about what I've found here. I can't believe you didn't think of me at the first sign of trouble. Why didn't you come to me in the first place?"

"Come to you?" she repeated on a boggled breath.

"Yes! Especially if Neal has been letting you down. I would've thought—would've hoped—that you'd have run straight to me."

"What an ego trip you men travel on!"

Hawkes's jaw tightened. It wasn't that at all. But he didn't know how to make her see. The idea that Valerie felt lost and frightened and alone for even one minute seared his heart. "I guess all this time...I thought Neal was taking care of you in his own way," he finally explained.

"I'm doing fine on my own!"

She was madder than ever, he realized as she stormed around the small pine-paneled room. No matter what he said, or how he said it, she was bound to twist it wrong. She so obviously was trying to prove her independence, while he was trying so damn hard to depend a little bit.

Their roles were reversed this time around. But the un-expected blows just kept on coming.

He hadn't thought this out at all. He'd simply seen an in and charged forward like a bull.

Was he going to lose the only chance he had ever had for a real relationship, just because he'd been too slow to recognize its value the first time around?

He'd felt emotionally paralyzed his whole life long, until she'd come along and struck a spark deep inside him.

If he tried to explain his change of heart, his awakening, would she take advantage of his weakness and seek revenge? These swirling fears caused him to backtrack a bit.

"Look, Val, forget what I said about wishing you'd called."

She lifted her chin like a petulant child. "Nope. You chose to be on the hook here and you're not going to wiggle off now." Valerie hovered over his seated figure with her nose in the air, but she managed to keep a keen eye on his expression just the same.

She was primed for anything.

Except perhaps for the flicker of relief that sheeted his features. She didn't know exactly what was on his mind, but he sure didn't want to storm back off.

"You wouldn't even dream of bailing out of this now that we've set it up, would you?" she demanded sweetly.

"I am going to see this through, all right," he announced with quiet firmness.

"Well, have sweet dreams." She charged for the door, yanking it open with gusto. "I'd have half a mind to slam this," she threatened in a hiss, "if I wasn't so damn thoughtful of everyone around here!"

"Hah!" he blurted out as the door closed. "Thanks for thinking of me!"

Chapter Four

"There's a man in here!"

Timmy Warner's eyes were round with wonder the following morning as he peered into the study.

"Let me see the man!" Tammy scooted down the hallway, a pink-and-blond blur in her furry robe and slippers. She stopped short in the doorway beside her pajama-clad twin. Together they ogled the huge form huddled under the covers of the sleeper sofa.

"See, I told ya."

Tammy's round freckled face brightened. "Where'd we get a man?"

Timmy scratched his chin in thought. He liked to have all the answers for his sister, but he was stuck this time. "I dunno yet."

"Is he our daddy?" she asked in a stage whisper.

"Maybe."

"He's got brown hair," she said hopefully. "Just like our daddy."

Timmy craned his neck for a better view. "His face is under the blanket."

"Not all his face...." she lilted in soft singsong.

With a telepathic look, they began to advance on the bed.

"His eyes are closed up," Timmy noted, peering over the innate form.

"Tight," Tammy affirmed. "When Mama's eyes are tight, we're s'posed to go away. Like quiet bunnies."

"Ah, we're only looking," he protested, edging a knee onto the mattress.

Tammy was right behind her brother, primed for a peek under the sheet. "Whiskers! Daddy's got whiskers."

"Every daddy's got 'em," Timmy explained with exasperation.

"Too bad his eyes are tight."

"It's not him," Timmy eventually declared with authority. He gave Tammy's bleak face a pat. "Don't be sad."

The child's breath warming his face brought Michael to full alertness. He'd been drifting in and out of semiconsciousness since the moment Timmy appeared in the doorway. Floating in a cozy comfort zone from which he had been reluctant to emerge. Dreaming in the half-awake world where vivid visions skimmed the line between fantasy and reality.

The sound of their young voices and their cloudy hovering figures had pulled him back to his own childhood, when he and his brother Jerry had been living under the same roof with their mother. They'd been too young to know how incompetent she was back then. They simply knew that they were alone night after night in their New York City apartment. And they knew that they could forget about the cold darkness if they talked to each other. So they'd shared their aspirations and ambitions until they fell asleep or until their mother returned. Eventually, when their mother didn't return at all one night, the welfare department stepped in to put them into institutional care. They were eventually separated in their teens, Jerry going to a home and Michael entrusted to Alexander. It had been aeons since he'd dreamt of Jerry or relived a snatch of his distant past.

"Whose daddy are you?"

The pair had gone from tentative whispers to jiggling. He cracked open a leery eye.

"Nobody's," he replied grumpily.

"We thought you were ours."

Yes, he had heard as much. And it shocked him down to his toenails. Neal had given him and the others at Cornerstone an entirely different impression. He'd been claiming to have an ongoing relationship with Valerie and the kids. Had contended their breakup was completely due to his inability to adjust to Valerie's traditional life-style.

It had been an outright lie.

Michael pondered this new twist. Neal had failed with Valerie and had totally dismissed her and the children from his life. But he'd lied about it, knowing how completely obsessed Michael was with her. Neal was frightened that Michael might be tempted to step into his shoes. And Neal had been right. It was his lasting bond to Valerie that had kept Michael from closing in sooner.

Their rivalry had reached a new low.

Another exclamation taunted him from the far corners of his conscience. Perhaps Neal was playing the protector. After all, they were both cut from the same mold: solitary characters steeped in dark secrets and buried emotions. Maybe Neal figured he'd already upset Valerie's life enough and was shielding her from a second renegade. If so, it was the only truly unselfish thing Neal had ever done.

That fact alone made the theory highly unlikely.

They were both self-absorbed men who'd grown up on the street and who had learned the hard way that only the selfish survived. They'd sized up each other over a decade earlier when Alexander had partnered them on a series of missions. They'd blended well, friendly rivals who excelled as a pair. Eventually Alexander had expanded their partnership, adding team players. Kim soon became a regular, and others came and went, including Valerie. The team concept had eventually eroded their friendship. Every team needed a leader, and Alexander had chosen Michael for the job.

The emulation had never damaged their Cornerstone missions, but the personal duels had become frenzied at times. Especially over women. Valerie had been the last of the bunch and had brought a sort of closure to that game. He'd bested Michael once and for all.

Michael had been paying the price ever since. Valerie had wanted him, courted him, offered him the ultimate prize: her devotion. But he'd turned her down, believing himself incapable of relating in an intimate way.

He'd gone on to find out he couldn't go on, not like before. She'd changed him forever, proven that he had a heart—he had to have one, because it was broken.

As angry as he'd been the previous night over her guarded, wary attitude, he understood it. She'd been justified in questioning his motives. Caring was a lot of trouble and the road to self-discovery was rough.

She'd even had the nerve last night to return with pajamas for him. Neal's old paisley pajamas. She said it was necessary decorum. He wanted to think that he was too tempting in his underwear, but he wasn't going to count on it.

It was bound to have been only an entrée to the discomfort in store for him, in her nest, under her house rules.

But she was worth it. Sharing a closeness with Val in both business and pleasure had been wonderful. He'd taken it all for granted, until it was yanked away from him. But he hadn't known any better back then. He would've made a lousy partner back then, but he was a better man now.

He could only hope that she would give him a second chance to make it right.

"Hey, you. Man!"

"My name is Michael," he announced, sitting up with a mighty, bearlike groan. He glanced over to the pair to see if he'd startled them away. He had. They'd jumped back a step and the girl was clutching the boy's pajama top. He finally had the drop on somebody around here.

Or did he?

His heart was thudding against his rib cage as he stared down the pair of cherub-faced blondes with the twinkling hazel eyes. The old childhood dream hadn't been as far-fetched as he thought.

These children could pass for his own! If he had children, which he most certainly didn't.

But what had he expected them to look like? Miniature Neals? Why even he and Neal could pass for brothers. So, presumably, could their offspring. It didn't really prove anything. Families were often mismatched-looking. Besides, he'd never perceived himself as a father. Didn't even know how a father was supposed to behave. It was one of those out-of-the-question issues he'd never examined. Still, it was impossible not to wonder....

It was totally ridiculous to even entertain the idea, he decided with a hard jerk the other way. And completely out of character. Could he be losing his blasted mind? One taste of Valerie and he wanted to claim credit for her children.

His solid reality base homed in on the one intriguing, undeniable fact that cut through the jumble.

The kids didn't look like him or like Neal. They looked like his brother, Jerry.

He rubbed his furrowed forehead, trying to somehow reason it all away.

Tammy's round face crinkled in suspicion. "Does our mama know about you?"

His lids sank. "Oh, yeah. She knows."

"She like you?" Timmy wondered doubtfully.

Michael rubbed his stubbled chin. "Are you kids five or twenty-five?"

"Five!" they chorused in exasperation.

"Can't you tell, Mike?" Tammy asked huffily.

"My name is Michael," he reiterated. Drawing his knees up under the covers, he leaned forward to study them with keen interest.

"Sometimes we call Mama's friends 'uncle,'" Timmy reported.

His dark eyebrow jerked. "You have a lot of uncles?" To his astonishment, they conferred, ticking off several masculine names.

He lurched in fear. Had she found someone new? Her choices had long ago extended beyond himself and Neal. Had she caught the eye of some literary type over at the college? He could only imagine how her phone rang and rang and rang. The thought of unknown competition compounded his other disadvantages. He wasn't one to fluster, but suddenly he knew exactly what the term meant.

"We gotta have uncles," Timmy went on to explain with a measure of authority. "'Cause we got the big *D*."

"You got the big *D*, Uncle Mike?"

"What's that?"

Tammy's lips puckered. "Dee-vorce."

"Guess there is only one big *D*, isn't there?" He rubbed his chin with a rueful expression.

"Well, you got it or not?"

"Okay, you guys." Valerie marched into the room. Her face was alive with complacency, but he was grateful for the bailout just the same.

"We're just talkin'," Timmy said defensively.

"Michael isn't accustomed to answering so many questions at one time," she explained.

"We always ask the uncles questions," Tammy whined. "He is one, isn't he?"

"I sure am," Michael interceded silkily, incinerating all traces of smugness from Valerie's startled green eyes.

She opened her mouth to object, then clamped it shut again. The plan was in place to behave like reunited lovers, and she had to keep up her end of the bargain. Especially in front of her children. She didn't want them to be frightened of Michael and she didn't want them to express doubt in the wiretapped rooms. They would have to really believe in Valerie's rekindled interest in Michael to make a good show of it. This problem did not have to overflow on them. They had a right to feel safe in their own home.

"We never had an uncle upstairs before," Tammy piped up. "You must be really special."

Valerie flushed under Michael's triumphant gaze. "Michael is truly unique," she improvised on a lilt. "Now, why don't you two go downstairs? Stephanie's on her way to the kitchen to whip up some pancakes."

The twins exchanged joyous smiles over the news. "See you later, Uncle Mike," they chorused, scrambling out of the room.

"Hey! Don't call me—" Hawkes cut himself off as their feet pounded out of earshot.

Valerie sauntered toward the bed, her arms crossed over her chest. Michael assessed her from head to toe. She looked fetching in simple blue jeans and a lemon yellow top. Capable and domestic. Queen of her castle. Maybe there was more to Saturday morning in suburbia than he thought.

"I don't remember you ever being grumpy in the morning," she observed.

"Well, I don't like being called Uncle Mike." It was the mention of the other uncles that really irritated him, but he wasn't prepared to deal with that weakness. "Tell them to call me Michael."

"You tell them."

"I tried." He tugged the pajama top over his head. "Do they ever listen? Do you have any real control?"

"They're five years old!" she scoffed, keeping her gaze leveled above his taut rippling chest. He was doing it all over again, stirring her up, causing a rainbow of emotions to flare inside her.

This was the one place she thought he'd never show up. The boring routine-driven home front. It was in direct conflict with his nomadic life-style.

"They can talk, so they can listen, can't they?" he argued.

"They're healthy and happy and good. And you can't blame them for getting a little excited over the sight of an uncle. They feel inferior because Neal doesn't pay them any mind. They think he's gone because they weren't good enough." When Michael's granite expression didn't waver, she made a fuming noise. "That's a pretty heavy load for babies to bear—babies who are just learning to spell their own names!"

Michael was accustomed to being referred to as a bastard. But it was the rare moment when he actually felt like one. Leave it to this redheaded siren to bewitch and bedevil him at the same time. He wasn't being deliberately difficult, he was just trying to digest it all. The idea that Neal had dumped them was so new. So unbelievable. Being brooding and cautious was a lesser sin than saying the wrong thing to her right now. Even he had the good sense to know that.

Moments passed and Valerie found she no longer had any patience for his patented sulky silence. "If you can't muster up some compassion for us, then you may as well march right back out of here. Leave it to you, with your temper and ego, to do just that!" she raved half to herself. "After shoving aside Kim, who genuinely wished to help me out."

With a sweeping motion Michael threw aside the covers and pulled Valerie onto his lap. His hair-roughened arm curled around her collarbone, but it was his penetrating gaze, hovering directly over hers, which really held her in place.

"Do you think I'd be sitting here in this mushy little bed, in these hideous pajamas, if I didn't wish you well in my own way?"

"That's just the trouble, Hawkes," she protested on a soft heaving breath. "You can't have it all your own way on a job like this. You've invaded a real, live family, with three little civilians—"

"And a real, live Professor Mom," he baited. His captive, now wedged snugly between his forearm and thighs, began to squirm under his tormenting treatment. But all she managed to do was bring them both a discomfort of the most delicious form.

"Saturday mornings around here aren't what you're used to." She curled her fingers around the forearm at her throat. "Parents don't just tumble into bed when the urge hits them."

"I'd swear you're the one trying to seduce me," he growled into the curve of her ear.

"Just trying to escape your trap." She yanked at his binding arm.

Michael bit back a shuddering breath. If she was the trapped little bunny, why did he feel like a caged lion?

"Let's call a truce," she suggested. "We can get this over with, if we work together like we used to."

Her words were a blow. She was already showing him the door at the end of the tunnel.

He set his jaw at a grim angle, studying her face as though it were a complicated map. It was all there, imprinted on her delicate features, the strength, the determination, the emerald-ice stare.

He'd have bought the package if it weren't for the hammering heart, the hint of fire flickering behind her rich russet lashes. She was ready to bloom, to burst wide open in his arms like a hothouse flower.

She still cared for him on some level. She might be fighting it with all her might, but it was strong enough to cause her an internal struggle. It gave him the courage to say something from the heart.

"Val, I...I always do exactly what I want. And right now, this is what I want to do. Where I want to be."

"But it's not like you to—"

"There's more to me than you know," he blurted out impatiently. "But you have no right to doubt me on the job.

Even my decision concerning Kim had its objective merits. She is of better use back at Cornerstone. She's the team's computer ace and can go over all your old case files with a keen, quick eye." He stroked the downy curve of her cheek. "You know that's how I operate. Each team player does the right job and does it well."

Her look was doleful. "But you do want to call all the shots."

"I want your trust. Like before." His mouth curved slightly. "There was a day when you really looked up to me. Even when I wasn't pinning you across my chest."

How bittersweet that he didn't deserve that privilege anymore. But even in all her pain and frustration she didn't have the brass to voice a fact already so devastatingly obvious.

"You're an expert in your field," she said carefully, "but this is foreign territory for you. Everything you say and do will affect my family long after you've gone."

She hoped for more starch in her voice, but it was growing increasingly uncomfortable in his lap. He was aroused. She could feel the rigid proof digging into the small of her back. But she couldn't afford to respond to the tremors running through her body. The time, the place, even her confused state made it all wrong. And she'd told him that!

But she secretly found it hopeful that he wasn't in complete control where she was concerned.

It edged the impossible man into the improbable category.

"Take the bad boy and tame him true," he crooned hotly in the curve of her ear, as though reading her thoughts.

"As if you'd like that!" The objection tumbled out in a desperate rush. She couldn't miss the flash of disappointment in his eyes as she shot off the bed like a Roman candle. What had gotten to him? The move or the words? As always, it was difficult to gauge what was happening behind his hooded gaze.

"It would be nice if you put a little effort into our supposed reunion," he advised, as he swung his powerful legs over the edge of the mattress.

"I shall," she promised, smoothing down her clothing. "On the condition that you treat the children with patience and kindness. And I mean Stephanie, too."

"She doesn't seem like too much trouble."

"She's fifteen years old." When he blinked in perplexity, she remembered he would need a thorough explanation, as though he were from another planet. "She is in the valley between girlhood and womanhood," she began, carefully weighing her words under his curious gaze. "One minute she's the vamp, the next she's the cuddle doll."

"What woman isn't?"

"Well, during the teenage years, the mood swings are deeper and more dramatic."

He clasped his hands between his knees. "Great."

"She's extremely unpredictable and remarkably insightful—"

"Sounds like somebody else I know," he drawled.

She shot him a quelling look. "It's just bad luck that she's involved. Our folks are abroad and she's in my care for the next several weeks."

"How much does she know?"

"After our little display last night, I'd say way too much!" Valerie bit her lip as she sought to salvage her pride. "She's known about you since our, ah, fling. She was nine years old at the time, and my parents have always been pretty open about everything. But none of them know that you dumped me like yesterday's news back then. I don't think they ever need to know that."

"So some privacy, some personal space, is all right," he taunted.

"Well, some is healthy. You happen to have an extreme case of hermititis."

"That isn't a real word."

"It oughtta be," she snapped back. "Look, I'm the first to admit that there aren't a lot secrets kept round here. But I don't want a repeat of last night, got it?"

He threw his hands in the air. "Okay, okay!"

"My parents didn't drop Stephanie off here for a summer course on sexy ninja techniques."

"You made that up too," he grumbled. Just a couple of orders and she had him going, just like she used to. The conservative clothing and the short bob of a hairdo hadn't totally tamed the lady inside. Good news really. He was glad to know that she still had the same spirit he'd fallen for the first time around. If he could just survive long enough to get into her good graces.

"So do we have a deal?" she pressed.

"You haven't scared me away," he purred with a keen, insightful eye. "I'll meet you downstairs in ten minutes."

She started for the door, then paused with an afterthought. "Oh, by the way, are you carrying?"

Not certain if it was good or bad, he reached under his pillow for his revolver. He held it up, only to see her mouth pinch. "Of course, the safety is on."

"I'm not keen on weapons in the house, Michael."

He lifted a heavy dark brow in genuine surprise. "You were a hell of a shot, loved the pistol range."

"That was a lifetime ago. My children don't have my training," she explained patiently, realizing that he genuinely wasn't following her line of reason.

"I've slept with a gun under my pillow for years."

"Not every night."

He smiled wickedly. "It's my habit to stash it under the bed for those rockier mattress moments. But you can believe that no one else, big or small, has ever managed to put their hands on it."

"Regardless, I'd like it on the high shelf of the closet," she tersely insisted.

"What if I refuse?"

"Then you will be out. Without delay."

"Okay, okay," he surrendered, realizing that this was one of those household calls she intended to win. "It'll be on the closet shelf when we're here. But I will be carrying, if and when we venture out. And I strongly advise you to do the same."

"No, I believe my standard ninja training will be enough, thanks." With that last comment, she whirled on her heel and marched out.

WHEN MICHAEL JOINED THEM in the kitchen, he looked like a whole new man. His coarse dark hair was tamed, his angular face cleanly shaven. He was wearing jeans and a red cotton pullover that molded to his frame with a tailorlike fit.

A wolf in uncle's clothing. Valerie felt twinges of trepidation and infatuation over the blend of images. Whatever his skin, he filled the room with an overwhelming masculine presence. It was an unmistakable man-of-the-house energy. He knew nothing about houses, but he was taking over hers!

And the fanciful Stephanie was picking right up on it. As Michael eased into a chair at the round dinette table, her little sister glided across the linoleum with a plate stacked with a half dozen enormous pancakes. She set it in front of him with a flourish. "Can I get you any favorite toppings?" she inquired in a tone thicker than the maple syrup already on the table.

"I'm not much of a breakfast eater," he admitted evenly, frowning at the mountain of food set before him.

"Me, either," she breathed with a huge smile. "I have to watch my figure." With an announcement she headed back toward the stove, her body and lush mane of hair swinging with every step.

"Please pour some coffee for him, Steph," Valerie requested, forcing a smoothness into her voice for the sake of the electronic eavesdropper. Sitting down beside Michael, she forked two of the cakes onto her own empty plate.

Michael reached for the syrup bottle under the watchful eyes of the twins.

"Big day, Uncle Mike," Timmy told him.

"Oh?" He leaned back as Stephanie delivered his steamy mug.

"Fish and shoes," Tammy squealed with delight.

Michael turned to Valerie for interpretation. Her jaw slacked in surprise.

"Oh, gosh. I completely forgot! I promised to take the children into Baltimore this afternoon, to Harborplace for new shoes and to the National Aquarium—"

"To see the fishies behind the windows," Tammy finished gleefully.

Timmy's eyes were round. "You know about Baltimore, Uncle Mike?"

"I've been there once or twice," he blandly replied, digging into his pancakes. "These are delicious, Stephanie," he commented a few moments later. His tone was laden with a surprise that would have cancelled the compliment—for anyone but a lovestruck teenager trying to please.

"Perhaps Uncle Mike doesn't want to do those things today," Valerie said haltingly.

"They even got whales," Timmy wheedled.

"I think it sounds like a wonderful plan," he assured. "It will be a chance to learn something," he added with a pointed look to Valerie.

Valerie immediately picked up the message. He was thinking that such a prearranged outing would make a meet with Alexander or Kim much less conspicuous. But what a relief it would be to lose him for a few hours. To sit quietly in the house with the security system on. To breathe a calm, sane breath and explore just what it was she wanted out of him now.

"Perhaps Uncle Mike already had plans for today," she ventured with a significant look. "We would understand if he wanted to go off alone for a while."

A chorus of groans filled the room.

Michael deliberately set down his fork and took her chin in his hand. He studied her amusement as she strained to keep her face steady. "I'm here to spend time with you, remember?"

"Make her say yes, Uncle Mike," Tammy urged.

"All right," he said huskily, his eyes holding hers. Her mouth sagged open as she read the raw sensual intent in his expression. He seized the opportunity to taste her sweetness.

They lost themselves in the moment, in the past, in each other.

Valerie had to admit, even to her own stubborn self, that this kiss was not for the sake of show. He still had the power to turn her legs to instant jelly and it felt so good...

"Say yes, Val," he coaxed silkily against her lips.

Valerie slowly sank back in her chair. "The kids are a handful in public. A huge responsibility."

"No, we're not," Timmy whined. "We can be good, if we try."

"I really want to shop today, Valerie," Stephanie put in anxiously. "I need summer clothes. You promised we'd stop at Chic City in the mall."

"You make us keep our promises," Tammy squeaked with raised brows.

Valerie's squinty look fell on each of them. "What about Saturday chores? There's a promise we all keep every week."

"We'll do 'em," they insisted.

"All right, then. Get going." She clapped her hands as they scrambled out of their chairs. "Pick up your toys, make your beds. I'll be up in a little while, to help you choose some clothes."

"I'll lead the upstairs team," Stephanie offered, taking the twins in tow.

Michael grinned at her as they hustled out the doorway. "So what I can do?"

She lifted her shoulders beneath her yellow top. "Can't think of a thing. We have our routine. Have to, to keep things running smoothly."

"Well, let me do one of your chores, then," he suggested sincerely.

Her smile was rueful. "Michael, I am going out to weed my vegetable garden out back."

"I can do that."

Her russet brows arched in doubt. "The plants are just beginning to sprout. Pulling out the wrong little green things could set me back to nothing."

Her insulting assumption, along with his painful childhood memories, caused him to visibly wince. "It just so happens that I know my eggplant from my cabbage."

"Really? You had a garden as a boy?"

"Sort of," he said quietly, averting his gaze. All his team players knew his background was stark, but she couldn't have a clue to just how bleak it truly was. And it wasn't necessary to share such things, either. It was depressing to talk about the death of his father back when he was a toddler, the institutional care he and Jerry had endured after their mother had finally abandoned them for the last time. But boy, did those places have their gardens. That produce hit the table each and every day, fresh or pickled.

But he would keep that information to himself. He was trying to put on a virile, capable, infatuating show, after all. He was trying to win Val back with the limited charms he had.

Valerie knew she'd taken a misstep, but hadn't a clue as to which one. When Hawkes clammed up, there was nothing she could do, except perhaps just give him a chance. Any major mistakes to her sprouting seedlings could be corrected by buying new plants down at the garden center.

Despite her resentment over his callous treatment in the past, she couldn't help feeling that old soft spot for him. There'd always been a perpetual pain inside him. It surfaced in the eyes more often now. Her yearning to help him heal was rapidly resurfacing, too, taking over her good sense.

"Well, the tools are out in the garage on a shelf," she said with forced nonchalance, standing up to clear away the dishes. Without a word he rose and headed for the connecting door.

"Oh, Michael?"

He paused with his back to her. "Yes?"

"Thanks a lot. It'll really help get us started ahead of schedule."

He lifted a hand in rejoinder and kept on walking.

He was the most solitary of men, especially when someone close struck a nerve. She'd been compelled to question him further, but it was too awkward with the microphones in place. He was so difficult to reach, with that natural guard up all the time.

Valerie couldn't help but watch him through the window over the sink as she loaded the dishwasher. He did know his way around a garden. He looked like a bull in a china shop, trapped in the small square of dirt surrounded by a low white picket fence. But as unsuited as he appeared, he was doing everything right out there. He was troweling the soft rain-damp earth between the rows of sprouts with practiced care, and he was pulling at only the weeds, tossing them in a pile out on the lawn.

It was an interesting sight. The way his muscles moved beneath his tight red shirt, the sheer power in his exposed forearms. He was obviously better suited for far more strenuous tasks. Still, he moved gingerly, watching where and how he stepped. He was at home somehow, at ease with the job.

Valerie had the grace to be a little ashamed of her instant doubt concerning his skills. Ten minutes later, she mustered up the mettle to tell him so.

The first thing she noticed as she eased through the glass patio door and onto her redwood deck was her sultry next-door neighbor, Beverly Tremain, stretched out in a lounge chair, soaking up the sun in a skimpy red bikini. Beverly shared Valerie's Big *D* status, but had no children. Lonely and manhunting, she too, had obviously been watching Michael, for she'd moved her lounge chair off her deck, nearer to the chain-link fence dividing their yards.

Envy and territorial feelings surged up inside Val.

Michael isn't even your man, she thought in chiding reminder. *If he decides to leap the fence and do a belly flop onto that lounge, it's his right.*

She forced a cheery wave to Beverly and moved in on Michael. Her quest for democracy proved nothing more than a fleeting idea.

"Now I know why you insisted on outside detail." She couldn't resist folding her arms across her chest with a knowing look.

"You know better than that," he murmured under his breath.

She sighed, scanning the sky. "Mmm, well . . ."

He rose to full height, still gripping the trowel. "Can't make up your mind whether you want me around or not, can you?"

His teasing tone made her feel young and silly and self-conscious. It was like the old times. The best of the old times.

He squinted at her in the bright sunshine, delight dancing across his face. "Good for ya, baby. Considering that I have all of those other uncles to worry about."

Michael's light banter was like a refreshing breeze. She couldn't resist joining in. "Maybe I should go put on my swimsuit," she silkily suggested.

"Maybe you don't need to. I can see you quite clearly right up here—" he tapped his temple "—with nothin' on. Any old time I want to. And I want to all the time."

Her pulse jumped under his knavish look.

If only he could let go and make it last.

If he'd only come back under his own steam when things were right, when her life wasn't in turmoil and under scrutiny. Maybe they'd have had a better chance of reaching each other, clearing the air.

But he hadn't. He took the dark, hard road back. Six years she'd sat here dreaming of him, and he'd returned now of all times!

"Well, I just came out to tell you that I shouldn't have jumped to the conclusion that you were ignorant about gardening," she offered in apology.

"Okay," he said simply, a grin splitting his face.

Valerie stared up at him for an expectant moment. But "okay" was all he was going to offer.

They were taking one final look at his handiwork in the garden when the twins scampered out onto the deck. "C'mon!"

"Come here," Valerie called across the lawn. "Help Uncle Mike wash his tools and collect his weeds." She turned back to him with a smug smile. "There are times when we all could use a bodyguard. Or two." With a significant look to the bikini-clad vamp next door, Valerie waltzed off toward the house.

As was par for the caregiver, Valerie was the last person out to the garage for the excursion. She'd taken extra time with her appearance, selecting a summery yellow culotte dress that drew out the orange highlights in her red hair and accenting it with white leather sandals and purse.

Instead of finding everyone strapped into the van as expected, she found Michael standing on her old rickety stepladder, struggling to bring their plastic swimming pool down from the rafters. Stephanie and the twins were hovered around the ladder, giving him ground support.

"What are you doing?" she blurted out in amazement.

"Chores, Mama," Tammy piped up, her head tipped way back to take in his every move.

"Bringing that thing down is not a chore."

"Sure it is," Timmy insisted. "He's gruntin', isn't he?"

"Yeah, he don't like it, so it has to be a chore," Tammy affirmed, her pigtails bobbing.

"Doesn't like it," Valerie automatically corrected.

"Whatever, Val!" Hawkes cut in. "Help us with this thing!"

"I shouldn't."

He gawked at her, clinging to an overhead beam for support. "Why not?"

"Because this is a scam," Valerie scolded, stepping closer to steady the ladder.

"Excuse me?"

"These two are conning you," Valerie clarified. "Don't you think that if I wanted that pool down, I'd have taken care of it?"

"Well, gee, I thought that maybe I'd hit upon something you couldn't do yourself." But as soon as the words spilled out, he knew how silly they were. They'd scaled buildings together, dived out of planes together. A molded piece of plastic stashed twelve feet off the ground wasn't going to deter her for a minute. But he'd just wanted to be useful.

At least the twins had been overjoyed—apparently for pulling one over on him!

They were actually capable of tricking him. Smart enough and savvy enough, and downright brave enough to push him around like a chess piece.

"They know full well that I won't consider any swimming until their ear infections clear up," Valerie went on to chide.

"I'm sorry, Valerie," Stephanie rushed to apology defensively. "I didn't realize there was a problem."

His face registered disbelief as he appealed to the tiny pair. "You midgets really do that? Use me?"

Their high laughter rippled through the garage.

It was Jerry's little-boy laugh, echoing over the years, ringing in his ears.

Michael looked at the twins through narrowed eyes. *First the faces. Now the laugh* Could he be their father?

He shook his head. That was hardly enough evidence to determine paternity.

He swallowed hard, as an awareness crept into his rock-solid reality base. It was quite likely that these two kids were indeed Hawkes. He gave it eighty-percent odds. No—ninety. He rocked on the rickety ladder as he played with the figures. His own fears were causing the indecision. No need to panic yet. He would reserve judgment until he had some concrete confirmation.

Did Valerie even know for sure? His body trembled as he wondered. Was she capable of such a deception? And who was she fooling? Him . . . or Neal?

"Might as well get it over with," Valerie announced abruptly, slicing into his thoughts.

He stared down at her with a mute expression.

"The pool, man. May as well send it down."

His face was beet red as he angled the plastic tub down into her arms.

Tammy clasped her hands with glee. "We got it!"

"But I will be the one filling it," Valerie assured. "Now get in the van. Pronto!"

Valerie followed Michael to the wall where he was replacing the ladder on its hook. "I warned you that this wasn't going to be a piece of cake."

He turned to take a good hard look at her face, desperately wishing he could read her thoughts. "You were right. This is a tough assignment."

"You won't underestimate them again, will you?" With a smirk, she headed for the vehicle.

He watched her glide away with a playful hip swing. "No," he murmured in return. "I'll be watching everything a whole lot closer from now on."

Chapter Five

"If anyone is on our tail, we'll give them a tour of the city," Michael declared as he pulled out of the service station several blocks away from Valerie's house. They were on their way to Baltimore's Inner Harbor, with a tankful of gas and a potential meeting with Alexander. Michael had used the pay phone inside the station to leave a message for the controller with his office assistant, outlining their itinerary for the afternoon. Alexander was planning to meet with them today.

"Hey, you got a tail, Uncle Mike?" Tammy inquired from the back of the van.

"I didn't see a tail on ya," Timmy said excitedly, wiggling on the bench seat he shared with his sister and Aunt Stephanie, to get a look at Michael's posterior.

Michael exchanged a wry look with Valerie. No wonder she'd stepped outside at the pumps to inquire about the call. These midgets missed nothing!

Michael had been happy to pass on the assistant's report. Valerie's eyes had instantly lit up over the news that Kim made progress in her computer case search. The agent had spent most of the night shifting through the data and had narrowed down the possibilities.

"Lots of tails at the aquarium," Tammy went on.

"You mean fins," Timmy corrected. "Boy, are those fish strong!"

Michael listened to the light family banter with new interest and perplexity. This was all so brand spankin' new, a novelty. The kindred concept was completely foreign to him. Alexander was the only father figure he'd ever known. And Jerry was his only living relative. But their jobs kept them at a distance most of the time. His brother was a foreign correspondent, living in Paris with a new wife. Alexander did take them to dinner several times a year, whenever Jerry was in the States. These get-togethers summed up his family interaction. Until perhaps now.

Personal thoughts of Alexander brought up another issue. Hadn't he spotted the Hawkes traits in these children when he rendezvoused with them at the grocery store? He must have! And he'd had the perfect opportunity last night at Cornerstone headquarters to tell him about it.

Instead, Alexander had tried to steer him clear of Valerie and the kids.

How dare he do that?

Michael gritted his teeth as he stared mutely out the windshield at the oncoming traffic. Alexander's betrayal added yet another blow.

Of course, everything with Alexander was secondary to his relationship with Valerie. He wanted to win her over now, more than ever. Even when he wasn't sure he could handle being a husband and a dad, he couldn't help but rise to the challenge of a new tomorrow. He wasn't getting any younger. And the idea of sticking to one lovely, compassionate partner was getting more enticing with each passing year.

But her tame, ritualistic world was so apart from the reckless, spontaneous life-style they had shared before. And she was so defensive about her ways, so specific on how she wanted things run under her roof. No guns. No disruptions in the lives of the twins. And here he was, perhaps poised with the ultimate disruption of all: the daddy issue.

How would she react to him in the dad role? She'd been hard-pressed to trust him with her garden! Secret-agent dad? Would she twist those words into something awful?

Little did she know that he'd been lying in wait for some opening, the chance to resurface in her life.

But the doubts festered in his brain.

Family men weren't made. Not at the age of thirty-eight.

He'd been on the move for as long as he could remember. First in his mother's care, then in institutional care, then finally in Alexander's care. He was in perpetual flight, frantically putting more and more space between him and his disappointing beginnings. How could such a fugitive ever hope for a happy ever after?

Valerie had been the only woman who had ever managed to leave a lasting mark on him. Make him think of tomorrows, of perhaps looking ahead with more than his next flight plan on his mind.

He'd denied the signals the first time. But he wouldn't make that mistake again, if given a second chance.

But would there be another chance?

She could logically claim that they were impossible together.

But there'd never been anything logical about them, then or now. Not back when he knew it jeopardized the harmony of their team. Not when he'd mourned her retreat and subsequent marriage to Neal. Not even now, when he knew damn well that Kim could've guarded her brood and Alexander could've done the case search—leaving him totally out of the picture.

He desperately wanted to give his relationship another shot. Despite the odds against him.

Maybe if he got her out of this dilemma, she'd melt. Just a little bit.

THE NATIONAL AQUARIUM was crowded. Valerie had kept her three charges in a tight circle as Michael paid their admission. She knew all the precautionary measures needed to make this work. Her Cornerstone training had begun to renew itself, putting her on alert, urging her to think several steps ahead. It was difficult to believe that this sort of ever watchful, overly cautious procedure had once been a way of life for her. She tingled with awareness and an old reckless spark. It was a clear-cut reminder of why she had found agenting so alluring in the first place, and why Michael still did. Missions held a certain amount of routine work, but there was always the possibility of the unexpected, a turn of events that made the game new and different.

Of course this was one of those circumstances when Valerie was hoping for boring—a safe, swift closure.

Naturally, the risks involved in the outing seemed so magnified with her own children. And Michael had given her further assurances at the gas pump. He didn't seem to think they were in any present danger. Someone was eavesdropping on her to find out something. If he had wanted her children, he would've had many opportunities to snatch them.

Cold comfort. Delivered with flat practicality.

It was the way a good agent measured a situation. He was the best for this sort of operation. The very, very best.

They toured the five-level complex, viewing the varieties of rare birds and reptiles and mammals. As they traveled along moving belts and ramped bridges, Valerie and Michael kept their eyes peeled for Alexander. This seemed like the perfect setting for a meet. It would be a huge chore to keep track of them in this tourist magnet. But there was no sign of the controller.

Valerie wondered just how much of the children Michael would be able to take. The twins were full of questions about all the different creatures and their habitats. They tugged at his sleeves and fingers, pushing him one way, then the other. Stephanie kept brushing into his solid shoulder with a wispy smile of apology.

It was a miracle he hadn't reached his limit yet. Or had he? Michael had to be stretched well beyond his regular tolerance levels, with the clinging, the invasion questions, the con job. So why was he going the extra mile?

To prove he was a better man than Neal?

Maybe it was a simple case of pride. He'd stormed in on her and didn't want to retreat a failure.

But he had claimed he was here with her because he really wanted to be.

And it made her lonely heart soar. The man was incorrigible, indifferent to a fault, but he was in so many ways simply irresistible.

The children began to tire after a couple of hours on foot so they settled back in the amphitheater for the thirty-minute program given by the aquarium trainers.

Valerie glanced over the heads of the youngsters ten minutes into the program to gauge Michael's mood. His chiseled profile was indecipherable. What the hell was going on his complicated man's brain? Her dream right from the beginning had been to pierce his shell, really get to know him. But he had dumped her before she'd gotten the chance. Or had he dumped her because she was succeeding at peeling back that hard top layer that kept him separate and alone?

Valerie fingered her smooth russet cap of hair, shaking away the questions. Michael revealed only what he wanted to reveal.

As they rose to leave the theater a short time later, Michael grasped her arm. "We may as well move on out of this place altogether," he murmured into her ear. "Alexander's not here."

Worry creased her lovely features. "Maybe he's having trouble locating us."

He shook his head. "With the flash of credentials, he could be inside their security area, scanning all the cameras, pinning us down in minutes."

She released a shuddering breath. "All of this for nothing."

"The kids are having a great adventure," he argued with a curl to his mouth, inviting her to take a good look. Small hands were tugging at his lightweight tan jacket to reclaim territory, blond heads bobbing for his attention. He didn't understand children, but he understood power. "I'm the hero of the day."

"More like the pliable chump of the day," she teased. "If they ask you to buy them the Baltimore Orioles, you'd better know that they mean more than the bird."

"Very funny." He shot her a sarcastic smile. "But believe me, I won't miss another trick."

Valerie was poised for further explanation, but Michael was already moving on, with two clinging children at his sides and a moony teenager at his back, dreamily clocking the motion of his leopardlike walk.

How could her life have turned entirely upside down in this short span of time?

They stopped for lunch at an Italian restaurant on Light Street and ordered two large pizzas to suit everyone's tastes. The atmosphere was cheery and informal, with wide windows offering brilliant sunshine and a view of the shimmering water.

As Valerie feared, the questions began to flow from the twins about Michael's link to her. She noted that Michael immediately stiffened under their scrutiny. She had the feeling he'd rather track an enemy down a dark London alleyway than confront these two curious youngsters with any personal details.

"Michael and I worked together years ago, before you were born," she told them in simple terms as the waitress was setting the pizza down on the large table.

"That job like Daddy's?" Timmy asked.

Michael waited for the waitress to move on before nod- ding in affirmation.

"We all worked together," Valerie went on to expound as she gave them each a hot, cheesy wedge of the pizza dotted with pepperoni. "Michael was our boss. And the man you met in the store last night, Alexander, was and is Michael's boss."

"You know our daddy," Tammy said. "Just like that old man."

Michael gripped his water glass tightly, taking a long sip. "Yes," he eventually answered.

"He must like you better than us," Timmy mumbled into his pizza.

"He sends us presents," Tammy put in, with their standby description of Neal.

"Yes, I've been along on some of those buying trips," Michael admitted.

Timmy leaned sideways in his chair, until his blond head was tipped into Michael's arm. "Tell him I don't like dolls, okay?"

"That clown he sent last month isn't a doll," Valerie protested. "Not exactly."

"Sure it is!" Timmy lashed back. "They're all crummy old dolls, even if they have a boy head and pants!"

"They're worth a lot of money." Stephanie sought to console them, raising a paper napkin to her nephew's chin.

Timmy leaned into Michael. "I don't care! I can't even touch 'em! They're too frugle."

"Fragile," Valerie corrected softly. "Let's just forget it for the time being. We're having a nice day in the city, and I'm going to buy you new tennis shoes."

The reminder brought fresh smiles to the pair. Michael couldn't help but be intrigued by the spectrum of emotions they could display in just a matter of moments. Excite- ment, frustration, joy, all bound together with a consistent, insatiable curiosity. Their little eyes were perpetually wide with wonder, choked full of innocence and sincerity that he didn't even know existed in the human race.

And they could be a part of him. A mysterious, glorious extension of himself.

As they lingered in the restaurant, hoping for a glimpse of Alexander, Valerie scanned the diners. She noted that there were a few people from the aquarium in the restaurant.

Michael angled his arm over the back of her green vinyl chair. "Noticed them too, haven't you?"

"Yes," she whispered, her green eyes earnest. "The older couple at the table near the rest rooms. And the young man seated in the booth near the entrance."

"Cute, isn't he?" Stephanie chirped with a sip of cola.

"You know him, Steph?" Valerie asked hopefully.

"Normally, you'd be crazed if a guy in his twenties was a friend," she retorted. "But no, I don't know him. Except from the aquarium. He seemed to pop up a lot over there. Do you think he's following us?"

Michael's mouth tightened. "If he is, he's an amateur."

"He's getting up to leave," Valerie noted tensely, fingering her napkin.

"Even a dunce would know we'd tagged him," Michael grunted.

"Gotta go, Uncle Mike," Timmy announced abruptly.

"Go where?"

His eyes fell to his plate and his voice to a mumble. "You know. The potty."

His dark brows jumped with apology. "Oh! Sure."

Valerie noticed the flicker of hesitation in his eyes as Timmy urged him to his feet. He didn't trust her alone for a moment. And she didn't like it. She deserved his faith.

Once the females were alone, Stephanie lunged halfway over the table. "Okay, so what gives with you two?" she asked in an excited gush.

"What do you mean?" she asked with strained levity.

"You know I mean Michael."

Valerie raked her fingers through her hair. "He's my old boss and friend."

"Yes, I remember," Stephanie said rolling her eyes. "That one before Neal. The hundred-hanky one. Little sisters like me aren't totally dense. Even at nine."

"Neither are five-year-olds," Valerie said, casting a significant eye on Tammy. So her family had understood the depth of her pain at the time. Even as a kid, Stephanie hadn't missed a single tear.

Tammy looked up from her pizza with innocent interest. "I'm five."

"We know it," Valerie said, giving her small soft hand a pat. "Finish eating."

"Why is he really back?" Stephanie persisted.

"To help us out," she insisted impatiently. "You saw how it was last night."

Her eyes glittered knowingly. "Boy, oh, boy."

"So you know the issues," she murmured tersely. "You know enough."

"But he didn't realize that you needed help at first," the teen probed with maddening persistence. "He showed up all mad at you."

"Sometimes people start out mad and change their minds."

Stephanie huffed. "Yeah, duh. But what's his game now?"

"When he found out we needed assistance, he cooled off okay?"

"But Kim was there to help. He sent her away. Valerie, you know what I'm getting at. How much of this reunion is acting and how much is real? I mean, Mom and Dad are really going to want to know."

"You are the nosy Warner, Steph. And I resent your attitude. You think it's impossible that I still might attract him. You think there has to be some other explanation."

Stephanie flexed her fingers with a dramatic moan. "He is just so hot. A zillion watts more than your regular dates. You never go out with his type."

"There aren't a lot of hot men to choose from in Ferndale," she said defensively. "Given the chance, I can still do...hot," she claimed with a petulant lift to her chin.

"You?" the girl hooted. "You spend your days in a classroom!"

Valerie's green eyes narrowed to slits as her temper simmered. "Hey, missy, I can do hot or be hot any old time I feel like it!"

"Darn right, baby."

Valerie flinched as Michael's heated affirmation touched her ear. She blushed with embarrassment. He had actually heard that last remark. And he was tapping his temple like he had in the garden, when he said he could imagine her naked any old time he wanted. How could such a pain in the neck cause her so much pleasure everywhere else?

"I feel like we missed something," he said with disappointment as he and Timmy slid back into their chairs.

Stephanie squirmed under his inquisitive look. "Well, I was just wondering about you and Valerie. You seem so mismatched."

Just as he suspected, she'd been challenging Valerie's charms when he'd walked up on them. And was Valerie ever defensive about it. The last thing he wanted to do was make her feel unsure or uncomfortable here in her own world. He wanted to make her feel good. Real good. So good that she couldn't bear to let him go.

Stephanie didn't know what she was saying. How could anyone not see a total fox when looking over Valerie? Sure, she'd grown more conservative with time. But that red wildcat he'd fallen so hard for was still lurking around the edges of her Professor Mom persona. He saw flashes of her old spark time and time again.

He'd been shortsighted to expect her to be the same siren she'd once been. Of course she was bound to settle down, take on her responsibilities. It had to have been extremely tough at first, coming back home with her job and personal life in tatters—not to mention single and pregnant.

Had she known from the start that she was expecting?

Had she let that louse Neal claim the babies, or had she tricked him, too?

Had she actually tricked anyone?

Hell, maybe they weren't his after all!

The questions tumbled over and over through his brain, increasing in number with every orbit. He wanted the answers, but he didn't want to destroy things by getting them. He had to wait for the right opportunity.

They finally moved on toward their last stop of the day, the Comfort Plus shoe shop in the Light Street Mall.

As they walked through the glass-enclosed mall, Stephanie tore her attention away from Michael's lean, corded body to point out her favorite clothing store, Chic City.

"Here's the place I told you about." Stephanie stopped in front of the store's window display to admire a sunsuit of blazing neon green, causing them all to halt in their tracks.

"Maybe another day would be better," Michael strongly suggested.

Stephanie paid his negative words no mind. "You promised, sis. And you know Mom left plenty of money for my needs."

Valerie appreciated Stephanie's point of view. She'd been so preoccupied this past week with her students' final exams that she hadn't paid much attention to her houseguest. And now there were these new, unexpected obstacles invading their quiet routine. She strayed from her contemplative thoughts to Michael who sent her a negative frown. The shoe store was their last possible point of contact and he was edgy to move on.

"There's nothing good in there," Timmy pronounced, with a stomp of his foot. "I don't wanna go."

Tammy extended her lower lip. "Me either, Mama."

"Guess you're outvoted," Michael declared with a glint of triumph.

"Why don't you take the twins up to the shoe store, Michael," Valerie suggested in counterpoint to Stephanie's mortified gasp. "We'll catch up."

"I don't like that idea," he said flatly, his expression sharpening.

She'd seen that look a hundred times while under his command. When he didn't like something one of them did, his eyes sheeted with chrome, his mouth thinned to a blade. How she'd followed his every wish back then, like a playful puppy anxious to please.

He had no way of knowing what pain that particular look now triggered inside her. He did know that she could never go back to being that starry-eyed, lovesick colt that he'd once dumped on. She answered to no one these days. And she was more than capable of taking care of Stephanie and herself in a clothing store for a few minutes.

"Michael," she began on a low, terse note, "I won't let you take over my life again. I won't."

"But this is a mission," he uttered with similar restraints. "And as lovely as you still are, I've found your temper to be the only quality you've managed to keep honed so far."

"That only goes to show how uninformed you really are," she purred. "I'm not half bad on the mat."

He lowered his head, to keep their exchange private. "Mat or mattress, what's the difference? I'd say we settled this question in the bedroom last night, butterfly. When I pinned your tush to the bed and spread your little wings—"

"I knew it was you, fool!" she shot back. "Ever think that maybe I held back on purpose?"

His chuckling reply was low and infuriating.

"Okay, so you won that tussle hands down," she mumbled. "But I've kept up on my defense skills. An edge I feel every woman owes herself. Besides, there is no sign of the man or the older couple. I think we overreacted."

"I say we stick together," he cut in sharply, eyeing the fidgeting kids uncomfortably. "Keep our defenses high."

Her eyes gleamed with new realization. "You're just chicken."

His features hardened. "Of what?"

Her eyes slanted down to the twins. "Of being conned again."

"That's ridiculous!"

He was bluffing. It was written right across his face like a big SOS. They scared him to death and he didn't want to handle them alone.

She pursed her lips. "I'm sure if you're on alert, they won't get the drop on you again."

"You really think I can't—" He broke off in a growl. "You've got fifteen minutes." He turned on the heel of his boot, clasping the small eager hands reaching for his.

"The shoes are a special order, so they're holding them for me," she called to the broad expanse of his back.

"Under your name or the children's?" he inquired evenly.

"Warner. Valerie Warner." With that saucy reply, she grabbed her sister's elbow and steered her into Chic City.

The funky store was geared for the teenage crowd, with loud, thumping music and wild, colorful outfits. Valerie scanned the shop for any oddball customers as Stephanie began to make selections from the jammed racks and shelves. Most of the shoppers were clusters of young girls, giggling among themselves.

They were in the shop for a good five minutes when she saw him again, the young man who had seemed to be on their tail all day long. Michael would have a fit when he found out they'd been followed.

If only she could solve this part of the puzzle herself. Then he couldn't call her incompetent.

For as mixed as her emotions were concerning Michael, she wanted his respect, his affirmation that she was indeed still on her game.

With store security being pretty tight back in the fitting area, Valerie felt it was the best place for Stephanie. Valerie grabbed a match to the neon suit Stephanie had admired in the window and urged her sister to take it to a stall along with her other selections, as her special treat. Satisfied that Stephanie would be preoccupied for a little while, Valerie began to stalk her stalker through the cramped, crowded shop.

Her heart picked up a tempo to match the store's thumping music as she closed in to study him. He was in his early twenties. He had no distinctive features really, aside from a large mustache. His hair was curly and black and his height and weight were average.

Their gazes connected for a long, drilling moment. Her green mother-hen eyes, full of fierce frustration over what was happening to her family, stabbed his deep brown ones, widening in surprise. Clearly, he hadn't been expecting her to make the first move. It gave her added courage. She advanced on him, pent-up anger propelling her forward.

He was so focused on her approach that he didn't notice a young customer coming up on his blind side with an armload of clothing. She barreled right into him full tilt. They both did a teeter in the honeycomb of racks.

"Hey!" The girl's yelp was theatrical, but she was agile enough to right herself. Against the man's chest.

With a grunt he lurched into a circular rod full of summer blouses. He reached out for the chrome tubing in an effort to steady himself and would've done so if Valerie hadn't rushed up to extend a foot beneath the heap of falling blouses to drive him to the floor.

It all happened within a matter of seconds. He floundered and he was down—with her foot pressed firmly into his biceps. She grabbed his wrist, swiftly dropping a blouse over her shoe so that it appeared that she was trying to help him up.

Naturally, the incident had attracted some attention.

"Oh, let me help you, sir," she oozed, digging her heel into his muscle. He was strong, she realized with a measure of trepidation. But if he decided to bring her down, he wasn't going to make it out of the mall. Not with uniformed security people strolling just outside the storefront.

A teenage clerk with frizzy black hair and sparrow legs came scurrying over.

"He's just a little dizzy," Valerie hastily ad-libbed, squeezing his wrist harder. "I'm just taking his pulse."

"Maybe we should call for aid," the clerk suggested.

"No, thank you," he croaked. "Just give me a minute."

Valerie said a silent prayer of thanks. Truce was written all over his face.

"I was told you'd be easy to approach," he complained, struggling to sit up.

She pressed her foot deeper into his chest muscle. "Don't move."

"This isn't necessary. I assure you I'm a businessman," he said with surprising modulation.

"You've been following us around," she accused in fierce undertone. "You could've approached me two hours ago, if you'd wanted to."

"I've been hoping to get you alone. To warn you."

She arched a thin russet brow. "About what?"

"About a traitor close to you," he explained quietly, craning his neck to look around.

"Looking for Hawkes, I take it."

"Yes. I'm taking a chance talking to you at all."

"I've had a hard couple days, mister," she said grimly. "What are you getting at?"

"I'm only doing my job." He gritted his teeth as her foot gave him a prod. "There's a male agent from Cornerstone who's been doing some dirty dealing."

"Who?"

"I don't know yet," he insisted. "Now let me up. I have instructions not to hurt you, but I am capable of tossing you across the room."

She decided it would be wise to step back. He wasted no time rising smoothly to his feet.

"Instructions from whom?" she prodded.

"It's not my place to say. Just watch your back." With a nod, he took long strides for the exit.

Valerie let him go without a fuss. He'd gone to a lot of trouble to speak to her, and he could've hurt her if he wanted to.

So he had been following them. He'd remained in the background till he could give her that disturbing message. It was the last thing she wanted to hear, of course, that any man from Cornerstone could be acting against her. There were only three males in question. Alexander, Neal and Michael Hawkes himself. She shook her head in forceful denial. None of them would harm her. They wouldn't!

Valerie noted that Stephanie had stepped up to the cash register with a sinful amount of clothing. Valerie swiftly moved up behind her.

"You try all that stuff on?" she asked.

"No, but it'll be fine. The last of the secret agents," the teen turned to goad softly in her ear. "They were chattering on in the dressing room about some woman tripping a guy. I knew it had to be you."

"It was that same man," she related urgently. "So if you ever catch a glimpse of him again—anywhere, anytime—let me know."

Stephanie intently studied her face. "What did he do? What did he say?"

"Nothing I really understand," she said with a forced smile. It would serve no purpose to alarm Stephanie with his message. Or to alert Michael just yet. Not that Michael could ever harm them. Not deliberately. Not at all!

But Valerie couldn't suppress the maternal fear creeping up her spine. The twins were all right, of course. But she just had to see them. She made a wild grab for Stephanie and her purchases and raced for the exit.

Chapter Six

"These shoes aren't colored!"

Seated in the shoe store with her arms folded across her chest, Tammy looked like a discontented pigtailed Cinderella. The young male clerk seated on a stool at her feet reddened. "But your mother specifically ordered these. Snow white canvas. With supportive arch."

Michael hovered overhead, with one eye on Timmy, at a round rotating display, and the other on the petulant Tammy, who looked more and more like her mother by the minute.

"Hey, Tim, c'mere."

Timmy's freckled nose wrinkled. "Why, Uncle Mike?"

"Because—" Michael's dark head snapped back to the squealing Tammy.

"He's tickling my feet, Uncle Mike! Make him stop it right now!"

"No, sir," the clerk sputtered beneath the towering man, attempting to capture Tammy's ankle. "Just trying to make a fit."

Michael gritted his teeth. Val had done this to him on purpose. To knock him off his high horse. Or perhaps to force his surrender. But he wouldn't give in. He wouldn't storm away from these infuriating miniatures, no matter how baffling and infuriating they became.

"Tim," he repeated firmly. "Come over here and try on your shoes."

Timmy trotted over to the row of hard vinyl chairs and plopped down next to his sister. "Look, Tammy," he said excitedly, waving a sandal in her face. "I found one with the toe cut off!"

Tammy grabbed the sandal and leapt up on her chair to gain height. "Look, Uncle Mike! Red and blue and yellow and a holey toe!"

Michael snatched the bright sandal and pointed to the chair. "Sit down!"

"I wanna see my toes when I'm walkin'," she informed him in exasperated singsong as she obeyed his command. "I want to wiggle my toes."

"In colored shoes," Timmy concurred with a firm nod to his blond head. "Primary colors."

"I don't like these tennies," Tammy sulked. But she did inch her foot back at the clerk under Michael's tight-lipped look.

As the clerk struggled to fit and lace the shoes, a man appeared in the doorway behind the cash register. Michael sized him up as he approached in a fluid, businesslike way. His hair was a rinsed black and combed back off his head, the color and style far too severe for his sixtyish age. He was dressed in a dark gabardine suit and white shirt, a red tie slashing the center of his chest. His tag read "manager."

"Oh, Mr. Withers." The clerk gulped as he stared up at his superior.

"Is there a problem, Robert?"

"No!" The clerk swiveled on his stool to peer up at Michael. "This is a manager from the home office. He's just doing a spot check on our store. There's no problem here, is there, sir?"

"No indeed," Michael agreed smoothly, rocking on the heels of his snakeskin boots.

Mr. Withers put a hand on the employee's shoulder. "Just the same, I'll take over this sale."

"But—"

"The commission will go to you, of course. And the stockroom is in dire need of your organizational skills."

The young man reluctantly rose from the stool. Mr. Withers swept down into his place. "So, children, what is all this ruckus about?"

Timmy leaned forward in his chair and peered at the manager. "Hey, we know you." He turned to confer with his sister. "The man from the grocery store. Right, Tam?"

Tammy crinkled her round little face for a closer look. "He painted his hair all black. Why'd you do that, mister?"

Michael leaned over Alexander's crouched form. "Can't even fool the kiddies anymore."

"I imagine you're finding that they're the toughest ones to fool," Alexander remarked with a plastic salesclerk smile. "Where's Valerie?"

"In a place known as Chic City."

"Is that wise?"

"She assures me that she is still quite capable of taking care of herself."

"Ah, I thought she might feel that way. Leaving Kim in place would've been wiser. A far more cordial mix."

Michael set his hands on his lean hips with a mean look. "I'm plenty cordial."

Alexander's smile was wry. "Hmm, yes."

He turned his back to the twins in order to shield them from his harsh words. "And I don't appreciate the scam you pulled on me last night. I want an explanation."

"In due time," Alexander said smoothly.

But Michael could see the trepidation in his eyes. Even Alexander didn't care to deal with his best agent when he was about to snap.

"This your store, mister?" Tammy chirped in interruption.

"No, just helping out for today," he replied mildly.

"Then you can tell Uncle Mike all about the shoes with the cutoff toes," Timmy urged with a grin to his sister.

Alexander rose from the stool to Hawkes's level. "Uncle Mike, is it? That was quick work."

Michael cleared his throat with an uncomfortable growling noise.

Alexander looked down at Timmy, struggling with his own pair of sneakers. "You have those on the wrong feet, son."

His small mouth dropped open. "Okay. Trade with me, Tam."

"No, he means you have your left and right shoes confused," Michael hastened to explain.

"Oh." With a shrug the child unlaced the shoes.

"Amazing how they always think in terms of two," Michael remarked.

"Yes, they are an intriguing little pair," Alexander agreed. "And how fortunate to have a lookalike always looking out for you. The way you and Neal were in the early years." Once the twins were properly fitted, he directed them to a full-length mirror against the wall.

"You shouldn't have gone to such lengths to keep me out of this," Michael muttered, his voice brittle with betrayal.

"Just trying to serve Valerie's needs the best way I know how," he claimed, his voice lanced with regret. "She discussed options, and you weren't one of them."

"I see."

"It's my guess she doesn't even suspect you could be their father," Alexander went on.

Michael jabbed a finger to his chest. "But I had a right to know. You should've told me."

"It's not like I've known for years, Michael. I discovered the fact only yesterday."

"And decided you'd play god and keep me away."

"She didn't want you or Neal. She wanted Kim."

"Still—"

"Still the mission should be your first priority," the older man said sternly under his breath. "There'll be plenty of time to hash out the rest."

Michael nodded, running a hand through his short brown hair. Alexander was right. First he would focus on keeping her safe, then he would focus on keeping her. "Have you come up with anything?"

The controller smirked with pride. "Oh, yes. It seems that Valerie's last mission is the one which has come back to haunt her."

"Prudence Manders." Michael pulled a grim smile. Great. He was trying to mend fences with Valerie and they were going to be forced to reexamine their time in Cancún under a microscope. He wasn't in the habit of looking back on his personal choices, wondering how he could have done things better. Now there was no chance of simply moving on anymore without a heart-wrenching exploration of what had happened between them.

The idea of Valerie wrenching his heart had him shuddering with apprehension.

"The gold pin is a promotional gimmick of Prudence's," Alexander went on to explain. "Seems she's on the verge of opening some sort of a resort clinic on Zapata, the island where she was held captive. The place is called Chapel Renew. It's especially for celebrity teenagers who have troubled personal lives."

Michael expressed surprise as he thought back on all the research he'd done on the immature television star before the rescue. She seemed like the type that would burn hot, then fizzle out. Apparently he'd been wrong. She'd come around from the hands of kidnappers, however."

"It didn't occur to us to examine the Manders file. Not at first. Poor Kim had profiled a lengthy list of possibilities before I managed to track the pin. But it was the middle of the night, and results are harder to come by.''

"You never know how these things are going to fall," Michael agreed. "It's inconceivable that Prudence would want to listen in on Valerie after all this time."

"That is a puzzler," Alexander mused, turning over the colorful sandal in his hands. "It always seemed a mistake not to track down her kidnappers, but it was the way the Manders girl wanted it. She was so shook up at the time, that Valerie urged me to respect her wishes and cut bait."

"We all felt the job was only half done."

"Neal called in from Dallas this morning," he went on conversationally. "Still on assignment there, you know. Wanted to see how Valerie and the children were doing. Seemed genuinely concerned."

"Genuinely curious is probably more like it," Michael muttered. "He's been scamming us with that devoted ex-husband routine of his."

"Valerie told me as much last night," he confessed.

"He doesn't care a whit about them. Hell, maybe he has doubts about the kids' paternity, too."

Michael swallowed back his fury. It was bad enough that Neal had deliberately worked to keep him away from Val. But he would hate to think that Neal had deliberately kept him away from his own children. Of course at this point it was all conjecture.

Alexander's look was pensive. "Has Neal ever met your brother? Would he have any way of knowing just how strong the resemblance is?"

"Maybe years ago. I don't remember for sure. In any case, he doesn't care about that family," Michael stubbornly maintained. "Valerie made that quite clear. So did the kids."

"Maybe he's just expressed himself poorly to everyone since the divorce, including Valerie. He may have side-stepped involvement in this situation because he knew Valerie would turn him down."

"He should be ashamed!" Michael shot back. "What kind of coward makes a commitment, then waltzes away? At least I knew I couldn't make it work."

Alexander expressed surprise over Michael's uncharacteristic flash of emotion. "Couldn't make it work," he repeated with inflection on the past tense. "What about now, Michael? Just how involved do you think you want to become in this domestic situation?"

"I don't know," he blurted out honestly, leveling a keen eye on his little charges, hopping up and down in front of a floor mirror several feet away.

"Some interest would be natural," Alexander gave him. "The chance to play house with a lovely ex-lover and those two delightful children. It's a slice of life you've never experienced before."

Michael could easily read between Alexander's lines: "Satisfy your desires, your curiosity, and get back to the business you're so suited for." The guiding hand of Control. He certainly had honed Hawkes in his own image, detached and self-serving.

"We really don't know how Neal feels about his family, not for certain," Alexander reiterated. "But it does appear that he's exaggerated his role on the home front. Surely you understand his ego. Neither one of you likes to admit weakness or defeat." His tone was wistful and stern, as though lamenting over his two roustabout "sons."

Michael's eyes narrowed. "Well, Valerie's welfare is most important here."

"Indeed. It would be a big disservice for you to shake up her home, the relationship she does have with Neal, then walk away from it all when the old rambling itch overtakes you."

Michael would never do anything so rash. It was why he was trying to be so damn cautious.

"Did you brief Neal on the Manders angle?" Michael asked, anxious to shift back to the safer territory of the mission.

"Yes, I brought him up to speed. He's puzzled, as well. Which reminds me, I have a printout for you, with all the info we could scrape together." Just as he was passing the folded sheet to Hawkes, the twins stomped back across the carpet.

"I don't like these," Tammy complained, extending her lower lip.

"We want to watch our toes when we're walkin'," Timmy explained.

"Quit smirking," Michael hissed in the older man's ear. "And help me out of this mess! I have to make them understand about the shoes. They're special order. With arches!"

"Why not buy them both kinds?" Alexander suggested mildly. "That will make everyone happy, will it not?"

Michael slapped him on the back. "Brilliant."

As Alexander was ringing up their purchases, an almost breathless Valerie entered the store, with Stephanie and their sacks in tow.

The twins rushed up, pulling her to the cash register. "Look, Mama, it's your friend," Tammy whispered with a crafty look. "But it's a secret game."

At the sight of her children safe and sound, Valerie's tense green gaze lit up and she breathed for what seemed like hours. But of course the twins were fine. She knew they were in safe hands. Michael could never do them harm. Not deliberately, anyway.

She felt a twinge of guilt over not trusting him completely for the short amount of time it took to run the distance between the two stores. But she couldn't help herself. The idea of letting someone else in—especially the man who had hurt her the most—seemed foolhardy and risky.

Michael watched the play of relief and apprehension on her face. She was probably happy to see Alexander, but still steaming over his overprotective move. He'd been so difficult about letting her loose for those few minutes. And apparently nothing had happened. Both ladies were still in one piece. He sauntered over to the register with new modesty, while Alexander briefly explained that they'd traced the pin to Prudence and that Cornerstone would be seeing her through the situation.

"So, is everything taken care of, Uncle Mike?" Valerie queried on a mischievous note.

"Arches are in the box, as are rainbow-colored sandals," he smoothly replied.

"He shops nice," Tammy cooed, giving Michael's arm a pat.

"Gee, they're usually a couple of little monsters in this store," Stephanie blurted out in wonder.

"All in the technique," Michael said with a dash of pride. "They cooperated fully, once I agreed to the extra purchase. Rewarding people in advance often inspires them to behave their very best." He shot Valerie a look, as if to be sure she picked up on the innuendo.

She did.

As remote as he could be, expressing his amorousness had never been a problem. Valerie flushed under his branding look, quickly busying herself with the children and the packages. What had he said this morning? Something about "taming the bad boy true"? Did he really believe she would attempt such a thing? Did he want her to? The task and its sensuous implications sent a tingle down her spine.

And now, after her collision with their stalker, she wasn't even sure if she should be trusting him.

But she so wanted to believe he was sincere. And her instincts were giving her the green light. Foolish needs were surfacing, too; the yearning for his approval, his interest, his affection.

She knew such fancies could be self-destructive. Her offers of hearth and home weren't a strong enough lure to turn him around the first time. And he'd been absent for six long years, without a word of contact.

Her emotions churned in contradiction.

Attraction and irritation.

Faith and suspicion.

Thankfully Kim and Alexander had made some progress on the case. She now knew Prudence Manders was spying on her. Apparently she'd sent someone from her Chapel Renew organization to bug her house and presumably the man to warn her today. His ineptness led her to believe that he'd been the one who'd accidentally dropped the pin in her kitchen.

There were so many nagging questions left; questions only one woman could answer—Prudence Manders.

"I CAN'T BELIEVE Prudence's nerve!"

Valerie made the proclamation later on that night, in the privacy of her own bedroom. Stephanie and the children were fast asleep and she and Michael were hashing out the day's events. Michael was lounging in a ruffled chintz chair near the window, watching her tirade with open disapproval. She knew what he was thinking, that she was leading with her heart rather than her head. But she couldn't help herself. Her patience was spent, taken over by feelings of anger and betrayal concerning Prudence. After being helped by Valerie through the toughest of times, the actress was returning the favor six years later by scaring the life out of her, by eavesdropping on her. Then she'd sent a minion to caution Valerie. What could that starlet be up to?

"I helped her, you know," Valerie went on. "Helped her put the pieces together after the rescue, so she could return to her show! And it saved her skin. She continued with 'Stepfamily Robinson' for another few years. Nobody ever found out about her wild personal life or the kidnapping attempt. She faded from the spotlight with a bundle of cash and the respect of her fans!''

"I understand your outrage over this invasion of privacy," he quietly acquiesced. "But you've got to keep a cool head."

Michael remembered that time after the mission only too well. From subjective and objective points of view. Valerie was out of his life from the moment the helicopter had deposited Prudence and his team back in Maryland. Per her request, she'd been promptly transferred to desk duty, her first assignment being to help see Prudence through her emotional crisis. It was the only period of time in his whole career that he'd avoided Cornerstone headquarters. Then in a flurry of weeks she and Neal had eloped. Then she'd announced her pregnancy. Then she'd disappeared from the scene to await the birth of her babies.

This turn of loyalties on Prudence's part didn't make sense. Everyone in their company knew just how special Valerie had been to Prudence. How heavily Prudence had come to rely on her. Valerie had seen the epilogue through on her own while the rest of them went on to other assignments.

That just might be key issue now. Valerie had been the only Cornerstone operative in contact with Prudence after the mission, the person in whom the actress confided.

"I'd like to go down to the kitchen right now and give her a piece of my mind into one of her crummy bugs!" Valerie raved on.

Michael recognized that wild-eyed look. Sea green eyes, churning troubled waters. Val was capable of anything when she reached this frenzied level—slapping him, quitting him. He couldn't bear either.

"We've gone to a bit of exertion to set up this charade and pretend that we don't know about the surveillance," he swiftly reasoned.

"I know!" Folding her arms across her chest, she paused to think. "But that was when the threat was perhaps very tangible trouble and not some troubled rich girl with a chip on her shoulder."

"This sure doesn't sound like the diligent psychologist who served on my team," he observed, hoping to reach her professional sensibilities.

Valerie's scowl turned thoughtful. "You're right, of course. It's the mother hen in me blowing off steam. True, telling her off over her own device might not get us any answers. But it would feel damn good."

Michael shifted uncomfortably in his chair. He was in the habit of playing with complacent women and working with obedient ones. It made duels like this one far and few between.

"I won't go on living this way," she said. "Prudence's eavesdropping days are over."

Michael raised his palms to halt her tirade. "How about a compromise? You agree not to chastise her over the listening system, and I'll disconnect it. That way, they may think it's just some technical problem. And we'll have some time to decide how we're going to proceed."

"All right."

He got to his feet. "I'll take care of it right now. On one condition. That you go in there," he said, his finger pointing in the direction of the master bath. "Fill the tub and take a soak. Relax. Study Prudence's motives."

"Now? In the middle of everything?"

He closed in the space between them and grasped her forearms. "Trust me, please."

A silence filled the air for a brief moment as Valerie struggled with her options. "All right. I'll—I'll take some downtime. Think things through."

True to his word, Michael went about his chore downstairs, methodically using the sensor left behind by Kim to double-check the placement of the listening devices. They weren't even top-of-the-line ones, he judged, as he twisted them into junk. Prudence had hired some help, but it wasn't anyone nearly as dangerous as he was himself.

It annoyed him that that spoiled-brat actress had frightened Valerie so and put Cornerstone on red alert. Of course, she'd be a woman now. Around twenty-three. The whys of the case buzzed around him like a swarm of angry mosquitoes. He'd be damned if he'd let that mixed-up kid get the best of them!

Michael couldn't get beyond the idea that perhaps Prudence had confided something to Valerie during their therapy sessions after the rescue. It would explain why she'd targeted Valerie. According to both Valerie and Alexander's report, Prudence had managed to hang on to the sterling reputation that the producers had honed for her. The success of Chapel Renew was leaning heavily on the fact that Prudence was a sterling example of a stable superstar reaching out to help less fortunate celebrities.

What a boost to her fading fame! Alexander's report had filled in many blanks. Apparently like many actresses before her, Prudence hadn't been able to make the transition from young pixie to sultry leading lady. Now her career was taking fresh direction with Chapel Renew. She'd always been loved by her public, but now she was garnering respect, as well. She was slotted for talk shows, she was writing some sort of healing book for all troubled teenagers. The grand opening of the clinic was tomorrow night, and it would undoubtedly be splashed across the national news.

But nowhere was there a hint that she'd had problems herself. Her new image was as phony as her old one, with perhaps a higher polish on the surface. Somehow, for some reason, she now considered Valerie a threat to her well-being. Only Valerie could decipher that part of the mystery.

VALERIE FOUND LITTLE comfort in her soak. Slipping into the steamy water was giving her a chance to think, but it only dredged up the frustrating tangles of the past and present. Prudence's case had never rested in her mind. It hadn't found closure as most of the others had. Yesterday's questions remained unanswered. The poor girl had no idea who had kidnapped her, nor did the Cornerstone Group. Presumably the motive had been money, but since the rescue was a success and the ransom drop was never arranged, the party behind the plot was never identified.

The memories hadn't stopped there. Valerie tried to stem the flow but failed miserably. She lolled in the warm water, reliving her breakoff from the company, her marriage to Neal, her pregnancy. It was possible to separate the rescue mission from her romantic triangle with Michael and Neal.

Why did this hopeless tangle have to hit her now, when her life was finally in order? Her job at the college was well-paying and satisfying. Her children were becoming more self-sufficient by the day, finally capable of communicating in a most delightful way.

Valerie emerged from the bathroom thirty minutes later to find Michael again seated by the window, so invitingly masculine in her frilly, little reading chair. She gave the sash of her white terry robe a tug under his frank, lazy appraisal. Desire danced in his eyes as he assessed her robe and its contents. Already agitated, she couldn't deny the knot of excitement twisting in her belly.

She was in her bedroom with an old lover who had taken her across the galaxy with his seductive skills. He was the kind of dynamite man every woman hoped to find under her covers one lucky night. All the passions he quelled in everyday living exploded in the bedroom.

He would be the perfect partner.

If one could spend a lifetime in bed.

How many times had her fantasies started with just this sort of scene? His huge body lounging in these cozy quarters, watching her parade around in a silky scrap of this or that.

In her make-believe world he was totally committed to her with a wide open heart. And he was rooted solidly in her life, because he could never bear to let go of her again.

What a silly romantic fool she was! Standing here like a nervous bride, wanting to believe in him all over again. He was trying so hard to do the right thing by them. But surely he could only compromise up to a point in the best of times.

"You keep your end of the bargain?" she asked, her voice quaking slightly.

"Yup. You can make all the noise you want. In privacy."

Slashes of red crossed her cheeks under his sexy look of invitation.

Valerie's eyes grew to saucers. "I know what you're thinking, Michael," she cautioned, her voice off-key.

"Can't blame me for thinking about that a little bit. But I do want to talk. Sit down, please."

She perched on the edge of the mattress, eyeing him guardedly. "You want to know what Prudence confided in me, don't you?"

He clasped his hands together between his knees and leaned forward, meeting her troubled eyes squarely. "Is there anything that might be haunting her now? Anything that could jeopardize her Chapel Renew project?"

"I don't think so. And even if she did tell me things, it's all confidential. She should know I'd never betray her."

"This girl has been sold out before," he reminded her. "Treated like an asset. Why, her own parents were using her as an automatic cash machine before she pushed them away."

Valerie nodded. "Well, yes. But I don't feel free to discuss the private things she told me."

"She is spying on you, Val!"

"That doesn't give me the right to sell her out," she argued. "And I imagine you already know everything I know.

The situation with her greedy, dysfunctional parents. The fact that producers were far more concerned about her clean image than they were about her. She mainly needed comfort, reinforcement.''

"I wonder if she knows that you were the only one who really cared about her in the whole messed-up rescue," Michael grumbled on a gentler note.

Valerie lifted her slender shoulders beneath the thick terry, inadvertently revealing a glimpse of creamy breast with the movement. He wanted to reach out, slip his fingers between her lapels and stroke her softness. She was so distracting.

"It was my function to care," she said, wrapped up in her own anger. "Alexander hired me with that specific duty in mind, to delve into motivation, make second guesses. I hope I didn't let anyone down along the way—but especially not Prudence. For all her privileges, she was one unhappy girl."

Michael released a long held sigh. What she said was true. She'd simply done her job. And he was guilty of sometimes taking that for granted while she was under his domain.

But how his appreciation for her had deepened once she'd yanked herself from his life. How he wanted her to care for him again in that warm, encompassing way of hers.

"I believe you, Val. But I wonder if you could be missing something, one small thing that has been magnified in her mind—"

"Face it, our lives don't intersect at all! This is nonsense!"

"Think harder!" he cut in sharply. "She's after you, woman!"

"Damn you, Hawkes!" she huffed. "If I say that Prudence didn't reveal anything else, believe it!"

He nodded mutely. "I'm sorry. I can do better."

She gulped back the rest of her lecture. "You can?"

He flashed her a sheepish look as she forced him into a corner. "You know what a hotshot I am," he began on a note of reluctance. "But coming into your world has really been an education. I was wrong to charge forward like Rambo, intent on proving you inept. You still can take care of yourself and your own." He pressed his lips together, studying his hands. "I have faith in you. No matter how impatient I get, how demanding, please remember that."

Valerie couldn't believe what she was hearing, couldn't believe the change in him over the past two days. With painstaking effort he'd tried to fulfill her laundry list of conditions. He'd given up his gun, humored her children, slept in her crummy sofa bed. All hopeful signs that in his own way he was trying to meet her halfway. She could only imagine the beating his protective armor was taking.

But why?

There had to be a goal. Could Michael actually be trying to make it in her world? Could he be hoping for a future here with her?

She thrilled at the thought—at the same time as she was consumed by guilt. She should never have kept what happened at the mall from him. He'd finally succumbed to her in humility—after six long years of waiting—on the very day that she'd kept her first secret from him, shown a lack of trust in him.

This posed a new threat to their renewed merging, she realized with dismay. If she had told him about the man right away, he'd know that she didn't suspect him. But she hadn't. For a moment she had been suspicious and frightened.

In hindsight, she realized that she mishandled it all, with the man, then with Michael. That man had gotten away far too easily. Michael would've gotten the truth out of him, whereas all she'd gotten was the short message he'd wanted to deliver. He probably had known everything they needed to know—and she let him walk off.

She should've told Hawkes right away, endured his annoyance, gotten it over with. But she hadn't. With the passing hours the blunder had grown in outrageous proportion. Now it was too late. She couldn't tell him at all anymore.

"So what do you say, Val?" he asked with husky uncertainty. "Do you understand? Do you forgive me?"

Valerie averted his gaze, twisting her hands in her lap. "You've always been way too hard on yourself. There's nothing to forgive. We're just from separate worlds, trying to manage the best we can."

He took a slow breath, trying to steady his jangling system. Some men expressed such thoughts all the time—but it had taken all he had to risk her rejection that way.

There was a shadowed reluctance in her small smile... What was she thinking?

He was so damn close, she inwardly lamented. His eyes were trained on her every facial muscle, to see which would twitch.

He had to be suspecting that she was holding something back.

What did she do now? Hoping for some breathing space, she stood up. He anticipated the movement and jumped to his feet as well. In a flash his hands were squeezing her forearms, his face was in hers, angrily searching for an answer.

"Don't!" she cried out in dismay.

"Don't care? Don't pry? Don't stay?" He shook her slightly, as though trying to jiggle loose the truth. "Tell me what's going on in your head. Do you still hate me for turning you down?"

"You don't understand—"

"Talk to me!"

"All right, all right. Just give me a chance."

He didn't have a second to spare, his nerves were so frazzled. But he reluctantly loosened his grip a little.

"I wasn't a crack agent at all today," she confessed in a small voice. "I don't deserve all your praise."

This was business? His gaze delved into hers with a piercing look that wouldn't let go. "What happened?"

"That young guy in his twenties didn't vanish like I thought he had," she explained in a rush. "He approached me in Chic City."

His hands skimmed her shoulders over her robe. "What did he do to you?"

"Nothing, really. He tripped and fell. He wasn't very smooth—"

"Smart enough to avoid tangling with me, though," he muttered with new understanding. "No wonder he lingered behind all those hours. He wanted to get you alone."

"Yes."

"So what did he say?"

She blinked, pressing her lips together. This was where it was going to get real touchy. "Michael, I don't want you to misunderstand—"

"Give me the chance to understand!" he snapped impatiently.

"He warned me to watch out for a male Cornerstone agent."

He muttered oaths under his breath. This was business, but it was a fateful roundabout revenge, too. She suspected him! He'd been laying it all on the line for her in the best way he knew how and she was wondering if he was the enemy!

"I should've told you right off—"

"You couldn't take that risk. Why, I might be the bad guy, right?"

"Wrong!" she cried back, blinking back the tears. "I didn't want to hear you say 'I told you so.'"

Michael jerked her close with a roar. "You suspected me, didn't you?"

She pressed her fingers to her temples. "No! I didn't know what to think!"

"Well, think again, because it isn't me!" He released her so quickly she stumbled back.

"I panicked," she confessed, righting herself against the nightstand. "It all happened so fast, I tried to get more information out of him, but he fled. I'm only telling you now because your compliments have made me feel ashamed. I'm not a crack agent anymore. I blundered with some key information. But I do want your trust and respect, Michael," she added on a plea. "It really does mean a lot to me."

"Has it occurred to you that Prudence sent that message to drive a wedge between us?" he demanded tersely. "Because she'd like to see me out of here, to see you alone and vulnerable again? Have you thought of that?"

"Yes. But he also could've been telling the truth. Now that we know which mission it is, we know exactly which agents we're dealing with. Naturally I thought of Neal, Alexander right away, but now we can add Manuel from the Mexican side to the list. All three of them actually came in personal contact with Prudence during the rescue."

"Don't forget me."

Wincing under his glare she went on in her own defense. "I believe in you, Michael, but I am confused. You've avoided me for six long years. Suddenly you're back, looking for intimacy."

"I've been aching to come back for the longest time," he angrily admitted.

"Why now, during this trauma?" she pressed. "I've been here forever!"

"Because the trauma brought out the truth. I shot over here in the first place on the excuse of straightening you out. It was just going to be my chance to look at you . . . maybe touch you."

"What made you decide to stay?"

"When I found out that Neal was really out of the picture, I understood that you were really free." *Not to mention that fact that I might be a father.* But he let that go unmentioned. That was for another talk, another time. If ever.

"But we've been divorced for ages!"

"I know," he conceded, staring at the toes of his boots. "But he's kept up the front that you're still close. That you got divorced only because marriage didn't fit his life-style. And of course I figured you'd hate me until the end of time."

Valerie always knew how hard it was for Michael to express his emotions. Now she knew how hard their separation had been for him all these years. As hard as it had been for her.

"I couldn't stay away anymore, Val. I've missed... I haven't been able to match what we...." He groaned in despair, running his hands through his thick thatch of hair. "Valerie, the very idea that you might think I could ever harm you kills me inside."

Chapter Seven

With a muffled cry, Valerie went into his arms. "I never really doubted you, Michael. It's so important that you believe me. Please." She breathed easier as she felt his arms encircling her.

They shared a long, hard hug, then an electric moment of communicating silence.

"I believe you," he murmured, fingering her soft hair. "It had to be a tough situation for you. Trying to prove yourself, only to have that jerk pop up again."

"It wasn't the agent in me that gave me the courage to handle him. It was my terminator maternal instincts."

"Yeah, I'm sure it was," he said with a warm twinkle. "Renegade Mom."

Valerie searched his shimmering blue eyes with a new inquisitive delight. They were an open window to his heart now. He was actually letting her inside. Her pulse quickened at the unspoken promises, the burning desires in their sparkling depths.

"What are you doing?" he asked, blinking in discomfort over her steady gaze.

"Shopping, savoring."

His lips curled provocatively. "So, what do you see?"

"Compassion, tenderness . . . lust."

He fingered the curve of her rich red hair. "Whatever you see, you put there."

"And what are you going to do about it?" she whispered invitingly.

Hawkes shrugged his broad shoulders. The red knit shirt he'd worn on their outing today was pulled taut across his wide, solid chest. Valerie couldn't resist moving her hands over his rippling muscles. The ripple passed clean through her, making her inner thighs quiver in longing. A small sound escaped her as she skimmed the waistband of his jeans.

"Whatever you want," he rasped. "I'm in your hands."

Her expression was wistful. "I don't expect you to think past tonight—I don't think we should even try."

Michael felt a surprising nudge of disappointment over her compliance. "I want you to believe in me all over again, baby," he rasped. "Is there a chance?"

"I'm more careful these days...."

His face fell.

"Let's start with this moment," she suggested gently. "See where it take us. I want you inside me again so badly." She captured his mouth with hers, delving deep and hungrily.

He kissed her back with a low moan. His thirst was about to be quenched. His goal of a half-dozen years about to be met. But an undeniable ache came creeping up his spine....

How could a solitary soldier like him ever keep this nested lady all to himself? It would take emotive action. The civilized scholars she mingled with these days undoubtedly knew all the right words and the right time and place to express them.

But they weren't more sincere, he reminded himself. She'd be married again by now, if even one of them had pushed all the right buttons.

The idea of any other man touching her again was inconceivable. But how could he stop it?

Even if he could say what he felt, she might not buy it. She knew better than anyone how hard he worked to avoid permanency. But this reunion seemed a prophetic twist of fate. He was most likely about to prove himself a windfall father, who was already captivated by the most glorious creature on earth—his childrens' mother.

"I've wanted this for so long," he uttered in ecstasy, kneading her shoulders.

Valerie smiled. Every revelation was an effort, she knew. And he seemed to be enjoying the process, testing his new feelings of affection, allowing them to surface and overtake him. She was flattered that they were centered on her. But she knew better than to dream bigger just yet.

Besides, making love to him tonight was a dynamite beginning. She, too, had found no one comparable.

Her hands moved at the small of his back, pressing their hips together with a wanton thrust. His strong arms swiftly closed around her, drawing her up against him. She couldn't help but tremble as the sheer power of him infused her. With a deep-seated moan of hunger, he buried his face in the curve of her hair. "Oh, baby, I was beginning to wonder if I'd ever get my way. Wondering if I'd ever have the chance to call you baby again."

"Please do, my darling." Grasping his face in her hands, she drew his head down over hers for another kiss. This one was far more urgent and Michael felt it too, for his tongue sliced into her mouth in hot, moist exploration, engaging hers in a tingling tango.

"I've missed you," she confessed on a hard, fast breath.

His eyes flashed with a sensual sheen. "We've wasted so much time."

'We won't waste any more.'

His sturdy body shuddered as her hands tugged at his T shirt, climbing beneath it to comb his matted hair with her fingernails. It was a dream. A happening. A second chance to relive a miracle. And it was all falling into place. Th chemistry and excitement of the previous time was heightened by a mutual caring.

This was what other people felt with their mates all the time, Michael realized.

Perhaps there was hope for him. Twenty-four short hours in this woman's new life and he was coming to an understanding about intimacy.

But the old fears continued to tap at the pane shielding his subconscious. To put so much in another human's hands still seemed so risky.

Michael had never felt so unprotected, not in all his years as a field agent. But it was understandable. What threat could be more dangerous than the one buried in the pit of his being? Rooted deep within, where a fragile vulnerability hid behind his bad-boy bravado, where memories of Valerie's sweet, pure adoration lingered like a painful wound. No enemy could ever hope to reach so deep.

He made a marked effort to quell the fears, drive them back into the darkness. He continued the loving with renewed energy, showering kisses along her jaw and throat, tasting and nipping in eager exploration.

The reward was worth the struggle with his demons. Miraculously, it was like his first time, with wide-eyed wonderment and a thirst for discovery. An ironic state, considering the fact that he'd gone through the motions of seduction more times than most.

Valerie tipped her head back with a lavish sigh as his mouth went on to cover every inch of her face, stamping his claim with a hot, wet trail.

His hands never stopped moving, skimming over the fabric of her robe, as though trying to guess the contents of an exquisitely wrapped package. Soon his fingers were at the tender flesh of her throat, sliding down the slope of her shoulders, peeling the terry cloth from her skin. The garment fell clear, landing in a heap at her feet.

"Professor..."

Michael stood at arm's length, appraising Valerie's body for the longest moment of her life. Michael's eyes traveled up the length of her legs, the flare of her hips, to her jutting breasts, imprinting every detail in his brain.

He was obviously comparing the past Valerie with the present one, Valerie thought.

She eagerly watched his face, hoping that he liked the changes. Bearing twins and breast-feeding them had left her curves lush and mature.

He liked what he saw, she knew. His lusty grin of approval made her quiver with anticipation.

His mouth quirked in pleasure over raw responses. With all that had changed between them, she was still open and sincere in her lovemaking. He reached out to her with a bolder touch, sliding his palms beneath the undersides of her breasts, measuring their new weightiness against his memory. He closed his eyes, and a low groan of pleasure rumbled in his chest. His hands moved over her rib cage and down her trim waist.

As his thumbs connected at her navel, her thighs quivered and parted.

A rough shudder shook him. He so wanted to be desired and appreciated all over again by this woman.

But more than anything else, he wanted to be unforgettable. He wanted her to feel the urgency that was turning everything he stood for upside down.

His eyes slid over hers with a roguish promise as his hand slipped down over her triangle of hair. Holding her in the crook of his arm, he rubbed his palm over her nest of crisp russet curls with a slow rotating motion.

"Michael!" She cried out in joyful surprise when he plunged a finger into her hot, slick opening. His roughened touch sent tremors through her feminine core, giving her a heavy, heated feeling down low. "It's been so long," she gasped in wondrous pleasure. Valerie set her hands on his shoulders and arched back reveling in his invasion, swimming in ripples of pleasure. She savored the sensations for a while, eventually clasping a stilling hand over his. "You have to catch up." With swift, shaky fingers she began to peel off his clothing.

Michael helped with the disrobing process, eager to feel her softness against his skin. With mighty arms he pulled her close. She wound her arms around his neck and buried her face in the hollow of his shoulder, lavishing in his scent, his feel.

His hardness against her belly was grazing temptation. Her body shook as he cupped her bottom and lifted her completely up off the floor, urging her legs around his waist. His mouth was wet and hot at her ear. "Bedtime."

With a graceful glide he brought them both down on the satin spread. He abruptly withdrew, but only to reach his wallet on the bedside table. He fumbled with it, reaching in a slot for the sheath of protection he kept there.

"Always prepared," she teased.

Michael offered no contest. His reputation preceded him, of course. He couldn't erase his past, only make the future better. "But I never wanted a woman more."

"I believe you, Michael."

With her twinkle-eyed encouragement, he rolled atop her sleek, creamy form, bracing his hands over her head. He hovered over her fragile, luminescent face for a moment, spellbound by the affection and need in her expression. He recognized that look from the previous time, but now he was smart enough to fully appreciate it. She was his light, the only glimmer in his dark, crazy world. He'd come full circle to understand.

If he ever wanted a woman of his own, this was his chance.

"You're thinking way too much," she softly complained, pressing her hips up to his. "Make love to me now."

"Soon, baby, soon." He wanted to make this last, to make it worth the six-year wait. He probed her gently at first, without invading. Even that touch sent electric spirals of pleasure through his entire system. If only they could live on and on in this moment, capture it forever and never come back.

Valerie's hands at his hips held him deeply inside her. She arched in urging, kneading his sinewy buttocks with greedy fingers. He picked up her rhythm and plunged inside her over and over again.

Locked together they merged the past and the present in a fevered rush.

They climaxed rapidly and thoroughly, with muffled sounds of satisfaction. Then, still entwined with one another, they collapsed together on the mattress.

Valerie closed her eyes, cuddling into the crook of his shoulder.

As hard as she tried to quell her anxieties, the truth of their real, separate worlds eventually crept into her afterglow. The gap between them was even wider than it had been the first time around. It was more than their different backgrounds this time. They weren't even in the same business anymore.

Even if he agreed to a personal commitment, it wouldn't be enough. There would still be his dark, perilous job. He'd still kiss them all goodbye, walk out the door and vanish for weeks at a time. Neal had been distant enough when he'd been making the relatively short commute to Cornerstone's Washington headquarters. There were so many secrets to keep, responsibilities and duties he could never share.

"What are you thinking about?" he wondered, stroking the curve of her hip. "You look way too concerned."

She released a hollow breath. "I think you know, darling. Our different life-styles."

Trepidation flashed through his eyes. "Already?"

"I cannot allow myself to ever get serious with an agent again."

"I don't care to take the fall for any of Neal's mistakes," he forewarned. "I would like to think you could regard me differently."

"Yes, in so many ways you are a different man. And I'll admit that I never loved Neal as thoroughly as a wife should. But all the love in the world wouldn't be enough to make it ever work out. You understand the life, the danger, the covertness involved. I am a mother of two precious children. I won't put them at risk to satisfy my needs. And I won't let them bond with a father figure who could slip off the planet just doing his job."

His throat tightened, causing his voice to croak. "Yes, they should come first." A selfish part of him wanted that coveted spot in her heart. But she was talking sense.

He too, wanted the best for those children. Especially since they might be his.

Again, he wondered if she knew.

She certainly was up-front about putting them first. Keeping their paternity a secret from everyone could fall under that same umbrella of responsible action in her mind.

No matter who fathered those kids, the last thing she wanted for them was a second secret-agent dad.

Valerie soon drifted off in his arms, her warm, gentle breath on his chest. Michael squeezed her close with a fierce possessiveness. He didn't know what he wanted to do about all of this, but he didn't want to pay for Neal's mistakes.

He wasn't Neal, dammit! No matter how much Alexander had tried to press them into the same mold over the years. Michael was a separate man to himself. He would take the rap only for his own blunders.

WHEN SHE AWOKE ONCE again, Michael was emerging from her bathroom, dressed in his jeans, T-shirt and snakeskin boots. She blinked and rubbed her eyes. The attempt to orient herself brought a tender crook to the corners of his mouth.

"May as well go back to sleep," he suggested, reaching for his wallet and keys on the nightstand.

"Where, what..." she trailed off groggily.

"I'm going out to make some travel arrangements."

She stiffened with alertness. He had to mean Mexico. For a brief spell, Valerie had forgotten all about Prudence, the danger, everything.

"I'm going to Zapata with you, you know."

He shrugged, straining to keep his voice casual. "I thought you'd prefer to stay here with the kids. I can handle this alone. Really."

She gave her head an adamant shake. "Oh, no, I intend to see this through. I have to confront her face-to-face."

"Okay, but only if you agree to practice some caution." His tone reflected a blend of sternness and relief. He was glad she was coming—it would mean more time together. But at the same time he was sure she'd be tougher to handle now that she was not a member of his team. "And I will have to be boss," he said. "Just like the old days."

"No problem. I'll get in touch with Kim. I'm sure she can handle the brood while we're away. The twins will be a little put out, but they'll have a familiar face in Stephanie." She struggled to sit up, her expression accusatory. "Good thing I woke up. You'd have made all the arrangements without me."

He leaned over to plant a kiss at her tousled hairline. "I was going to wake you up before I left."

"Oh?"

"I was." His amused smile disappeared as quickly as it had come across his face. He pulled open her nightstand drawer.

Valerie took one look inside, at his gun lying atop her address book, and groaned. "Not this again. Aren't we safe and sound with the security system on?"

"We have to take that warning you got seriously. I hate to consider it, but somebody at Cornerstone might be untrustworthy. There's always that chance. You know it happens in our business."

"Neal is the only one who knows how to crack this—" She cut herself off in midsentence. "You don't think— He couldn't pose a real threat to me, could he?"

"I don't know!" he snapped back, resenting even the scantest amount of faith and hope she might still have in that louse.

"Hey, why can't you just make the plans from my telephone, now that the bugs are neutralized?" she asked. "You staying on would be the ultimate safety precaution...."

The offer was enticing, but he had to refuse. "I want to pick up the tickets tonight, and I want to do some digging in the file room."

"But why?" she asked on a yawn.

Because I want to know more about Neal. I want to know his blood type, his medical history. I want black-and-white proof about those children. The kind of objective proof I've always demanded in everything.

"Michael?" she prodded.

He snapped out of his reverie. "I'm just reaching out for leads, any information that can put us closer to the truth." He leaned over and gave her a pat. "Just keep this gun by your side until I'm safely back in bed."

She made a clucking sound of regret. "I'm afraid it's back to the foldaway in the study for you."

"But I thought I could spend the night now," he said. "All night— Oh, never mind." With a helpless gesture, he moved toward the door.

"Wait!"

He turned on his heel, a glimmer of raw hope in his eyes.

"Would you mind picking up a couple cartons of milk at the convenience store?"

"Is that necessary?"

"If we're going out of town, it is. The kids need three glasses a day."

"All right," he grumbled, flipping open his wallet to count his bills. "But it seems unfair. I feel like a domesticated animal without a domicile."

"Don't be silly," she scoffed. "It's only milk."

"Only milk.... Nobody else would get away with this!"

Valerie watched him exit with a measure of melancholy. It was the sort of territorial response she'd always wanted from him. And now that she had it, she didn't know how they could possibly make it work.

If he'd shown these positive signals the first time around, they might have started building a life together back then, kept their goals streamlined, maybe even had their own children.

Valerie didn't want to change the life she'd built for herself. She just wished there was an easy way to include him in it.

THE CORNERSTONE BUILDING had that middle-of-the-night deserted feel as Hawkes rode the elevator up to the clerical suite. There was the regular skeleton crew seated at the bank of computers. Madge, a plump, middle-aged, brassy blonde with a razor-sharp tongue and years of experience behind her, was the first to spot him.

"Evenin' Hawkes," she greeted cheerfully. "Didn't expect to see you. Considerin' your current assignment," she added with an impish wink.

"As if you're ever far from my thoughts," he intoned.

"With that charming Valerie in your hands?" She snorted in disbelief. "By the way, how is she?"

"Perfect."

And Madge was perfect. She was a friend who'd never suspect him of a thing. He promptly laid out what he needed in airline tickets and hotel reservations.

It took a lot of self-control, but he stood around with a casual air, making small talk for a few minutes. Luckily no one ever expected much banter out of him.

He eventually made the announcement that he wanted access to the file room.

He realized that Madge had the power to ban him. Especially in the middle of the night, when there were no clerks on duty.

"You'd have to dig around on your own, you know," she forewarned.

He made a careless gesture. "Sure, sure. No problem."

Madge made moves to launch her large form out of her chair.

"Just give me the keys, Madge."

She frowned at his extended palm. "It's not procedure."

"It's off-hours," he wheedled, favoring her with a wink this time. "And it would expedite matters. I could do my research, while you get hold of those tickets for me."

"All right. Suit yourself." She dropped the key ring into his hand. "I'll need thirty minutes or so."

That was all he would need, too.

Like the rest of the Cornerstone complex, the huge file room was under twenty-four-hour surveillance. Hawkes kept his demeanor relaxed and loose as he entered, switching on extra lights. He moved between the towering cabinets, extracting a small notebook and pen from the inside pocket of his tan jacket. He didn't imagine that anyone would think twice about discovering him now, or later on videotape, but he did have a method of diversion in mind. He would start in the personnel section, checking out Neal's file, Val's file, plus several more at random, moving from cabinet to cabinet with a consistent level of nonchalant interest.

He was after blood types, health records, anything he could cross-check. It could be as simple as Neal's blood being an incompatible match for the twins. That would be the black-and-white proof he needed.

He began to open drawers, his large, blunt fingertips skimming the labeled file flaps. He was jubilant to find the twins were included in Val's records. There were logs right up until her divorce from Neal. How efficient of Alexander. But Hawkes knew the controller hated to lose her. Despite the bluff Alexander and Kim had run on Michael concerning Val's lagging capabilities, perhaps Alexander held a secret hope that she would return to the fold one day.

It seemed highly unlikely that Alexander would pull a fast one on Valerie or any of them.

But he had tried to keep Hawkes away from Valerie and those children. Alexander was no longer worthy of Michael's unquestioning trust.

Minutes ticked by as Michael painstakingly made bogus inquiries along with the pertinent ones, jotting small notes out of the camera's range. He saved Neal's file for last. One swift perusal down his medical records confirmed that the all-too-common type O-positive blood ran through all their veins. He curled his fist for a brief frustrated moment. Dammit! It had seemed like such a good idea. He scanned the rest of Neal's medical history with a quick, half-interested eye, looking for...

It was there after all. Real paternity proof. Far stronger than blood type.

The truth hit him hard. He felt his gut clench and it was all he could do to remember the surveillance camera trained on his every move.

He slowly closed the folder and returned it to its rightful slot. It took all his self-control not to stop then and there. He pulled several more files and pretended to examine them.

He eventually moved on across the expansive room to the case files, to look up the Prudence Manders mission. He didn't bother with any diversionary tactics here. It would only be natural for him to wonder about any new developments.

He slapped the file down on the cabinet top, slowly paging through its contents. He didn't know what he was looking for, perhaps some slipup, something out of kilter, a person in the wrong place at the wrong time. If Alexander hadn't wanted something made public, he'd have yanked it by now. But there was still the chance of finding some stray fact that could click right.

Fifteen minutes later he had nothing new. Valerie's own reports made for the bulk of the paperwork. The only thing set in his mind was what a superb job she'd done with the actress. He replaced the file and locked things up.

Madge was idly waiting for him when he returned to the clerical area. "Bingo!" she called out, a fleshy arm waving the tickets high above her large hairdo.

"Bingo is right," he agreed.

Chapter Eight

Valerie woke up again around three o'clock in the morning to find the nightstand drawer open and empty. Presumably, Michael was back and asleep on the sofa bed. She decided to double-check.

Dressed in an orange jersey-style nightshirt, she silently glided down the hallway toward the study. The banker's desk lamp was on and the bed was open and rumpled. But the room was empty. She checked the closet, quickly spotting the gun up on the shelf and his clothing hung on the rod.

He was on the loose in those ugly print pajamas, she thought smiling. Well, if he was having a snack, he would have to share it—along with any information he might have come across.

She almost breezed right by him as she padded on toward the staircase. There he sat in the twins' room, on the wooden toy box wedged between their child-size beds. In the glow of the clown lamp's light, he appeared to be carved in stone, with his elbows resting on his thighs, his profile trained on the children.

She bit back a delighted laugh. The paisley sentinel.

"Michael?"

Her whisper startled him. He straightened his spine and his head snapped to the doorway.

"Didn't mean to scare you." She kissed his cheek as she sat down next to him on the cedar chest.

He flashed her a wry smile in the shadows. She'd borne his children without his knowledge or consent, seeped into his very soul with her capacity to nurture—and she didn't mean to scare him?

"They look like bookends, don't they?" she noted in a proud hush.

"Yellow-topped hurricanes," Michael marveled softly.

He'd been studying the two small forms huddled beneath the covers for a good long while. Trying on his new fatherly role for size. Laying claim to them in a private, instinctive, harmless way. It was so easy to do now, as they slept on in solitude.

He couldn't believe the night-and-day difference in them. Sleep had transformed the rambunctious pair into heaven's tiniest angels.

Wispy lashes fanning pudgy, freckled cheeks. Puckered lips. Small, even breaths. Tiny fingers splayed on pillows. All with a golden crown of Hawkes hair.

Wonderful, miraculous images.

Imprinted in his mind forever.

A tear crowded the corner of his eye, surprising him, frightening him, forcing him to face his past mistakes.

If he had said yes to Val six years ago, they would be a family right now. She'd have made it work one way or the other. She was so young and eager to please him. And willing to marry an agent.

It was his fault that Neal had been that agent, that husband, the man who'd taken credit for this pair.

Valerie caught a glimpse of his hand stealing up to his eye. What was going on inside him? What lured him in here, leaving him in this pensive limbo?

Her heart soared with the obvious possibility. He was weighing the value of their family unit. Trying it on for size, in his characteristically deliberate way. Wondering if he could cope.

"You don't have to guard them this way, you know," she said, giving him a plausible out.

Her voice again drew him out of his trance. "Oh, yes, I know. I was just passing by and couldn't help checking up on them, getting a look at their space." He followed her gaze over to the shelf displaying Neal's dolls. He knew of several of them already, purchased in toy stores across the globe. Delicate porcelain heads with soft fabric bodies. It seemed like an odd way to treat the kids, but perhaps the dolls were better than no gift at all. At least the children knew they were remembered on occasion.

"Maybe when this is over, you can say something to Neal about a more appropriate gift," she suggested hopefully.

His jaw tightened with resolve. "I'll take care of him."

"I arranged things with Kim. She'll be here tomorrow."

"Good."

Another lapse of silence followed. Valerie was about to rise when she felt his stalling hand on her knee. "Yes, Michael?"

"They're a huge responsibility, aren't they?"

She drew a hesitant breath. "Yes, of course. But the rewards are a hundredfold."

"Too bad they don't come with an instruction manual."

"Even if they did, I'm sure people would misinterpret the directions," she declared dryly. "The idea is to do your best. Child rearing is supposed to be a joy."

"My mother sure didn't enjoy it."

Valerie smiled in sympathy. The confidence only confirmed what she'd long suspected. "I'm so sorry, darling. But fortunately it is possible to break the family traditions that have harmed us."

"Guess a man can do anything, if the reasons are right," he whispered.

"Something to think about," she murmured in return.

With a light kiss and three long strides he was gone.

It wasn't until Valerie was snuggled back beneath the covers that she realized that she hadn't asked about his trip to Cornerstone, or whether he'd remembered the milk.

HAWKES WAS STANDING at the bathroom mirror Sunday morning with his razor poised over his lathered face when he felt a presence, heard the creak of a hinge. In a split second the door bounced open and Timmy's image joined his in the glass.

"Hey, Uncle Mike!"

Hawkes whirled round with heart-pumping ire. "Don't you know—" He cut short his words with a deep restraining breath.

Timmy continued to regard him with hesitant hazel eyes. "Know what, Uncle Mike?"

"Don't you know better than to sneak up on a guy?" he queried quietly.

Timmy blinked in confusion. "Huh?"

He didn't understand. But children didn't know better about something unless you told them, did they? It was why they were always asking invasive questions, poking into personal places.

He hadn't meant to snap, but there seemed to be no private haven in this big, rambling house. He'd never felt more claustrophobic, not even in the tightest hiding spots.

The boy had caught him at a bad moment. He was in his soldier mode, immersed in the mission ahead. Going over their travel plans, second-guessing Prudence Manders, fretting about Alexander and Neal and Manuel, wondering if one of them had turned. Michael knew he didn't belong around civilians when he was working. It was his practice to remain aloof and mechanical.

It saddened and frustrated him. But he knew his limitations better than anyone.

Besides, he'd spent the night thinking about the kids, even dreaming about them. The news would probably heal the disappointment in his son's eyes, but he couldn't tell him.

"I'm accustomed to a little privacy in the morning," Hawkes stated firmly. "Okay?"

Timmy blinked in perplexity. "Huh?"

"Shut the door, Tim," he clarified. "Please."

The boy's blond head bobbed in comprehension. "Oh, get it. C'mon, Tammy," he called out over his shoulder. "You heard what he said."

Hawkes turned back to the mirror with a grunt of relief, raising his razor back to his jaw as the door clicked shut. But he gave himself a jab with the blade when he again focused on his reflection. The door was indeed closed, but the twins were standing on the *inside,* intently peering at him.

"We never seen a man shave before," Timmy announced.

Hawkes inhaled deeply, setting the razor on the marble vanity with deliberate care so as not to wound himself further. "This wouldn't be a good time for your first look," he said gruffly. "I'm in a hurry—"

"Oh, sure, you big, old bear," Tammy scolded. "You're gonna take our mama away! Well, you can't just do that. I would be bad. Bad man."

His mouth formed a grim line. The idea of Valerie pinning this trip on him pricked him harder than the blade had. He spun around on his bare feet and advanced on the small pair. Their small freckled faces tipped up to confront his thunderous one, then dropped down his muscled chest, to where his jeans and huge hands squeezed his hipbones.

"You just can't have her, Uncle Mike," Timmy mustered the courage to say.

"She is our mama," Tammy squeaked huffily, lifting her chin in a haughty gesture reminiscent of Valerie.

What the hell was the matter with them? Hawkes wondered in confusion. He'd been the hero yesterday. Now there wasn't even a trace of the old spark in their open, little faces. They were desperate and frightened, and just plain mad.

The realization that he didn't want his children to ever be angry or disappointed in him hit him with swift, sudden force. "Just what did your mother tell you?" he asked evenly.

"Nothing," Timmy admitted. "We heard her tell Stephy that you were going away."

Hawkes rubbed his cheek in contemplation, inadvertently spreading the blood from his small wound. Hadn't they ever been separated from Valerie before? "Stephanie will be with you, and a nice woman named Kim—"

"But if you take her, we won't have a mama or a dad!" Tammy broke in tearfully.

New understanding hit him squarely in the gut. What a blockhead he was! They thought Valerie was going off on Cornerstone business as Neal did. Neal had done it and disappeared from their lives. Hawkes squatted on his haunches so he could communicate on their level. "We're just going on a little trip," he explained. "A—a fun vacation."

"A honeymoon?" Tammy wondered with new sweetness and a hopeful smile.

"No—no, not exactly," he stammered, heat rising from his neck. "But it's just for a rest. She'll be back before you know it."

"We can come," Timmy informed him. "We're done with kindergarten."

"Not this time, buddy. I've already got our tickets."

"Well, what about next time?" Tammy eagerly demanded, clapping her small hands.

Hawkes blinked in disbelief. They were so sharp, it was tough to keep up. He felt an ever growing respect for Valerie and all other caring parents. They faced this challenge day after day. They took on the huge responsibility of raising their youngsters with the proper balance of love, patience and strength.

Sacrificed their privacy, their life-style, for the good of all.

He just didn't know if he could handle it, given the chance.

But he could set this one small issue right. Try to ease their minds about Valerie's absence.

Some quick, flashy consolation prize would do the trick. A bigger swimming pool. A day in the city. But he wasn't going to cop out by making promises he didn't know he personally could keep. How many times had his own mother lied, made assurances she had no intention of honoring? The list was endless. There had never been enough of anything, material or spiritual. But how she'd doled out the promises. Empty, stalling promises. Even the last night, when she had stuffed her personal items into a sack, she'd promised to be back by morning.

He never wanted his own children to feel as totally abandoned and worthless as he had.

"I'm sure your mother will find a way to make it up to you when she gets back," he said. He drew a breath of relief when they didn't take note of the singular reference keeping him out. He just didn't know what he and Valerie were going to do about their circumstances. He wanted to be extremely careful.

In a spontaneous move, Tammy cuddled into his chest. "Sorry I yelled."

"I'm sorry she yelled, too," Timmy chimed in, patting his bare shoulder and grinning from ear to ear.

Hawkes's throat closed as they fussed over the small cut on his face. They were sorry. And they truly liked him, without having a clue to who he really was. It was so flattering. How many fathers could say they had passed the same test?

The father test. It was more than likely unique to every man. There were undoubtedly different ways to best serve one's own children.

In his case it might mean stepping aside, shielding them from his own cold heart. He couldn't put them through the motions of accepting a second father, only to be disappointed all over again.

Somehow, he hoped to come across fresh insight to show him the way.

'IT'S TIME TO LEAVE, VAL!"

Valerie rolled her eyes later that morning at the sound of Michael's impatient refrain. She was still flying around her bedroom in her panties and strapless bra, collecting some last-minute items for the trip. She glanced at Stephanie, seated on the bed beside the suitcase, shaping her nails with the file from Valerie's travel kit.

"Tell him I'm coming," she directed fretfully, digging into a dresser drawer for some spare stockings.

"I have to do everything!" the teenager huffed, popping up off the mattress. "Val's coming!" she hollered out the doorway.

Valerie paused to glare at her. "I could have done that."

"Exactly," she said in disgust, giving her short white shorts a tug over her bottom before bouncing back down on the bed. "I'm sure he's getting tired of hearing it from me."

"Look, I'm sorry you're trapped here for the next couple of days."

Stephanie's grimace softened. "I know. It's just that there's a big party tonight. You had said I could go—"

"Before all the trouble started," Valerie pointed out. "There'll be other parties. And you can't very well expect the twins to stay here alone with Kim. She's a stranger to them, and she's not exactly strong on motherly qualities."

"I noticed that the other night," Stephanie conceded.

"And even if we were going to be here, you're under house arrest until we clear up this matter."

"I know you're right," she said, stuffing the file back into the leather manicure case. "But it still burns."

"I'm sorry."

"Okay, okay," Stephanie raved with a dismissing gesture. "Just do yourself a favor and figure out what you're going to do with this guy."

Valerie was just pulling her sundress over her head when her sister's direction hit home. She regarded Stephanie with openmouthed surprise. "Just what do you mean?"

"Remember our talk at the pizza place yesterday?" she lilted, flashing a coy grin. "If you want to be hot, this will be your chance, without the monkeys tugging at your shirt."

"It's a bit more complicated than that," Valerie objected, pausing at the dresser mirror to run some bright red lipstick over her mouth.

Stephanie leaned forward, propping her chin in her hand. "Yeah, right."

"The attraction isn't the problem. We have that nailed down."

"It's about time you married again. Use that tropical moon to lure him in."

Color tinged her cheeks. Sure. A simple and easy plan to a dream-struck fifteen-year-old. But saying "I do" was only the beginning. Michael would still have his career. And his career would profoundly affect anyone close to him.

She strongly suspected he'd never let anyone close enough to really get in his way, force a compromise out of him.

She couldn't fathom why he was making this supreme effort to blend into their world, when the end seemed so near. The solving of this mystery with Prudence would be a closure to his official assignment. Another assignment would no doubt follow. He would be saying goodbye all over again, as he had in Cancún.

Unless he could find it in himself to make a fresh start ere in Ferndale.

But could he make such a dramatic change? Give up his resent job for something more stable? The idea had taken oot the night before, sometime after he'd left for Cornertone. The loss had hit her hard, made her realize just how uuch she wanted him.

But a career change for such a man as Michael was on a ar with an organ transplant. His operative role was a maor part of his identity. He lived and breathed his job. He'd een so proud of himself this morning, when he'd shown her ie tickets, explained how he'd charmed Madge for entry ito the file room. Even that little trip had been a kick. She adn't seen it that way, especially considering that he'd ound zilch in Prudence's records. Still, Valerie was wise nough to understand that it would have to be Michael's lea. His decision.

But Stephanie was right. This trip was bound to make a ifference one way or the other. The clock was ticking on his ecision. And he had to know it.

HEY WERE WAY BEHIND SCHEDULE.

Michael paced the square entry-way, frowning as he lanced at his watch. He'd been timing every phase of this endoff, from his shaving adventure, right through their nidmorning brunch. They should've been on their way to ie airport by now. He'd been packed and dressed in his haki slacks and white muslin shirt for nearly an hour. And 'alerie had seemed on the brink of readiness for half that me.

Here she was, finally, drifting down the staircase with the ther bag.

Suddenly it seemed worth the wait. She was a dream in er polished-cotton dress, her hair fluffed prettily at her hin.

"I'm ready."

The twins pounded down the hallway from the back of the house, charging into her arms. "Don't go!" they chorused.

The statuesque Kim was close behind the pair, wearing an easy grin and white sweats. "I could go in your place, Val," she offered.

"Yeah, let the big girl go," Timmy urged with shiny eyes.

"Uncle Mike said it's not a honeymoon, Mama," Tammy wheedled. "Let's go on a honeymoon instead."

Michael watched the scene with a fretful outlook. The last thing he wanted to do was disrupt this household. Especially for his own selfish desires.

"C'mere a minute, Val," he said, taking the tote bag from her hands.

She squinted at him. "Where?"

"Excuse us." He took her by the elbow and guided her out of the children's earshot, to the dining room.

"I know what you're going to say!" she hissed in frustration.

He raised his hands helplessly. "I feel like a heel, taking you along."

"Well, don't, I insist."

"Please reconsider. Kim can easily take your place. The results will be the same."

Her eyes grew round. "Well, thanks a lot!"

"You know what I mean. Prudence will answer to us."

"I'm going for me, Michael. I need closure on this."

He rubbed his chin, battling his temper. "I am going to call the shots all the way," he reiterated. "I want to make sure you understand."

"Yes!" She understood only too well. He was at war with himself. He wanted to enjoy her company in the tropical setting, but he also wanted to singlehandedly handle the mission. He respected her to a point, but he still expected to run things like always.

"It's time to go." He took her arm.

"I know. You're the one who's holding up the show." Without another word she marched back to the entryway to make her goodbyes.

Chapter Nine

Michael and Valerie had no trouble clearing Mexican customs at Cancún International Airport later on that afternoon. They appeared to be just another married couple on holiday with their forged birth certificates, light luggage and friendly smiles.

Michael had assured her that the phony identities were probably not necessary, but rather a bonus precaution. It might give them an element of surprise concerning the Manders camp, and it would keep the government from wondering just what Cornerstone was up to in their country.

The name of Hawkes set off automatic alarms world round.

Valerie couldn't count the times she'd almost tossed out all the false identification she had used so routinely during her months with Cornerstone. Michael's face had lit up with the news that she still had everything.

She hoped his complacency would last for the duration of the trip. She didn't feel like a subordinate agent under his wing anymore and didn't want to be treated like one.

They paused inside the terminal building to change some American money for Mexican, then joined the other travelers wandering outside in search of transportation into the city. It was a hot, sticky day of a sort so common to the area. The sky was bright and the air heavy.

Valerie slipped on her sunglasses against the sun's glare, scanning the rows of buses and taxi lined up in the street. "Are we renting? Hitching? Busing it?" She turned to Michael, who was also perusing the vehicles clogging the thoroughfare.

"Lined up even better service than that," he replied with pleasure as he spied a large white town car pulled up at the curb a short distance away. "Follow me." He grabbed her elbow and with swift steps he moved her through the crowd. The trunk popped open as they approached. Michael swiftly set their garment bag and tote inside, closing it again with the heel of his hand.

Valerie took one look at the vehicle's dark tinted windows and balked at him. "Are you sure—"

"Positive. And be sure to act surprised and delighted."

"Rather than what?"

"Surprised and annoyed."

Before she could protest further, he whisked open the back door and urged Valerie onto the seat. Taking a last look into the crowd to ease his mind, he ducked inside and closed the door.

"¿Cuánto cuesta a Cancún?" Michael leaned forward to ask the driver.

"Two hundred American dollars."

"What!" Valerie exclaimed. "That's robbery."

"No, baby, it's Manuel Castillo," Michael explained with a laugh. "Good to see you again, *amigo.*"

The small, dark man at the wheel turned around, flashing a grin in greeting.

Valerie's spine and smile stiffened simultaneously. Cornerstone's top man in Mexico. And the top man on their suspect list.

No wonder Michael wanted her to act delighted, when he knew full well she'd be irritated. It was so like Hawkes to

draw potential enemies near for a long, hard look. And he'd
kept it from her so she could not protest. Manuel had probably been briefed on almost everything they had, too. That
would've been the only way to draw him in.

"Manuel! How have you been?" She forced pleasure into
her voice.

"Good, Valerie." His narrow face taking on a roguish
look. "Happy to see you two back together. *Hado.*"

"Destiny?" Michael dourly translated in query. "Aren't
we in a sentimental mood."

"Merely insightful," the native claimed with a chuckle.

Valerie felt a flush rise up the slender column of her
throat. Manuel had witnessed their parting scene after the
rescue. Her slap to Michael's face. His decision to stay on
in Mexico. Most likely, Manuel had helped him drown his
sorrows that night.

Michael had always spoken of Manuel in the most glow-
ing terms. He was one of the few agents that Michael openly
and genuinely seemed to like. And Valerie had always
agreed. The foreign operative was efficient and pleasant and
easygoing. He was joking around with them now, as though
their lovers' quarrel was the biggest issue of the day.

"I arranged your room," Manuel went on to report as he
merged into the traffic headed for town. Valerie suppressed
a gasp as he steered across lanes on the congested freeway.
The people of the area preferred a slow-paced life-style—
unless they were behind the wheel of a vehicle, it seemed.
"Oleaje Hotel."

The scene of their previous loving—and their revealing
afterglow conversation. Valerie bit her lip, turning to gaze
out the window at the open fields beyond the highway. She
would never forget how Michael had dismissed their lovemaking with casual gratitude.

It would be silly to linger on such memories. Forgiving
was far more important than forgetting. And she could forgive. Sometime during the night, as they had sat together in

the twins' room on that toy chest, she had become absolutely certain that she could put the past behind her—if Michael could make a reasonable offer for the future.

Michael got the gist of her mood and gave her knee a comforting squeeze. "Everything will be all right."

Manuel spotted the exchange through the rearview mirror. "Something wrong with the Oleaje?"

"Not at all," Michael smoothly assured him.

"I usually set up operatives there. Alexander prefers it to—"

"It's the best," Michael broke in. "You register us under our passport names?"

"*Sí.* Mr. and Mrs. Pratt. Though it doesn't seem necessary. Prudence Manders shouldn't be any trouble."

Michael and Valerie exchanged a look in the back seat. Manuel's tone reflected an avid interest in the situation.

"So, what can you tell us about her Chapel Renew?" Valerie inquired.

"We call her place the *palacio,*" Manuel explained "The big opening tonight is like a *festividad.*" He jammed his palm against the car horn to protest another driver's lane change. "She bought that whole island you know, with some other American investors. Has provided many jobs for the locals. They ferry back and forth from the peninsula every day. Everyone loves Prudence. Her old 'Stepfamily Robinson' show is still very popular here."

"I imagine she's a local heroine of sorts," Valerie surmised.

"*Sí.* That is why I am so anxious to help you. So nothing is spoiled for my people."

Valerie absorbed the explanation with an open mind. In all fairness, it made sense. Perhaps Manuel was just what he claimed: a concerned citizen and a loyal agent.

"Hope we can crash her party without too much fuss," Michael said with a poke to Manuel's shoulder.

"Got everything arranged," Manuel assured him. "Cruiser. Passes. You're all set."

"Good man."

"It still amazes me that nobody here or anywhere else ever did find out about her affair with Chet Winston or the kidnapping plot," Valerie mused, intent on a probing expedition.

Manuel nodded. "Cornerstone did a great job. Saved her nice little buttock."

The passengers exchanged a wry look. Manuel liked to play a bit with the English language.

"Seemed wrong to let the case die without pursuing those kidnappers," Michael grumbled.

"I think I could've made headway on the Zapata end," Manuel said, matching his disgruntled tone. "But Alexander pulled the plug and that was it."

Valerie listened quietly as they complained about the frustrations of unfinished business. She understood, but again, she no longer felt a part of their espionage club.

This assignment was only a means to an end to her. A way to salvage the new world she'd worked so hard to create.

Could Michael, now seated beside her in vivid animation, ever find a satisfying niche in everyday routine?

They reached the Oleaje Hotel a short time later. It was still the jewel of the luxurious hotel zone, just as she remembered, an ultramodern skyscraper on platinum white sands overlooking the emerald green Caribbean Sea.

Manuel rolled up the curving drive to the entrance, where a uniformed bellman whisked open the curbside door. Valerie emerged from the vehicle, waiting for the bellman as he retrieved their suitcases from the trunk, allowing him to escort her to the glass doors. Michael took long strides to follow, pausing under the red entrance awning when Manuel called out to him.

"You forgot your camera case, sir!"

Michael had been expecting a case of some kind from the contact. He slipped it over his shoulder as though it were his own. "Thank you very much."

"Just want you to know," Manuel uttered quietly. "Neal Henderson is here in Cancún."

The tightening of Michael's jaw was his only visible reaction. But the fresh fury concerning his friendly rival swept over him like a storm off the sea, surging through his system with typhoon velocity.

"I didn't want to tell you in front of Valerie. Thought it might dim your romantic plans."

Luring Valerie away from her ex-husband and all those other "uncles" once and for all was certainly on his mind. But so was confronting Neal to clear up some personal loose ends. Feeling Manuel's eyes upon him, he thanked him for his discretion. "How long has Henderson been here?"

"He arrived this morning. Probably a coincidence. He said it was a vacation."

Michael pushed his wind-tossed hair from his eyes with an angry swipe. "Some vacation. He's got to be here because of us. Alexander updated him on our plans."

"But he did not follow you," the Mexican protested.

"Oh, but he did," Michael muttered. "Just had lighter baggage."

"But you traveled light," Manuel pointed out.

Manuel couldn't begin to know the sort of baggage he meant—the securing of Valerie's home front, taking measures with the children. He wouldn't have understood it himself last week. He would have scoffed at the idea of buying milk at the neighborhood convenience store, just so no cereal would go down dry. His life was changing, and no one who knew him as a rogue agent was about to understand.

"Neal easily anticipated our next move and managed to get here faster," he explained shortly. *"¿Comprende?"*

Manuel nodded, taking his straw hat off his head to wipe the sweat from his forehead. "I told him nothing, believe me."

"You met with him?" Michael asked, a new edge to his voice. The admission could go either way. Manuel could be sincerely on his side, or he could be setting him up.

Manuel shoved his hands into the pockets of his baggy shorts, staring down at his worn sandals. "I picked him up from the airport, too."

"Is he staying here?" Michael demanded in a growl.

"No. At a hotel downtown." A long silence fell between them as Michael absorbed the development. "I'm just doing my job," Manuel said defensively.

"Yeah, I know. Contacts. Loyalties. We're all in the game."

Manuel looked affronted. "You know you're more than a contact, Hawkes. You're a real *amigo*."

"Thanks." A shadow of a smile crossed his face. Manuel had never let him down. He owed him some faith. "Did Neal say anything useful?"

"Asked if I'd seen you lately."

"There's a game," Michael scoffed.

Manuel appeared bewildered. "I suppose he is jealous," he suggested. "Valerie was his woman—"

"She's mine now," Michael cut in forcefully with a clenched fist.

Manuel grinned knowingly. "She's worth a fight."

"Yes." Michael blinked, shell-shocked by his own fervent claim to Valerie. Like all his possessive feelings for her, it had come directly from the churning juices in his gut, completely bypassing his brain. But staking a serious claim would mean using his intellect above all else. Desires weren't going to cut it this time any more than they had last time. He'd have to do some heavy thinking, lucid planning before he opened his big mouth to her. "I'll take the room key now."

Manuel dug into his pants pocket, extracted two matching hotel keys and set them in Michael's open palm. "I'll wait for your call at home."

"Wait right here for me," Michael countered to the other man's surprise.

"Don't you want to stop for a siesta?"

Man, did he ever! He longed to make love to Valerie on neutral territory, far away from all her domestic responsibilities. But the opportunity to clear the air with Neal without Valerie at his side was too important to overlook. "I want you to take me to Neal. Give me a few minutes to make my excuses to Val."

"Blame it on me," Manuel offered.

"I have every intention of doing so." With a slap to the Mexican's back, he strode into the hotel.

Valerie was strolling round the airy atrium lobby. She moved with the grace of aristocracy, a cool blue vision in her royal-colored sundress. Sunshine poured through the ceiling windows high above them, gilding her cloud of bright red hair with a coppery crown.

Michael descended the short bank of marble stairs to join her. Together they wandered toward a fountain surrounded by chairs, out of the earshot of the bellman watching over their bags. He gathered her into his arms for a nice, long kiss. Anyone watching the couple would swear they were honeymooning tourists.

"What's going on?" she asked in a rush of impatience.

"Oh, Manuel has a problem with some local operatives," he lied, forcing direct eye contact. "Wondered if I could help him out."

Genuine concern furrowed her forehead. "Maybe there's something I can do. I'm a pretty good negotiator."

"Mmm, don't I know it," he said scorching her ear with muzzling breath.

"Well?" she pressed.

So when had paltering gotten so damn tough? Michael rested his hands on her bare shoulders, gently massaging her creamy skin. "It's sort of personal," he slowly improvised.

She frowned in confusion. "The operative problem?"

"No, baby, no. It's just Manuel's masculine pride. In this culture, the male generally doesn't run to the woman for help."

She wrinkled her nose. "You don't think this is some sort of trick, do you? Is that why you're passing me off? Because it could be dangerous?"

"No, baby, this is separate from us. Alexander has mentioned this conflict in passing, so I know it's real. And," he added with a bolstering smile, "I think we can trust Manuel."

"All right," she dropped her arms from his neck.

"C'mon, let's get you settled in our room—"

"Just me?" Valerie looked outside, her face crumpling. "He's waiting for you!"

Confident that he was doing the right thing, the only thing, he forced a careless smile. "Yeah. Won't take but an hour. I'll be back in plenty of time for the trip over to the Island of Prudence."

Michael tipped the bellman and grabbed the bags himself, whisking Valerie onto an elevator.

They rode up to their room on the eighth floor. Like the lobby, their suite was sun drenched and decorated in cheery pastels. Valerie gazed out of the large window onto a panoramic view of the sea and down at all the suntanned beachcombers, remembering how it felt to be one of them, dreaming of tomorrows.

Were she and Michael any closer to a happy ending this time than they were the time before?

Michael disappeared into the bathroom for a few minutes. When he returned, he was dabbing a towel to his damp face. "Why don't you take a little nap while I'm out?"

"I'm surprised you're even trusting room security to me," she said saucily.

"You'll have the necessary backup." Michael tossed aside his towel and set the camera case on the bed. Valerie knew it held weapons even before he pulled out the pair of pistols.

"One for each leg?" she quipped.

His mouth hardened to a grim line as he sat down on the mattress to strap a gun to his calf. "Look, I understand why you don't keep weapons around the house—with the children and all—"

"I vowed that I'd never again arm myself for any reason," she interrupted adamantly.

His frown turned mocking. "Have you forgotten how to use it?"

She reared back in affront. "Of course not!"

"Have you forgotten who's boss on my missions?"

"No. But this isn't like the old days, Hawkes. I'm a civilian now."

She flounced by him in a huff, the hemline of her dress taking flight. His position on the bed gave him easy access to her legs. His arm snaked out under her dress and grabbed a handful of bare solid thigh. She froze in place with a squeal as his fingers dug into her leg muscle. He held her fast, his blue eyes glittering clear through her.

"Call yourself what you like," he invited softly. "But there is nothing remotely civil about me on duty. You knew the terms from the start."

Her eyes grew as she absorbed his penetrating gaze. His fingers remained clamped in place, sending streaks of heat spreading through her flesh. He was driving home his point with an unforgettable brand.

"For the time being, you are back in the field, playing by the same old rules."

"You're just fishing for any excuse to be the boss of me."

His face gleamed wickedly. "I'm too old to dream tha big. And you're very foolish to be testing my patience."

Her features crinkled. "But I thought we were coming t some new level of understanding."

He made a rumbling sound. "You actually thought yo were going to twist me around your finger, didn't you?"

"No!"

He squeezed her harder. "Yes, you did!"

"Well, maybe," she confessed in an annoyed snap.

"Behaving myself in your home was a huge reach for me But don't believe for a second that I can be manipulate outside your turf. You can either follow my lead or I wi arrange for your escort back home. Make a choice and stic to it."

Valerie scowled into his finely chiseled face. "We'll do your way."

He released her with a satisfied grunt. "Good. You ma as well relax for the time being. I'll be back before you kno it." With several measured moves, he was out the door.

VALERIE PEELED OFF HER dress and laid it across the foot o the bed. But a few minutes on the mattress convinced he that she was in no mood for a nap. She raided the min fridge for some soda, then sank down in a chair by the wir dow. She sipped her drink slowly, clicking on the TV wit the remote control for company. She divided her time be tween the screen and window, trying to steady her nerves.

She'd learned a valuable lesson moments earlier.

As hard as he'd been trying in her home, Michael coul change his spots back in a heartbeat.

And sadly, he seemed far more comfortable as the u tamed rogue.

Where would it all end?

Or more to the point, how would he end it all? Ho would he get away?

Valerie eventually rose again, taking the time to carefully npack their formal attire for the island reception. She hung er gold lamé dress with Michael's dark linen suit and white hirt in the closet and stared at them with a wistful sigh. heir clothes looked wonderful side by side.

Amazingly, the hour passed rather quickly. But Michael ad not returned as promised. The same old scoundrel. Only e could make the rules and only he could break the rules.

In a fit of frustration she paced round the elegantly styled oom in her lingerie. She was so anxious to speak to Pru- ence. She wanted to scold her and grill her, shake some ense into her.

Suddenly the sharp ring of the phone cut through the oom, making her jump. Michael wouldn't want her to an- wer it. She resisted temptation for three peals before rawling over the bed and lunging for the receiver.

"Mrs. Pratt?"

"Yes," she responded guardedly to the unfamiliar fe- 1ale voice on the line.

"This is Juanita at the reservations desk."

"What can I do for you?"

"I am a friend of Manuel's," the voice explained. "I 1ake his arrangements here at the hotel. Cornerstone ar- 1ngements," she added in a faint voice.

"Oh?" Valerie's heart began to pump wildly. Had some- 1ing happened? Had Michael managed to get entangled in local skirmish?

"There is a man lingering down here in the lobby," she :ported. "Has been in and out all day long. He finally ap- roached one of the clerks at the desk with several photos. ou and Mr. Pratt were among them."

"I see." Valerie bit her lip in panic. "Can you describe im to me?"

"Tall. In his twenties. Dark hair. Mustache."

It sounded like the man who had approached her in th mall. So he had moved on to Prudence's turf as well. He ha to be one of her men.

"I must apologize to you, *señora,* but the clerk con firmed that you are here."

Valerie clenched the receiver in panic. "Did she reveal m room number?"

"She could be fired if she did so," Juanita replied eva sively. "But she is from a struggling family, and may hav taken a bribe. In any case, I thought perhaps we coul switch you to another room."

"No, Juanita. I don't believe that will be of any help t me. But thank you for the warning."

Valerie dropped the phone into place with a shudder Where the hell was Michael? He shouldn't have run off t play troubleshooter for the locals. It seemed like such a unnecessary exercise. Cornerstone had a capable operatio: here. Michael just had a compulsive drive to play hero t everybody. The work was in his system like a fever.

A fever hotter than his burn for her.

With bitter resolve, she decided she would have to han dle this inquiring stranger in her own way.

Perhaps he was an ally, as he claimed.

No matter what his loyalties were, Valerie was convince that a meeting was inevitable. He was already on the look out for her. Which was fine. He could put her in direct con tact with Prudence.

The idea that he might be on his way up to her room sen a nervous jangle through her system, however. She didn' want to be trapped in this hotel room with him. A publi place would be much safer.

With lightning moves, Valerie slipped back into her dres and low-heeled sandals. She grabbed her purse, scanning th room for her key. It was right beside the pistol on the bed She paused in contemplation. Michael had been right abou the weapon. It was part of the field, a tool of the trade. An n this situation, a way to balance the odds. With a quick wipe, she stuffed them both into her bag.

Valerie took one of the glass elevators down to the main evel, using the ride to observe the people moving through he lobby below. There were a few young men who fit the general description sauntering round the spacious atrium area. The floor had become more crowded as the dinner our grew closer. There was a lot of traffic near the pool ntrance and the two restaurants.

With a tight grip on her purse, Valerie began to wander hrough the crowd.

"Good afternoon," a deep, familiar voice murmured lose to her ear.

Valerie's heart jackhammered in her chest as she turned ver so slowly to find herself facing the man she'd encounered in the mall. He was dressed in white-and-navy nautial clothing and looked far more at ease in these urroundings. She wouldn't be getting the best of him, as he had in the teenage clothing store.

"You were inquiring after me?" she asked calmly. "On Prudence's behalf?"

He lifted a brow. "You've been doing your homework." Then on a sad sigh, he added, "I was hoping you wouldn't be the one to show, today of all days."

"The one what?" she demanded tersely.

"The Cornerstone agent to pop up on the day of the reception. I've been stationed here for hours, with instrucions to head off anyone from your organization who might ry to crash the island tonight. And believe me, I have the manpower to do the job." He nodded to several burly men tanding in different areas of the lobby. They nodded right ack.

Valerie pursed her lips. This backup had to mean that Prudence was truly frightened and expecting trouble. "You ugged my house," she accused in a gamble, "and I don't ven know your name. That doesn't seem fair."

"My name is Andy Freeman," he said smoothly, no' bothering to deny her accusation. "I've worked closely witl Prudence for a few years now. Manage her affairs. Anc greet visitors sometimes," he added, gesturing to his sea worthy attire. "I staked you out only out of desperation."

Valerie gazed at the California-issued driver's license h¢ produced, then into his steady brown eyes. He seemed quit forthright. "I am her friend," Valerie assured him with ex asperation. "If she wanted to speak to me, she should'v¢ called."

"She's had some hard times. Trusting comes hard."

Valerie shook her head, more bewildered than fright ened. "Why is she once again concerned with Corner stone? That was six years ago."

"It's not for me to say—"

"Don't start that again," she snapped. "I was enjoyin¢ my own little piece of heaven until your stunt hauled m¢ right back into the fray. I want my life back. And Prudenc¢ is going to give it to me—"

"Tomorrow would suit her better, after the reception."

"I want to go home tomorrow," she shot back.

He raised his hands. "If you were here alone, she'd hav¢ more faith, be more flexible."

They were bothered by Michael, just as they had been i¢ the mall. But they were wrong about him. If an agent wa¢ causing Prudence trouble, it was someone else.

"Well, I'm here alone now," she argued. "At least g¢ Prudence on the phone for me. That can't cause any harm.'

To give him his due, Valerie realized that he was trying t¢ keep her at ease. He maintained a nonthreatening distanc¢ from her as he beckoned her over to a bank of telephones "The cordless telephones have been a miracle to the is land," he explained over his shoulder as he lifted the re ceiver.

With her hands clutched to her purse, Valerie stood b¢ while he spoke to two different people over the line i¢

Spanish. "Yes, Prudence," he blurted out in sudden English. "It's me. I have Valerie here beside me now. No, she is alone. I don't know where Hawkes is—"

At this point Valerie took the phone and identified herself.

"So you did come" was Prudence's abrupt greeting.

"Oh, yes. I'm here all right. Here to find out why you invaded my life!"

"I'm the one with the problem." Prudence sounded defensive.

Valerie took a deep breath, using a soothing tone which frequently calmed the twins. "Let's talk it over. Face-to-face."

"I want to trust you, Valerie. But what is Hawkes doing in your life again?"

Valerie held the receiver close to her mouth, struggling to keep her voice low. "He moved in to protect me from an intruder. Who, as it has turned out, is your Mr. Freeman."

"Oh."

"Can you see the circle I'm running in? Your trouble came first, overflowed into my quiet space. I don't get any of it, Prudence. After all I did for you, you can at least supply me with an explanation."

There was a long pause on the line. "You'd have to come here. Alone."

Valerie thought of Michael—their plans to attend the reception together, his orders for her to remain in the room. "Hawkes and I could come tonight—"

"Oh, no," she interjected angrily. "It has to be just you and me. Like before. Who knows? In the end you just may be very grateful that he isn't around to hear."

Valerie recognized the uncompromising edge in the young woman's voice. She reluctantly agreed to the terms, then gave the receiver back to Freeman. He listened for a short time, then hung up.

Valerie absorbed the full impact of what she'd just done. In her quest to be a caring psychologist, she'd made any surprise visit with Michael an impossibility. He was good, but even he couldn't tear past a half-dozen burly men who were expecting him.

He would be livid. But he couldn't possibly begin to see this from her professional point of view. He regarded Prudence as a lingering assignment. A troublesome loose end who was making Valerie's life hell.

Valerie viewed Prudence as a victim of circumstance, a daughter forced into the limelight by ruthless parents. A pawn in the hands of her producers. Idolized by millions. Loved by no one.

Michael knew these things, but would never allow himself to care the way Valerie did.

"I have a boat waiting for me," Freeman prodded. "At the public docks. Right down Kukulcan Boulevard. We can be on Zapata in thirty minutes." When she still hesitated, he added, "There is nothing to fear. If you don't like the ride, you can plug me with your pistol." They both looked down at her small heavy purse with a glimmer of understanding.

"I'm pretty good with a gun," she stated with a hint of pride.

"Cornerstone trains their own well," he conceded simply. "I promise not to tempt you."

"I would like to leave Michael a message here at the desk—"

"No message," he cut in with the shake of his head. "It's part of the deal."

"But—"

"I can have you back here in ninety minutes," he cut in hurriedly. "You may even be back before he is."

Ironically, as she perused the lobby this one last time, it was to make certain that Hawkes wasn't in sight. "All right, Mr. Freeman. Lead the way."

"Please call me Andy," he invited, extending his arm. "After all, I've been listening to your intimate family conversations for a couple days. And following you longer than that. To me, it seems like we're old friends."

Valerie smiled tightly. To her, it seemed like a just reason to plug him.

Chapter Ten

Michael looked at his watch for the umpteenth time that
hour, then stared down at the glass of dark beer set before
him on the bar. Manuel had dropped him off at the cantina
across from Neal's crummy little hotel, promising to go
fetch the other agent pronto. That had been four beers ago.
Or an hour, depending upon how one measured time.

Michael's tolerance for alcohol had always been a whole
lot higher than his tolerance for people. And this waiting
was ticking him off big-time. Was it another game of
Neal's? A betrayal on Manuel's part? Michael didn't believe in much. A certain amount of justice, perhaps. And
Valerie. He did believe in her. His features softened in the
smoky dimness as he thought about just how rare she really
was. How kittenish she was in his arms.

The images could only be best described as a soft spot at
a time like this. And it was vital that Neal not sense even a
trace of weakness in him tonight.

Night. It soon would be dusk in Mexico. He should've
been back by now. Valerie would be waiting, wondering.
But there were questions he needed to put to rest. His own
wondering was a top priority right now.

The door to the cantina opened several minutes later,
bringing the last rays of daylight and Neal Henderson inside. He looked very much like his nemesis at the bar, aside

from the fact that he was a bit huskier, a bit rounder in the face and a couple inches shorter. Neal easily spotted Michael seated on a stool, then gestured to a small table back by an ancient pinball machine. Michael ordered two more beers and brought them back to the table.

"Sorry to keep you waiting," Neal drawled, drawing half the dark liquid down in one swallow. "Manuel had some trouble finding me on the beach."

Michael bit back the rage bubbling up his throat. "What are you doing here?"

Neal shrugged, pointing to his wild print shirt. "Vacation, man!" When Michael's glower didn't dim, he sighed in surrender. "Okay, so maybe I was a little curious about Valerie's dilemma, too."

"Not curious enough to handle it yourself, though," Michael snapped.

Neal winced. "I should've stepped in when Alexander called. Would've stepped in to stop you," he admitted. "Just didn't think you'd have the guts to show up either."

"Yeah. Anything to keep me away from that house," Michael muttered, thinking of the front Neal had kept up after his divorce from Valerie, pretending that they were still close. All to keep him at a distance....

"Val and I had something once," Neal blurted out with a measure of pride. "There were good times."

"Couldn't stand it for the long haul though, could you?" Michael taunted softly.

Neal curled his fists on the small chipped table. "No, dammit, I couldn't stand it then. Can't stand it now. Valerie is the sweetest thing on earth. But I just couldn't keep it together with her."

Michael leaned over the table into his face. "And I finally figured out why."

"Because agents like us can't be housebroken like those fuddy-duddy teachers at Val's college," Neal suggested.

"That's a bunch of crap," Michael uttered on a low, menacing note. "It's because those kids are mine, damn you!"

Neal erupted in laughter. A high, bitter, self-loathing sound. "So you really do finally know."

"About the case of mumps in college that left you sterile? Yeah, I know."

Neal slipped his glass between their noses and slurped. "It was in my file all the time. What finally tipped you off?"

"Those two are the image of my brother, Jerry."

Neal heaved in disappointment. "Well, I was afraid they might resemble somebody. But you didn't seem to have much of anybody. Aside from that brother." He slammed his glass back down, wiping the foam from his mouth. "Guess my luck was bound to run out sometime."

Michael seized his shirt collar with an enraged roar. "Your luck ran out when you divorced her!"

"I've never been lucky with her," Neal blared back. "The best I could do was keep you away. Keep you from having her. That's the luck I mean."

"That's why you married her? To win?"

One look into Neal's glazed brown eyes told him it was true. It was the rivalry, the challenge, the thrill of the hunt.

"I finally beat you at something," Neal confirmed snidely. "You cherished her, desired her, but she chose to be my wife. Mine because you couldn't bear to take a chance on matrimony."

Michael released his collar and sagged back into his chair. When had their rivalry gotten so out of hand? Perhaps he hadn't noticed, because he was so accustomed to winning.

"Well, you know the rest," Neal went on. "The victory began to lose its appeal after a while. I'm not cut out for that sort of domesticity. We tried. Had some pleasant times. But it never took off. I was only punished instead."

"How were you punished, Neal?" Michael bit out savagely.

He rolled his eyes, swallowing hard. "She called out your name in her sleep sometimes. And those kids were a royal pain, of course. A constant reminder of your potency. So you see, in the end, you aced me out again. Marked her heart for life. Left twin reminders of just how capable you always are." He stared down at the foamy residue in his glass.

"But does she know?" Michael demanded harshly. "Does she know that they're mine?"

Neal's gaze lifted slowly, a glimmer of triumph spreading across his padded features. "You haven't discussed this important matter with the lady yet?"

"No."

"So you're wondering if Valerie steered me to the altar knowing the paternity...." Neal's lips curled as he savored the last-ditch discovery.

Hawkes pounded the table, causing it to quake. "Yes! Is she playing games with me? Does she know I'm the biological father?"

"I'll bet that's tearing you up inside," he goaded with fiendish satisfaction. "Maybe she just can't bring herself to trust you with the truth. Maybe she doesn't think you deserve a chance to play papa."

Michael could feel the last thread of his control slipping away. A brilliant flash of red-hot rage blinded him and his fist shot out, connecting with Neal's chin. His head snapped back against the wall behind him. Michael was across the table in a flash, sending their glasses crashing to the floor. He grasped his surrogate brother by the collar, with swift, savage fingers.

Neal opened his eyes again, his features dripping with hatred.

They were paralyzed together in time, for one jolting acrid instant.

Their alliance, their brotherhood was dead. Destroyed forever.

Michael abruptly released him. After delivering a second knockout punch.

He sat there for another moment more, gazing at Neal's slumped figure through a blur of hot, salty tears. This was the sort of emotional impulsiveness he'd suppressed his whole blasted life. He hated himself for weakening, for losing control. Still, he decided, it felt good to deliver some justice to that farce of a father. Because despite Neal's claims to the contrary, he really hadn't been punished enough.

Michael rose with effort, staggering toward the exit. He paused at the bar to gesture to the inhuman heap at the table. "Figure out the damages. It's his turn to pay."

He stood out on the busy darkening street, searching for a taxi. He realized that his hands were shaking, his whole body was quivering. Valerie had ripped off his armor, leaving him totally sensitized in an insensitive world. He felt absolutely naked.

Stuffing his hands in his pockets, he began to walk.

TRUE TO HIS WORD, Freeman delivered Valerie to Zapata with swift efficiency. Chapel Renew boasted its own private landing, nestled far away from the public access area. Their cabin cruiser was met by several security men. Freeman graciously helped her onto the large wooden dock, then ushered her to a waiting jeep.

As Freeman maneuvered the vehicle through the dense jungle vegetation, Valerie took in the area with wonder. This poverty-stricken island had been transformed into a tropical paradise. And the timing was perfect for an atmospheric first-time peek, with the lavender-and-coral sunset streaking the sky. There was still plenty of untamed land full of animals and overgrowth, but all the standing buildings were freshly painted and roofed and the roads were paved for comfortable travel.

"Prudence has worked to keep a secluded natural feel to the island," Freeman offered in conversation. "But there is a new prosperity here. Many of the islanders now work at Chapel Renew. Once we start accepting guests, more employees will be hired. Poverty will be wiped out completely. So this clinic really has a dual purpose—healing young, broken people and giving the locals an opportunity to earn a decent living."

Valerie suspected that Freeman was trying to cast Prudence in a most favorable light, stress the importance of her work. But why involve this professor from Maryland at all?

The chapel sat on the small hill, a few miles from the water. Adobe construction on a bed of clipped green. The compound itself was smaller than Valerie had expected but imposing just the same. A self-contained fortress of white stone and red tile, enclosed by a high, impressive privacy wall.

There was a guardhouse at the gate. The wrought-iron doors swung open at the sight of Freeman behind the wheel. He proceeded up the winding paved path. The grounds were beautiful in the last light of the day. The wild vegetation had been tamed behind the walls, spurting fountains and colorful gardens set beneath the huge, ancient palm trees. The front of the building did indeed look like a chapel, with thick columns and a stained-glass entrance.

Valerie followed Freeman inside, taken aback by the hushed beauty of the reception area. The decorations were undoubtedly local handicraft. Colorfully woven rugs on the cool tile floor. Impressive pottery displayed on shelves. There was a young Mexican woman in a lovely full-skirted dress, behind a polished mahogany desk off to the side of the room. Her round brown face lit up at the sight of Andy Freeman.

"Prudence is expecting us," Freeman announced, returning her smile.

"*Sí*. She is waiting in her quarters for the *señora*," she replied, gesturing to a bank of tiled stairs.

Freeman escorted Valerie up the steps and along the hallway. He knocked on the last door. Prudence answered it herself, still the elfin figure with the curly raven mane and huge violet eyes. In her skimpy floral shorts and lacy halter top, she still appeared the ageless teenager.

"Come in, Valerie. Please."

Valerie's brows jumped a little. Please was a new word to the starlet's vocabulary. Valerie accepted the invitation, immediately noting that Freeman was no longer at her side. The room was a bedroom, done in Prudence's bold contemporary tastes. Bright aqua carpeting, chrome furniture, wild meaningless paintings—and stuffed animals in every nook and cranny. There was still a lot of little girl in Prudence. Valerie vowed to keep this in mind as she struggled with her temper.

"You've come a long way since we rescued you from that *palapa* down the road," Valerie ventured in conversation.

"Yes," Prudence agreed, managing a small smile. "I enjoyed destroying that hut. The circle is very healing to me. You saved me here. Now I will be saving other troubled celebrities."

"Noble cause," Valerie assured, strolling around the room. "Not one career memento in the room. It appears you've put your past behind you."

"I have a whole new life now," Prudence shot back, with a defiant lift to her chin. "The television grind was never my idea of a good time."

"I have a whole new life, too," Valerie confided, her tone sharpening. "Or I did until you invaded my home, my privacy. Tell me, Prudence, how on earth could our lives possibly intersect at this point in time? It's been nearly six years since we last spoke. I live in a small, sleepy college town, where an average date is a movie and tradesmen still extend credit. Please tell me, just where do you fit in?"

Prudence took the blowing questions with impressive maturity. "I didn't mean to upset you, Valerie. I just panicked. You see, someone from your operation is trying to blackmail me now. He has some pictures of me in that hut, drugged and vulnerable—and horrible!"

Valerie's eyes grew in astonishment. "You thought I was involved?"

"No, no," Prudence assured. "You've got to believe I didn't. Besides, it's a man, and I'm pretty certain he's acting alone."

"You could've just called me," Valerie said in reprimand. "I would've gladly stepped in to help."

"I didn't even want you involved," Prudence lamented. "I didn't want to draw you into the danger. It was Andy's foolish idea to plant the bugs in your house. He convinced me that it would be a long shot, but that somebody might call, let something leak. We didn't think you'd catch on so easily. But you came home early that day. Surprised Andy. He fled before he could right things again."

"And left a Chapel Renew pin behind," Valerie put in.

Prudence lifted a sable brow in surprise. "That was careless of him. But he is more of a manager than anything else. He took on the job just because there was no one else I could trust." Under Valerie's disgruntled look, Prudence went on in her own defense. "Of course the next thing I knew, Hawkes was back in your life! It was a shocking twist I didn't understand. But the timing was sure suspicious. One week a huge demand is made of me, then he shows up. I just didn't want to see you hurt."

"So you instructed Freeman to warn me in the mall."

"Yes. I didn't know Michael Hawkes was on hand to protect you until you told me so today on the telephone. You sounded very cozy over the mikes. And Hawkes was trying so hard to please you. I grew to fear that maybe he was trying to recruit you into his plan against me, because you know me the best of all of them. I have always been so

grateful to you for your support. I didn't want to see you pu
in jeopardy. Can't you see, I just wanted to keep you safe
through this! Without letting Hawkes or any of the other
agents close."

"It seems we were swimming in a sea of misunderstand
ing," Valerie said with a heavy sigh. She sank down on the
edge of the bed.

"The blackmailer wants three million dollars," Pru
dence blurted out angrily. "I don't have it, even if I wanted
to pay him. Every nickel I have is invested in this project."

"Have you considered just calling his bluff?" Valerie
suggested. "So what if the world knows you had an affair
with Chet Winston? Your 'Stepfamily Robinson' father
daughter relationship is history now. Who cares if people
discover that you were kidnapped and brought to this very
island? I don't think making revelations about your mis
guided youth is going to damage your clinic."

"It isn't that simple, Valerie! Believe me, you'd be better
off just going back home. This trouble doesn't concern you
It never did."

"I'm not budging until I have some answers," Valerie
insisted with a single stubborn nod.

Prudence sat down beside her on the bed. She took Val
erie's hands in hers and searched her face with desperate vi
olet eyes. "Guess I'll have to trust you all over again, won'
I?"

"I have earned your confidence," Valerie said on a gen
tler note.

"My secret could rock this whole project."

Valerie nodded, squeezing the starlet's slender fingers
"I'm here for you. Just like before."

"Those pictures aren't just of me in an embarrassin;
state," she confided with a swallow. "The kidnappers ar
in those pictures, Valerie. My own parents."

Valerie closed her eyes with a heavy breath. Suddenl;
everything was so much clearer.

AT THAT VERY MOMENT Michael was opening the door to his hotel room. The lack of light alone wouldn't have troubled him much. He knew for a fact that Valerie had been exhausted, she easily could've fallen asleep. But he had a keen sixth sense for human presence. The room was an empty black hole, beyond a doubt.

Where could she be?

He flipped on the light switch to find everything tidy. But things were arranged differently. The camera bag holding the guns was empty. Valerie's little leather clutch purse was missing. The garment bag was unzipped and open on the bed.

What did it mean?

He made a careful perusal of the room, discovering the clothing in the closet.

But the lady was a tougher find. She had vanished.

Hawkes took closer inventory of everything, discovering that the blue sundress and shoes she'd worn on the flight were missing, along with the purse and gun. Checking his own gun in his ankle holster, he darted back out the door.

The reservations clerk was the victim of his wrath.

The small plump woman named Lorena quivered under his interrogation. "I am so sorry, sir. I do not know of your wife."

A second woman, taller and cooler, with her sleek black hair pulled back in chignon emerged from the back office. The tag on her navy jacket read Juanita. Hawkes recognized her as a link to Manuel. She recognized him for the Cornerstone madman he was.

"I will handle Mr. Pratt, Lorena," Juanita murmured, steering the woman out of the way.

"Where is Mrs. Pratt?" Michael demanded, rapping on the counter between them.

Juanita told him about the man with the mustache. About Valerie meeting him right there in the lobby. His temper smoldered with her every revelation. And burst like a dam

over the facts she did not have. "You didn't hear any of
their conversation?"

"Not much. She seemed to know who he was. From the
start, when I called up to your room with a description."

"The guy from the mall...." he muttered to himself.

"From the Flamingo Plaza?" she queried in bewilderment.

"No, never mind," he said dismissively.

"I did hear him mention the public docks," she offered
with further thought. "Promised to be back in ninety minutes."

"Thanks." With a grim nod, he darted out the door.

As FREEMAN WAS HELPING Valerie back into the cruiser a
while later, a stream of boats could be seen crossing the water toward the island. Among the guests, Valerie knew there
would be a fair number of reporters. Without any urging
from her escort, she immediately went below to the cabin.
A single snapshot could arouse curiosity over her connection to the superstar. And Prudence had understandably had
her fill of uncomfortable photographs.

As Freeman piloted the craft back to the shores of Cancún, Valerie was left with her musings. After all the negative thoughts she'd had about Prudence, the woman was
only trying to shield her parents from kidnapping charges!
Much to Valerie's relief, Prudence had kept the ties severed
from the couple—had done so since way before the kidnapping. Which, of course, had been the motive behind the
snatch. The Manders couple felt they were being cheated
and wanted a continued share of Prudence's profits. Greed
gone wrong. As greed was bound to do.

Valerie and Freeman discreetly parted company on the
public docks, once they reached shore. It was the pickup
spot for the reception guests, so Valerie's discretion was
again needed. She didn't give Freeman another glance, as
she approached the well-dressed throng.

For a second time that day, a man crept up behind her. For the second time, she whirled with surprise.

The look in this one's burning eyes told her she was in more jeopardy than ever. But the torment behind the fire gave her insight. He was on assignment as he claimed back in the room, but he was a wreck about it. But it didn't matter. Getting him to admit he was a wreck about it was bound to be impossible.

"If you really were still on my team, I'd have you for breakfast," Michael growled in her ear.

"Is that the first thing you have to say?" she gasped in disappointment. "Not, are you all right?"

"I can see that you are!" With a squeeze to her bare forearm, Michael steered her off the pier.

There were many well-known faces in the crowd. Television stars, news anchors, reporters. Valerie recognized them in a passing blur, taking only the scantest moment to appreciate the star power, the support Prudence obviously was garnering. She found she couldn't focus beyond Michael and his energized fury. He was as steamed as she'd ever seen him.

They finally reached the sidewalk running along the well-lit Kukulcan Boulevard. Valerie swiftly wrenched free of his grip.

He hovered over her, his choleric frown driving deep lines between his brows. "You know what I said about following orders. One more slipup and you're out."

"Okay, I'm out!" she sassed back. "I'm going back to my room to retrieve my things."

"What?"

"I am going home," she verified. "I cleaned up this mess myself. So you're off the hook. With me and everything else!"

Chapter Eleven

Valerie's proclamation hit him like a blow to the chest. He steered her off the sidewalk and under a cluster of palm trees on the pier property. "You can't just walk away from a debriefing," he charged.

Her heart fluttered in hope. "Why not?"

"Because..." he faltered. "Because I expect an explanation!"

Valerie grew indignant. "Since you're going to act like an egotistical machine about this whole matter, you can dig for your own answers!"

Hawkes balled his fists at his sides. She had no right to be furious. He was the one who'd returned to the empty room, been forced to fear the worst. And now she expected him to dig for all the answers. He quite honestly didn't know where to begin. There were so many questions about the mission and about the twins.

If she knew those children were his... If she had kept that secret for six long years... If she had lain with him all over again in the most intimate way, deceiving him all the while... He would go ballistic.

"Machines don't have egos," he finally fired back in a sputter.

"How about robots?" she said on the uptake. "Only something mechanical would attack my logic right now. Only a machine wouldn't care about my well-being!"

He was no good at these emotional duels. But if he didn't care, he wouldn't be standing here, bickering with her like a bewildered teenager. She knew that, too. "Tell me what happened," he pressed. "Through Juanita, at the hotel, I understand some of the hows, but I don't understand anything else."

Valerie glowered at him in disbelief. Where was her compassionate lover, her paisley-pajama knight? There wasn't a sign of him in this callous taskmaster.

"Val, I don't know what's gotten into you," Michael chastised with steely resolve. "But I expect a rundown on what happened. I put my faith in you on this one—after you'd been out of action for years. I deserve some answers. At least on the mission."

At least on the mission? Valerie turned the odd remark over in her mind. She didn't understand it. But she did realize that he wouldn't back down until he got his report. He was only behaving true to himself. She had expected way too much."

"I don't like your attitude that there's a right party and a wrong party here, Michael."

Michael rubbed his neck, briefly closing his eyes. "Well, the dynamics between us haven't made for the best working conditions," he mustered the nerve to admit. "There's no room for emotional upheaval on the job. But we already know that, don't we?"

Valerie sighed hard, turning her face away from some people passing by on the sidewalk. So he was saying goodbye. He knew he had to make a choice and he was making it. "I'll fill you in," she said in a small voice.

"Let's walk back along the beach," he suggested. When Valerie nodded mutely, he escorted her back toward the busy pier, angling toward the shoreline behind the hotels.

The blackened sky was beautiful with its slice of moon and smattering of stars. They peeled off their shoes and moved barefoot along the wet sand. The ocean was wild and pulsing, the cresting waves silvery in the moonlight. The surf pounded the shore, sending foamy curls of cool water over their feet and ankles.

There were a few other couples strolling through the fine powdery sand, most of them looking more at each other than at their tropical surroundings.

Valerie swallowed hard. All the pain and disappointment of their first fling was flooding her like a huge wall of water off the sea. And it was happening all over again. She'd hoped for something better, only to be smacked down again.

"What compelled you to set off on your own this afternoon?" he asked, slicing through the silence in an almost conversational tone.

She recognized the remote tone. He was struggling with his own temper. The more distant, the tougher his struggle. He sounded at least a thousand miles away already. She went on to explain the sudden call from Juanita. The moment of indecision. Her intention to meet this man on neutral territory.

"But you got into a boat with him," Hawkes protested.

Valerie bristled. "He convinced me. Prudence convinced me. And I had the gun," she added in her own defense.

He nodded approvingly. "Your only responsible decision."

"I don't expect you to understand or approve, but I went there more as her counselor than anything else."

"Is this all privileged again?" he erupted in annoyance.

"No. I managed to convince Prudence that you could be trusted." When his profile hardened even more, she released an exasperated sigh. "I don't think you get any of this. She wouldn't have confided in us, had we shown up together at the reception. It was me alone or nothing. I wasn't even allowed to leave you a message. She considers the Cornerstone Group her enemy now. And quite frankly, I don't blame her."

"So what triggered this whole thing?"

Valerie briefed him on the blackmail photos of her with her parents. The demand for three million dollars.

He was openly surprised. "She show you the photographs?"

"Yes. They are genuine. The blackmailer wants to sell her the negatives for the one lump sum."

"How long has she known that her own parents were behind the plot?"

"She said she began to have some flashbacks in the hospital after rescue. I imagine my therapy sessions with her helped loosen some of those painful scenes hidden away in her mind. Once the drugs wore off, she apparently remembered quite a lot."

New understanding flickered in his eyes. "So that's why she didn't want us to go in search of the kidnappers."

"Yes. It was a bigger scandal than her affair with Chet Winston."

"The whole things's ironic, considering that no one was supposed to take pictures during the rescue."

"Probably was a red flag to an enterprising person," Valerie surmised. "Somebody took a relatively small gamble, hoping it would pay off big someday."

"Neal and Kim were both playing tourists with cameras around their necks," he recalled grimly. "And Manuel could've taken shots many times over."

"This certainly isn't Kim's style," Valerie was swift to object. "Her family is moneyed. She's in the espionage trade for thrills alone." A fact that made Valerie extremely happy that Kim was the one in charge of her twins. "And Prudence said it was the same man on the telephone all three times. She got the impression that he was acting alone. And let's face it, Michael, Cornerstone agents in general are pretty self-serving. Why would anyone with the negatives need or want a partner?"

"You've hit a lot of good points." With a satisfied grunt, he named Neal as his favorite suspect.

She bit her lip, hating what she had to say. "Don't leave out Alexander. He was on the island with us, too."

Michael understood her hesitation. Alexander had always been his trusted mentor. But he had let him down bigtime this week. It had seemed bad enough when Alexander had tried to steer him clear of Val, after seeing them in the grocery store. But after looking into Neal's file, Michael realized that Alexander knew all along that Neal was sterile, that those kids were his.

On an objective level, he understood the controller's motives. Alexander didn't want to lose him to Valerie. He'd groomed Hawkes as the ultimate agent. Keeping him a sharp-edged loner would be to Cornerstone's benefit. But subjectivity had crept into his system, his very soul. He could never go back to being the solitary man he had once been.

Of course, Valerie didn't know about this breach of faith, so Michael chose his words carefully.

"In his favor, Alexander did supply us with a rundown on Prudence. But of course, he would have to play it out, even if he is guilty."

"And he is arrogant enough to believe he can trick us all if he wants to," Valerie put in. "And he is always looking for fresh funding for the organization."

"How does Prudence plan to proceed?"

"I don't know. She doesn't have the money to pay. I imagine she's hoping her own staff can pinpoint the blackmailer and perhaps get hold of those negatives."

"Yeah, sure, like that clown who bungled the bugging of your house."

"Well, at least he is loyal to her," Valerie pointed out.

They soon found themselves on the beach behind their hotel. They stood silently for a moment in the stiff, balmy breeze, gazing out to sea. Valerie was satisfied that she'd given Michael the accurate report he wanted. If he was going to leave her all over again, she hoped he'd make the break clean and quick.

"I'd like to help her somehow," Michael said unexpectedly.

Not the line she expected, but she couldn't help but be impressed by the offer. "You can't blame her for seeking outside help. People independent of Cornerstone."

He released a hollow sigh. "What she needs most, however, is an inside man like me. All this unfinished business leaves me with a sour stomach. My team let her down. I'd like to clean it all up."

"Offering to help would be a very generous act," she admitted begrudgingly.

"It's selfish, too," he confessed. "I need to know who the culprit is, for my own peace of mind."

She flashed him a wan smile. How nice to know he could admit to a need. But it wasn't the need that affected her.

"I guess that settles things, then," she said with forced lightness. "Good night." Valerie made a move up the sand, but Michael swiftly snaked an arm around her waist. He drew her up against his length, cupping her chin in his hand.

"You can't really be serious about leaving tonight," he rasped off-key.

His body was as tight as a vise. She could feel every contour against her softness. His face was just as hard, devastatingly handsome, poignantly earnest.

"There's nothing for us, Michael. I'm going back to my warm comfort zone. Where I belong."

"What if I belong there, too, Val?" he challenged. "Are you going to let me in?"

"Can't you see we're hopeless?" she said. "Our lives could never mix again. Why, a few hours together on a mission and we're miles apart. Can you even begin to imagine spinning between the two worlds? The cold soldier one day, the nurturing family man the next?"

"I know they're separate—"

"They're oil and water, Hawkes!" She clenched her fists at her sides. Why was he torturing her this way? The lines drawn between them couldn't be more clear.

Michael could feel the reins of restraint tugging inside him, as they had back in the cantina. Neal, Val and the kids. His feelings for them merged in his belly in a mighty tidal wave of emotion, until he was on the verge of explosion.

"You can't give up the career you've built, the identity you've honed," Valerie went on, unaware of his rocky state. "So what do you care if I leave now, to recapture my own wonderful place? What's it to you, anyway, Michael?" she wailed into the wind.

Their eyes locked for a long, searching moment.

"It's everything, Val," he said finally. "Lord help me, you and your children are everything."

She balked at him, pushing the hair from her face. "How can that be?"

"Kiss me and find out."

He dipped down to plant his hard, hot mouth on hers. His hands combed every inch of her back, from her bare shoulders, down the length of her billowing sundress. They feasted in the sensations for a long, delicious spell.

"I love you, baby."

Finally, the words she'd been longing to hear. "I love you, too, Michael. Maybe it would've gotten us going last time around, but it isn't enough anymore. I'm sorry."

"I understand about your commitments. The baggage involved. You've just got to hear me out, honey."

She tilted her eyes expectantly to his.

"But not here," he said. "We're going to get all dressed up, have a nice meal. Our future deserves that kind of fine beginning."

MICHAEL INSISTED on a new and different place to have their dinner. He kept calling it a celebration, but Valerie was determined to reserve judgment. After a diplomatic conversation with Juanita at the desk, he did manage to elicit the name of a nice, cheery spot; a small, unpretentious restaurant outside the hotel zone, with a live band, local specialties and brightly dressed waitresses.

As Michael watched Valerie slide into the wooden chair opposite him at the dark corner table, he couldn't help comparing her to a flame, with her blazing red hair and sleek body encased in gold lamé.

And Valerie couldn't help but note how dangerously appealing Michael looked in his black linen suit, his shower-damp clipped brown hair and his strong angled features. Irresistible but seemingly unattainable.

She'd barely had a chance to wonder about his proposal. They hustled back to their room to change and make a call home. She put in a call to Kim while Michael set out his dinner clothes. Everything proved to be fine back in Ferndale. The time-zone change put them hours ahead, so Stephanie and the twins were asleep.

Naturally, Kim wanted an update. Michael had coached Valerie on what to say. The official story for now was that Prudence's ploys had been nothing more than a case of the jitters. That the star was afraid Valerie might be planning to talk to the press about their therapy sessions, once Chapel Renew's grand opening became news. It was a passable explanation. It was common knowledge that magazines and TV news programs paid top dollar for good gossip on people like Prudence. Valerie assured Kim that it was all over.

Michael had briefly spoken to Kim as well, asking her whether Neal had been in contact there at the house. He explained that he'd learned through Manuel that Neal was a bit jealous over Michael's reappearance in Valerie's life.

Valerie had listened intently to the exchange with a measure of surprise. Neal didn't give a damn anymore, did he?

Then, Michael had gone on to instruct Kim to keep the house buttoned up and keep Stephanie at home, just to be on the safe side. It all seemed a little too territorial, but Valerie marked it up to jitters. Michael was alive with electricity. But just what he planned to do with the voltage was still a mystery.

A waitress drew Valerie out of her reverie when she approached the table with their margaritas. They were giants, fishbowls with salt-edged rims.

"I think you've overdone it, Michael," she said with a dry chuckle.

"This moment can't be overdone, baby," he murmured once the waitress moved out of earshot.

"What are you getting at?"

His eyes gleamed in the dim light. "I want you to marry me."

"What?" she gasped. Leave him to spring something like that without a plan! "That isn't fair. You know I can't go through another marriage like the last."

His hand stole across the table to hers. "It won't be, Val. I—I'm going to quit my job."

Valerie's brows jumped. "Quit Cornerstone?"

"Yes. I understand that there is a clear-cut choice to be made. I've come to realize that it would be impossible to leap in and out of the soldier mode. The kids demonstrated the point all too well this morning, when they surprised me in the bathroom. They didn't understand why I was so cool at first, and there's no reason why they should have to. No man can live in a revolving door between darkness and light and make good on both sides.

"And you and the kids deserve the best. You need a stable, dependable husband, and the twins need a hands-on father."

"Think hard about them especially, Michael," she cautioned. "They can't bear to weather another failure. They blame themselves for Neal's terrible behavior."

"But I am not Neal. I hate the comparison."

"Just the same, I feel I'm forcing you to make a decision you don't really want to make—"

"I always do exactly as I want to," he said. "And I want us to marry." He paused to study her tremulous expression. "It's what you want from me, isn't it? It is the ultimate proposal, isn't it?"

Valerie closed her palms around the glass in front of her, lifting it to her mouth for a long draw. The salty, tangy taste of the drink juiced up the currents already running through her.

She smiled with cautious optimism, licking the coarse grains of salt from her lips. "It's always been my dream that we be a family."

"Great!"

"But I insist you slow down."

He regarded her in bleak appeal. "We've wasted enough time as it is."

"Still, I suggest we start with an engagement."

"How long do they last?"

"A couple months should be telling."

He released a low groan, drumming the tabletop with impatient fingers.

"And I want you to take a leave of absence, rather than quitting outright. You must have a lifetime of leave coming to you. Take some of it. Hang around our house. Explore your career possibilities."

"That doesn't seem necessary."

"Oh, but it is. Let's find out if you're cut out for residential living. If you're not, you'll still have the option to walk away."

"You're sounding too much like a mother hen," he complained.

"Michael, I believe that you want me," she said softly. "How much, is the question. The sacrifice would be great.

But I am flattered, thrilled that you're recognizing your abilities for loving."

Michael sat up straighter in his chair. He was doing that, wasn't he?

"Okay, baby, we'll do it your way."

Valerie picked up the menu at her elbow. "Let's order some food. All of this racing around has left me starved!"

VALERIE WAS IMPRESSED the next morning, to find that Michael was still determined to help Prudence out of her dilemma.

While Michael began to pack their belongings for their return home, Valerie attempted to reach Prudence for him by telephone. It took some coaxing, but Prudence eventually agreed to speak to him. Valerie sat cross-legged on the bed in her cotton nightie, watching Michael prowl the room in his snug cotton briefs with the receiver clamped to his ear. For the next twenty minutes he grilled Prudence with questions and made security suggestions. With the promise to keep in touch, he hung up.

"You told her she could reach you at my number," Valerie balked.

"It's where I intend to be," he explained matter-of-factly. "If you want me..." He moved toward the bed, his eyes on her crossed legs tented beneath her thin nightie. Sensations stirred deep inside her belly as he knelt on the mattress and began to kiss her legs, peeling back the barrier of cotton fabric.

Valerie ran her fingers through his thick head of hair as his mouth branded the tender skin of her inner thighs.

"You still want me around, don't you?" he huskily asked, inhaling her scent with open ecstasy.

"It's just that your giving her my number, Michael... I symbolizes permanency."

"Call it squatters' rights," he crooned, pushing apart her legs.

"I think you should go back to your own apartment,
_"

He lifted his head up and looked at her through half-
lded eyes. He'd expressed love and intent to commit. How
uld she doubt his purpose under her roof?

"Take the leave, look for a job," she went on. "Secret
gents from both the private and government sectors have
und new niches in security companies, private investiga-
ons. Take the time to look into it, see if it fits. Stay loose,
lichael."

"But I want to be trapped," he said huskily. "Inside
u."

It took all her resolve not to melt against him. "I will
ver forget the look in Neal's eyes during the final months
our marriage. The stormy disappointment, the bitter
are of a trapped animal." When he opened his mouth to
otest, she promptly continued. "Yes, you are your own
an. And I think we'd like to keep it that way."

"But if I'm not living with you, how—"

"We'll have lots and lots of dates."

Astonishment sheeted his features. "Huh?"

"I want you to court us, Michael." A light of humor
arkled in her eyes.

"But I'm already in at your place! I'll just keep camping
it in the spare room," he rushed on persuasively.

"But the kids—"

"I want to be around them!"

Her face lit up with pleasure. "I'm so glad. But no mat-
r how good your intentions, we still have the bonding
inger. And that, as you well know, is the only danger left.
don't need your bodyguard skills anymore. Just your
dy."

He shuddered as her hand dipped beneath the waistband
his briefs, her fingers nesting in his coarse hair. He im-
ediately swelled against her hand. "Dammit! Let's just go
t a quick Mexican marriage," he croaked. "People get

quickie divorces here. The process for unions must be ju:
as fast."

Valerie smiled wryly, thinking that she'd have leapt a
such a proposal six years earlier. "Let's just catch our fligl
home, get settled. You can help Prudence trap her blacl
mailer. Then we'll see, okay?"

"You're getting your way through very manipulativ
means," he growled, spreading himself over her on the bed

"Just so I'm getting it," she uttered with a bewitchir
gleam. "Just so I'm getting it right now."

WITH THE TIME CHANGES and some early morning loving
it was nearly four o'clock before Michael and Valerie foun
themselves back in Ferndale.

Michael eased his Firebird up the driveway, stopping sho
beside Kim's car. Stephanie was circling the open empt
garage on her ten-speed bike.

"You're back!" Stephanie called out cheerily to Valer:
as she stepped out onto the concrete apron. "Can I go o
now?"

"Yes, go ahead," she said with a wave.

Stephanie rolled up to her sister. "Kim said everything
okay. I'm glad."

"We never were in peril, it seems," Valerie explaine(
steadying the bike by its handlebars. "So life should fa
back into normalcy."

"You can fill me in later. So what about James Bond?'
She craned her neck toward Michael, who was busy takin
the luggage out of his trunk.

Valerie beamed as she tested the words on her tongue
"We're engaged."

"Yes!" Stephanie made a jerking motion with her arn
as though she were pulling down a slot-machine lever. Va
erie recognized it to be the latest teenage craze for expres
ing joy. With brief congratulations to Michael, Stephan:
rolled down the driveway and down the street.

They entered the house arm in arm, to find Kim seated at the kitchen table playing solitaire.

"We're home," Valerie announced brightly, setting her purse on the counter.

"And without another checkup call," Kim marveled with teasing sarcasm.

"One was plenty," Valerie said. "We got the job done and got back without a hitch."

"Amazing how kooky Prudence has become," Kim mused as she collected her cards. "Imagine, bugging your house, to see if you were thinking of giving a tell-all interview."

Valerie didn't dare look at Michael for guidance, fearful of arousing Kim's suspicions. She didn't enjoy keeping the real facts from her, but they'd decided to include no one.

"She apologized for the invasion," Valerie explained smoothly. "And I admire her total dedication to the Chapel Renew project. She doesn't want to see her image spoiled by her wild ways of the past."

"I guess we've seen nuttier over the years," Kim conceded, returning the deck to its box.

Michael set their bags on the floor and unbuttoned the collar of his pale blue oxford shirt. "Home sweet home."

Valerie nudged an elbow into his solid stomach. "Huh. Operator."

"That's me," he confessed grandly, wandering over to the refrigerator. He knew Kim's eyes were widening with the scene. He would tell her as much of the truth as he could.

"Where are the twins?" Valerie wondered, gazing round the kitchen.

Kim pointed to the back yard. "Out there. In their pool."

"What?" Valerie shrieked. She whirled on her heel, shoved back the patio screen and charged outside.

Michael took an apple from the crisper and shut the door with his hip. "Didn't Stephanie tell you about their ear problem?"

"Sure."

"So?" he chided. "What were you thinking of?"

The blonde rose up, nearly meeting her boss one-on-one. "The pool's empty."

He took a cracking bite into the apple. "What?"

"No water," she enunciated grandly. "They're playing pretend. Spaceship or something. I dunno. Does it matter?"

"Oh, yeah," he exclaimed brightly, moving over to the door. "I've got to see this."

"You do?" With hands planted on her hips, Kim blinked in perplexity.

"Great," he crowed, "they're conning her this time with that same pool. Isn't that sweet?"

"Guess it is," Kim agreed with a shrug. "Everything must've gone really well between you in Cancún." Her brown eyes twinkled.

He tore his eyes away from the three-sided hug taking place out on the lawn. "All is very well. Val and I are going to give it a chance. We're engaged."

"Wonderful! I don't know which of you is more off the beam, but enjoy."

"We can make it," Michael maintained with a scowl.

Her mouth turned dolefully. "With your life?"

"I'm taking a leave of absence, for starters."

"Taking the family for a test spin?" she inquired saucily, moving over to the chair where she'd stashed her tote bag and jacket. "You are a rogue."

"It was her idea," he swiftly corrected. "I wanted to marry right away. She's the one who put on the brakes."

"Smart girl. But, then, she's been through the pain of failure once already."

"Thanks a lot, Kim."

"Hey, I just don't want to see either of you hurt." She gave his back a pat.

The trio bounded back through the screen door just as Kim was slipping the strap of her tote over her shoulder.

"You gotta go, Kim?" the twins asked.

"Yeah," she replied with a dramatic sigh, kneeling down to accept their hugs goodbye.

"I imagine you'll be wanting this spare garage-door opener now, Michael," Kim wagered, digging the remote out of her jacket pocket.

"He isn't going to be a live-in," Valerie explained with a smirk.

Michael's sigh was wistful. "No, we're starting this relationship all over again. At the courting stage."

Kim nodded. "Ah. I see. Well, 'bye, all."

"What's courting, Uncle Mike?" Timmy asked, sidling up to him.

"It's when you treat a favorite girl in a real nice way," he paused to explain. "And you keep your own apartment."

"Can you court Timmy, too?" Tammy begged, cuddling up to his arm.

His throat closed as he gazed down into their fresh, upturned faces. "I think so," he croaked, drawing them flush against him. He looked up to find Kim leaning on the counter, watching with gentle approval.

Nothing had ever felt so right. He wouldn't let them get away. He just couldn't.

Chapter Twelve

Valerie made a quick, simple meal of hamburgers and macaroni for everyone that evening. Then she settled down in the family room with Michael to watch the news. The previous day's Chapel Renew reception had indeed made the national reports. Prudence was briefly interviewed, as were several of the famous guests—child actors who'd grown up with problems. The Renew program was praised for its innovation and Prudence for her past television work. There wasn't a hint of scandal.

"I feel like we did the right thing all the way," Valerie said.

Michael nodded. "You did your part, now I'll go on to do mine."

A short time thereafter, Valerie felt compelled to send a heavyhearted Michael upstairs to collect his gear. Taking in hand the luggage they'd shared for the trip, he climbed the stairs one last time to sort through everything that was his, transfer it to his tote. Timmy was right on his heels, zooming into the study, unzipping every bag.

"What's this stuff, Uncle Mike?"

Michael turned away from the closet to find the boy pulling his antiperspirant out for inspection.

"Deodorant," Michael replied shortly.

Timmy popped off the cover to take a whiff of the solid stick. "It's different from Mama's. Hers has a ball inside. Better show Tammy this. Hey Ta—"

"Tim, you don't have to—"

"Why not?"

Michael took a deep, settling sigh. He wasn't accustomed to anyone touching his things. And he was so tired.

To his relief, it was Valerie who answered Timmy's summons. "Get downstairs to dry those dishes, mister!" she directed.

"Oh yeah. I forgot." Dropping the deodorant back into the tote, he trotted for the door. "Mama can help you."

"We'll just see about that!" With a low growl, he dropped down on the sofa, pulling Valerie down on top of him.

"You're stalling...." she accused in lilting singsong.

"I'm courtin'," he corrected. "You know, trying to treat my favorite girl in a real nice way."

She scanned his weary features with a wistful look. "I hope the kids aren't getting to you already. They can be pesty. Even I feel the need to run off and hide for a little while."

"Really?" His expression brightened. "I needed to hear that. I was beginning to believe I was hopelessly defective."

She traced her finger along his jawline. "No, just hopelessly human."

The warmth of her smile and touch affected him like sunshine. She just couldn't know the twins were his. Not with those glimmering green eyes sparkling with trust and compassion. He was glad she wasn't deceiving him. But it did put the burden of revelation on him. She couldn't supply him with the truth, because she didn't know the truth. He would have to tell her he'd fathered the twins. Tell her before Neal told her. Before Alexander let it slip.

She would absolutely kill him for the sin of omission.

Valerie suddenly grimaced, stiffening in his arms. " hated lying to Kim."

Hawkes kissed her pouty lower lip. "It was the fair way to handle it. We agree that Kim is guilty of nothing. Drawing her into this mess wouldn't have been fair to her. We would've had to solicit her silence. Demand all her loyalty. She would've felt torn between us and Alexander. Believe me, it just wouldn't have been right."

"Yes, of course." She burrowed her face into the softness of his shirt, then rose to her feet again. "I really should go back downstairs and see how things are going."

"Okay."

Valerie was just putting away the last of the dishes when she heard Michael's roar from the upper floor. "Stay here," she directed the dumbfounded trio tersely racing back for the stairs.

Michael was waiting at the top of the staircase. "C'mere! Quick!"

Valerie followed him down the hallway, surprised when he rounded the children's doorway. She scampered after him, stopping short in the spacious room.

"Just look at this!" he shouted in dismay, gesturing to the half-open drawers and toy-tossed floor. The only inch left untouched was a high shelf with the showcase dolls on it.

"Michael—"

"Who would do such a thing?" he repeated incredulously.

"Whatsthematter?" Tammy asked in an excited babble, racing up behind Valerie. She clung to her mother's legs, making a rash grab for her favorite baby doll, lying face-down on the floor.

"What's goin' on?" Timmy demanded, charging into the fray.

"Just look around you!" Michael roared. "I'm sorry you had to see this," he said on a quieter repentant note, kneel-

g down near Timmy. "Sorry I blew my stack. But the idea
f somebody getting in here while we were away..."

Timmy's round freckled face crinkled in confusion. "See
hat? I don't see anything. What's he mean, Mama?"

Valerie looked down into Michael's distraught blue eyes
nd suppressed a laugh. "Darling, this is the norm. No-
ody tossed this room—nobody but these two little muf-
ins."

"Huh?" Michael's square chin sagged a mile.

"The children played in here. They messed it up them-
elves."

"But it was spotless just the other night—"

"I make them pick up. Kim obviously didn't. But they
ill be cleaning it up tomorrow," she said in a parental tone.

"He thought a robber did this," Stephanie gloated from
he doorway, nibbling on a strand of flaming hair.

Hawkes flushed profusely. With a pat to Timmy's blond
ead, he rose to his feet. "Sorry I— Well, I just didn't un-
erstand."

"It's all right," Tammy said.

"See, Uncle Mike," Timmy whined, gesturing to the only
ndisturbed shelf. "There's the dollies I was telling you
bout. If you could just tell my dad not to send me those
nymore. I could use a fire truck, instead."

Michael glanced grimly, once again, at the porcelain fig-
res. Now he knew for certain that Neal was doing this to his
on out of petty spite. Thankfully, Neal had left this house
efore his bitterness drove him to really damage these chil-
ren. "I'll put a stop to it," he assured. "And I'll get you
he truck myself."

"Wow, I'm gonna like courting," Timmy rejoiced, clap-
ing his hands.

"I wanna court, too!" Tammy piped up, trailing Hawkes
ack to the study.

As promised, Valerie discussed the entire situation wit
Stephanie later on that night over a wedge of chocolate cake
Without betraying Prudence's confidence, she explaine
that she was in trouble and had tapped into Valerie's life t
see if she could lead her to the source.

Stephanie was piqued over the very idea that someon
would use her big sister that way. But she was relieved tha
it was all over.

Valerie assured her that their life would be back to rou
tine tomorrow. They all had a leisurely summer ahead.

Everything would be the same. Except, of course, fo
Michael's masculine presence in their household. She wa
engaged to be married again! To the right man this time
And there was also Valerie's sacred conversion on the sub
ject of home protection. Andy Freeman's little invasion ha
given her new faith in her security system. Never agai
would she trudge up to bed—as she was about to do now—
without making certain it was activated. Ferndale was stil
safe enough in her mind. Unfortunately, there were n
fences at the city limits to stop the unwelcome outsider
from cruising right on through.

Valerie went over to the Ferndale College campus th
following morning to close up her office for summer break
Stephanie, behaving like a bird set free, made arrange
ments to spend the day at the beach with her friends. Th
twins accompanied Valerie to the campus, shaking hand
with her contemporaries, playing teacher at Valerie's hug
wooden desk. They had lunch out at a pizza place on cam
pus, then headed for home sometime after one o'clock.

The twins were tired and cranky, informing her in thei
own way that they were far behind in their sleep. Despit
their protests, Valerie put them down for a nap. She the
proceeded to change into comfortable summer grubs, de
termined to bring order to her very disorderly house. Sh

was just beginning to sort through her papers on the kitchen table, when the telephone rang.

To her amazement, the caller was Neal.

"You sound surprised to hear my voice," he said in a hurtful tone.

"I am surprised," she admitted, continuing to sort through her papers. "What do you want?"

"Wondered if you made it back all right." When she paused in silence, he added, "From Cancún. Alexander told me you were going."

"Oh, I see." Just what did Neal want from her, she wondered.

"Hey, I care about my family's safety," he shot back defensively. "We both know that it would've been uncomfortable for me to move back in."

"Yes," she agreed, her throat tightening. He could be the one blackmailing Prudence. Or he simply might be jealous of Michael's renewed interest in her. In any case, it would pay to be cautious.

"So, Prudence explain why she was giving you trouble?"

"Prudence was just a little mixed-up," she answered casually. "I believe we've come to an understanding."

"Well, glad to hear it."

Valerie stopped shifting round her papers, giving the conversation her full attention. "Is there anything else, Neal?"

"So how are our children?" he asked pleasantly.

"Fine. Exhausted. I just had them over to the college."

"So they're sleeping?"

"Yes. You didn't want to talk to them, did you?"

"Will they be napping long?" he asked, sidestepping the question.

"I don't know." Since when did he care?

"Sounds like you're settled in for the afternoon."

"I suppose so. Being a single parent takes enormou commitment. Goodbye, Neal."

Valerie slammed down the receiver with a huff, tucking rich curve of red hair behind her ears. She froze for a mo ment, thinking that she'd let her temper get the best of he with her ex-husband. It would've been far shrewder to drav him out, trick him into a possible link to the blackmail.

But it was too late.

Michael called later on in the afternoon from Corner stone, as she was loading the washing machine. Her ton was abrupt, for she was still fretting over her blunder witl Neal. Michael insisted on an explanation. She told him th truth. He was relieved that she hadn't pressed Neal. And h mentioned looking into an even more sophisticated secu rity system for her house, that Neal wouldn't be able t crack. Valerie was about to protest the notion that Nea would even want to return, when the front doorbell rang Michael let her go with the assurance that he was on his way to Ferndale.

When the bell chimed a second time Valerie smoothed he rumpled shorts, tugged at her tank top. She just couldn' imagine who would be at her door in the midafternoon Probably a salesman...

JUST AS MICHAEL WAS setting the receiver back in place o the intricate console atop his desk, Alexander breezed i through the door.

"I just heard an ugly rumor," the older man said, with out even sparing a greeting.

Michael tipped back in his chair and regarded Alexande with a flinty expression of his own.

"No costumes today?" he asked the controller, eyeing hi sober black suit and starched white shirt. "No dotty-pro fessor look, no slicked-back shoe salesman?"

"Looks like you're the one in costume, Hawkes." Alex ander jabbed a finger at Michael's T-shirt and denim cut-

fs. "So it is true. You're taking some sort of vacation.
ithout discussion. Without permission."

"That's right, sir. I am taking some leave. I have a truck-
ad saved up and it's about time I tapped into it."

"What about the Prudence Manders situation?"

Hawkes lifted his massive shoulders. "I left a report on
ur desk."

"My grocery list is longer! What do you mean, she's fin-
ed with Cornerstone?"

"Exactly that. As I explained, she was insecure about the
ings she'd confided to Valerie after the rescue and she
erreacted. It never really involved us, at all. It was the
erapy sessions she had with Val. It's taken care of, believe
e."

"Yeah, that was what Kim said you told her, too."

"Nice debriefing with you." Hawkes returned in mock
rtness.

Alexander's eyes hardened behind his spectacles. "Are
u finished with Cornerstone, too?"

"Frankly, I don't know what I'm going to do," Michael
turned quietly, rubbing a finger over his unshaven face.
You keeping the secret about my kids, Alexander—that
as a dirty thing to do."

Alexander leaned over the other side of the desk to face
m squarely. "You seem a hell of lot madder about it now."

"I am, dammit! A little shopping through the personnel
es told me that Neal has been sterile for years."

Alexander reacted without even a flicker of his steely
ze. "Oh. Well, it hardly seemed necessary to confess, once
u got your own look at them. And how was I to know
u'd give a damn?"

"You knew I gave a damn for her. Knew that if I ever had
chance with anybody, it was with her. And all these years,
e's been raising my kids!"

"You cared nothing for such—"

He pounded the desk. "Freedom of choice, Alexander
This is all about freedom of choice."

Alexander heaved a mighty breath. "I'm a selfish father
I admit it."

"You are a selfish bastard," Michael corrected flatly
"Perhaps a selfish keeper. But you are not my father! If you
knew the first thing about fatherhood, you'd have sent me
to my children. Instead, you tried to steer me away.
Swinging his leg to the floor, he sprang to his feet, meeting
Alexander nose to nose across the desk. When he spoke, h
words were sheathed in a brittle coating of ice. "I've turned
this over and over again in my mind, in an attempt to be fair
To understand and accept what you did. But I cannot. The
idea that you would've denied me the right to know my own
children leaves even my hard heart cracked in two."

"Then I made a huge mistake," Alexander diverted his
eyes, obviously uncomfortable with the admission. "I mis
judged you. I put myself in your place and made the wrong
call."

"Maybe if it had been another woman," Michael went
on. "Hell, I just don't know! But Valerie has forced me t
tap into my emotions, and I've discovered that I do indeed
feel very strongly about a lot of things. She and those
kids…" He closed his eyes, enjoying a warm infusion over
their images.

"It bored Neal," Alexander challenged sharply.

The remark hit another raw nerve, this one far more sen
sitive than the others. Michael was sick to death of the
comparisons, the friendly rivalry Alexander had always en
couraged between him and Neal. Michael's gaze delved
deeply into the old man's, hoping to forever brand his men
tor with his viewpoint. "I am not Neal. No matter how hard
you tried to hone us into a prototype unit, we are separate
people. I do not owe you anything anymore. Any generous
ties you've extended me have been repaid a hundredfold."

"All right, then, take your leave. Play house. Decide what you want to do. Just don't let your anger at me destroy your career. Don't—" He cut himself short as Michael pulled a red fire engine and a pink teddy bear from behind his desk.

"Gifts for my kids," Michael said tersely. "Have a good afternoon."

With that, Michael walked out the door, leaving Alexander openmouthed, the last word dying on his lips.

VALERIE HAD ANSWERED the doorbell to find a stranger on her front step.

A man in his mid-thirties, athletic build, with a head of thick blond hair, a roundish face, with a pale complexion reddened by the sun. But it was the eyes that held her fast—deep hazel and full of sparkle.

Valerie peered at him through the screen door, rapidly searching her memory for a connection. He had a warm, familiar quality about him....

"Hello, I'm Jerry." He smiled expectantly with the introduction. "And you must be Valerie?"

"Why, yes," she said, breathlessly. She again ran a hand through her disheveled cloud of hair, and looked down at her short shorts and skimpy tank.

"I got the call from Neal yesterday," he went on to explain pleasantly through the screen. "Something about being an uncle...." He paused once more, waiting for a signal of understanding.

"I am so sorry, but I am completely lost here," she confessed with a helpless laugh.

"There must be some mistake," he said with a loose shrug. "You certainly didn't give birth recently."

"I didn't know Neal had a brother," she confessed sheepishly.

His chin dropped a fraction. "My name is Jerry Hawkes. I'm looking for Michael. He's my brother."

Valerie gaped at the man. Of course he was.

"I heard that Michael was a father. And I must say, the news got me aboard a plane but fast. But you don't seem—"

"I do!" she interrupted. "I do believe I understand. Please, come in," she invited falteringly. Then, in an effort to sound lucid, she added, "Michael insists I be careful with security these days. So I had to make sure..."

"So you do know Michael rather well, then."

She smiled dazedly into his full, comforting gaze. "Oh, yes. Or I thought I did."

Jerry took her arm as she teetered dizzily.

"Shall we sit down here in the living room, Jerry?"

"Yes, of course." He eased her down beside him on the tapestry sofa, with solicitous care. "I've shocked you somehow."

He exuded an open gentleness so opposite that of his remote renegade brother. But his manner seemed so natural, so appealing. As it should, considering that he was the image of her own children!

"So you were saying something about Neal..." she began, wringing her hands in her lap.

"Oh, yes. Michael has spoken of him often. We actually met once a long time ago. And I know his boss, Alexander, a little better."

"I see." She saw only too well. Each new fact sliced through her heart like a shard of glass. Anyone from Cornerstone who knew this man knew that Neal Henderson was not the father of her children.

Michael Hawkes was.

Bitterness coiled in her belly like a snake. And they had all kept the secret of paternity from her!

"Have you ever met Kim Krenz?" she questioned. She had to know who'd deceived her. "Has she ever seen you in person?"

His eyebrows rose. "No, I don't think so."

"Good." One true ally left.

"I recognize her name, though. Is she a femme fatale I should avoid?" he teased.

"Why, no, of course not," she hastily assured, a bit of humor reaching her own eyes. "I do want to explain everything, Jerry. But it is so important that I first understand some things."

"I'm beginning to feel like the family pariah."

"I'm sure not!"

"But you knew nothing of my existence, did you?"

"No," she confessed. "Michael has never discussed his background with me."

"And for good reason." He clasped his hands together with a sigh. "Not a lot of good stuff to discuss."

"I suspected as much."

Jerry gazed round the cozy living room. "Does Michael live here?"

"No. We've had an off-and-on sort of relationship over the years. And to tell you the truth, it feels rather off again right now."

"Why would Neal Henderson direct me here? Claim I was an uncle?"

No wonder Neal called to see if she was going to be home. He wanted to make certain Jerry's visit hit the mark. "Neal Henderson is my ex-husband," she sought to explain, clenching her fists in her lap. "My cruel, petty, selfish... you see we all worked together for Alexander some years back. I fell in love with Michael and ended up marrying Neal when your brother rejected me. Michael's been back in my life, and Neal, no doubt in a fit of jealousy, sent you here. Not because he wanted you to see Michael. But because he wanted me to see you."

Jerry rubbed a hand over his bewildered face. "I'm more confused than ever."

A sudden noise turned their attention to the open stair-case behind the sofa. They shifted on the cushions as Timmy and Tammy descended the stairs in their bright summery outfits, wrinkled from their time in bed.

Jerry took one look at the faces of the twins and said, "Now I see." He turned to Valerie. "And you're seeing it for the first time, too, aren't you?"

Valerie nodded mutely, her eyes moistening.

"Can we be done sleeping?" Timmy asked.

"We're all done with cranky," Tammy assured with a sniff.

"Come here," Valerie said softly, struggling to keep the tears at bay. The sleepy pair padded barefoot across the thick carpet, pausing before the adults seated on the sofa. "Jerry, I want you to meet Timmy and Tammy."

"You a uncle, too?" Tammy asked.

Yes, an authentic one, Valerie thought to herself. To the children she said, "He's Michael's brother."

"Aw, sure, then you're an uncle, too," Timmy declared with a sound nod.

"You wanna be?" his twin asked.

Jerry smiled at them. "Of course, I do."

What a coward Hawkes was! Declaring his love for her and all the while allowing these children to go on believing that Neal was their natural father. All because he was too chicken to face the music.

Suddenly, another disturbing alternative came to light.

Maybe Michael wanted these children more than he wanted her. Maybe they were the reason for his grand plan at seduction.

Maybe Michael wanted ready-made heirs. Healthy, happy heirs. He wouldn't have to start at square one this way. What a stroke of luck for an apprehensive father. He'd had the chance to move in close, decide if the setup was for him.

"You two sure are nice and grown-up," Jerry complimented the twins.

Tammy giggled. "Not too big to sit on your lap."

Jerry drew them onto his legs. "Whoa, heavy!" He re-
ased a mock groan.

"You got kids, Uncle Jerry?" Timmy asked.

"Everybody should," Tammy told him affecting the
isdom of an elder.

"I'm going to have babies," Jerry explained. "I married
lovely Parisian woman just a few months ago," he added
r Valerie's ears. "And we already know we are expecting
vo. Apparently twins run in the..." he trailed off crypti-
lly.

"Your babies gonna run, Uncle Jerry?" Timmy won-
red. "We'd sure like to see that, wouldn't we, Tam?"

"You betcha!"

"We'll just see." Jerry ruffled their blond heads.

"Do you live in France?" Valerie asked, hungry for de-
ils.

"Yes, I have for many years." He inhaled in hesitation.
I can assume that Michael has behaved rather strangely in
ese circumstances. Perhaps if we discussed things—"

"Is Uncle Mike coming?" Timmy cut in excitedly.

"Yes, he'll be here for dinner," Valerie replied, too shell-
ocked to correct him on his manners. "Go wash up and
'll start cooking." The children scrambled off with
hoops of glee. "Please stay for dinner, Jerry."

Jerry smiled, giving her hand a pat. "I'll help you pre-
re it. We'll talk and try to understand that brother of
ine."

Chapter Thirteen

When Michael swung his black Firebird into Valeri
driveway early on that same evening, he was surprised
discover a boxy gray rental car already parked off to the le
Armed with his gifts for the children, he took quick, lo
strides up to the houses, entering through the front do
with his own key.

"Val?"

No one answered his call, but light, laughter and coo
ing smells radiated from the hallway off the kitchen. T
combination was like a cozy, warm magnetic field, bec
oning him into a safe paradise called home.

"Hey, I—" Michael stopped short in the doorwa
dumbfounded by the image of his brother setting pla
around the table with his children.

"It's 'bout time," Tammy huffed with hands on hips a
cute, exasperated housewife noises. "We've been keepi
the meat loaf warm over a hundred minutes!"

"I don't like it hard on top," Timmy scolded over l
shoulder, as he set out the silverware with care. "But I l
it's too late!"

"I bet it is, too." Michael released a lungful of air, me
ing Valerie's glare with a mixture of defiance and sheepi
ness.

"You got us toys!" Timmy whirled round to do a double
ake. "My fire truck, Uncle Mike!" He raced over and took
t from Michael's numb arm. "And the bear's for you,
ammy. It's pink." He thrust it into his sister's arms.

"Thank you," she said, cuddling the furry animal. "This
s our uncle Jerry," she went on in a matter-of-fact intro-
uction.

"He's your brother, too," Timmy informed him.

Michael's eyes skirted from the table to Valerie, standing
t the stove. "Hi, honey," he ventured off-key. "So you and
erry have finally met."

She smiled sweetly. "Yes. The children always can use
nother uncle, can't they?"

Michael offered Jerry his shaky hand. The robust fair-
aired man gave him a bear hug instead.

"Better fix this, idiot," he uttered in his ear.

"Yeah." He gave Jerry a hearty slap on the back as they
roke free.

"Well, we may as well eat," Valerie announced, turning
ff the stove burners with a sharp twist of her wrist.

Michael sank his towering frame down into one of the
ow-backed chairs. The children were on him like light-
ing, their new toys in his lap, their small fingers skimming
is muscular arms.

"This courting works fast," Timmy said excitedly.

Tammy kissed his cheek. "We got a new uncle and toy."

Michael set a shaky hand on their blond heads. He'd
ver felt more in jeopardy than he did at this very mo-
ent. It was amazing how circumstances could creep up on
man. Never in a million years had he expected anything or
yone to dislodge his shield of indifference.

Everything he could ever need was right here in this room.
nd she could take it all away. In a snap, she could deny him
e dream they had worked so hard to lay out.

"MAY AS WELL GET THIS food on the table," Jerry sug
gested jovially. Moving over to the stove, he murmured er
couragement in Valerie's ear. "You can do this. For th
children's sake."

They all went through the motions of the meal. Jerry too
charge of the conversation, steering it one way, then a
other. Valerie appreciated it. She just couldn't cope with th
emotions flooding her. Jerry engaged the children's help i
cleanup, giving Valerie and Michael the private time the
needed. Concerned that the children not hear a word of the
confrontation, Valerie ushered Michael out back to th
deck.

The evening breeze was warm, but Valerie felt the need
wrap her arms around her shaking torso.

"You hate me."

"It's so like you to assume so, Michael," she shot bacl
"Of course, I hate what you did to me. It's all taken me b
surprise...." Her mouth fell open as she sought the prop
upbraiding.

"You have a right to be angry," he assured her stiffl
pacing around on the planks.

"It's the hurt you don't want to deal with," she easil
surmised. "I feel used."

"But I never meant to—"

"Look at this from my point of view," she cut in fiercel
"You charged into my house to show me up as an incon
petent agent. Then you discovered your children—no dou
a novelty even to a hard-hearted soldier like you—and d
cided to stick around and eavesdrop on us, in a way f
sneakier than Prudence did."

He stared down at his shoes for a moment of contritio
"It's the truth. But only part of it," he hastily added, on h
startled cry of pain. "For the first time in my life I w
afraid," he confessed in disbelief. "I saw Jerry, my chil
hood, my legacy mirrored in those children, and I sudden
felt that I had a personal stake in this crazy world. I didn

now if I was even capable of caring. But I knew it was time to find out." He turned to make eye contact, but Valerie turned away. With a growl of frustration Michael closed in, pinning her around. Despite her sputtering, he held her fast against him. "Believe me, I've come to realize that I can and do care. For you and the children."

Her eyes moistened. "Why didn't you tell me they were ours?"

"Because I wanted black-and-white proof first—"

"Oh, come on," she snapped. "One look was enough."

"Well, I went through denial, I suppose. Couldn't believe anything so wonderful could've come from me. But the shock wore off, truths surfaced."

"You told me you loved me, and you couldn't tell me that, too? Why not just blurt it out all in one breath?"

"I was paralyzed with confusion. And I wasn't sure if you already knew."

"What!" she exclaimed, exploding with fresh fury.

"I figured that maybe you knew all along, that you hoped I wouldn't make the discovery. With my record, the odds were that I would grow bored and disappear again."

"But you saw how hungry those kids are for a male figure in their lives. You've come to understand how Neal has disappointed them." She shook her head sending her rich red hair tumbling into her face.

He cleared his throat, but it didn't cut the husky edge from his voice. "I figured that maybe you thought I'd do even worse than Neal did."

Valerie sniffed, peeking at him as she pushed the hair out of her eyes. The revelation obviously took effort. There was real strain on his chiseled face. She had to admit that his explanation did make some sense, on a logical level. But she wasn't feeling reasonable. She was feeling hurt, duped, foolish and extremely insecure. He'd made love to her, shown signs of real commitment. and he'd kept that secret.

"I suppose Jerry told you specifics about our child hood," he said.

She exhaled, trying to calm herself. "Yes, I know that you barely remember your real father. You've certainly been the victim of circumstances—"

"I don't ever perceive myself as victim," he cut in sharply.

"Well, maybe that's part of the problem. Maybe you should come to terms with your frailties for a change. No one is invincible."

But he'd always believed he was. As long as he was in command of his space. Indifferent to his environment. The fact that she had broken him like a wild stallion was such an obvious fact in his mind. Wasn't that enough for her?

"We're all victims sometimes, Hawkes," she went on in his stoic silence. "Admitting when we're knocked down deliberately getting up again—that's the reality of living."

He blinked, staring into the dark starry sky. "Maybe so."

Valerie gritted her teeth. He was still grasping her arms in a sure, viselike grip. But his answers were, as always, angry and indefinite.

"Are you forgetting that I campaigned to move in here?" he asked on a note of desperation. "I've been trying to do and say the right things, come to some crossroads. And I was going to speak to you about the twins...."

"I wonder when," she shot back.

"Just how did Jerry end up here in the first place?"

"Neal meticulously arranged it," she replied bitterly. "He called Jerry in Paris and told him he was an uncle. That's why my efficient ex even called here this afternoon, to make certain I was going to be home."

His mouth tightened dangerously.

Valerie nodded. "He must've gotten a lot of pleasure out of spoiling your game, hurting me with one last slam."

Michael absorbed the news with a rush of outrage. "He so badly wants me to fail with you. I just cannot believe the epth of his resentment. The way it's brewed all these ears...."

"He was asking about my visit with Prudence, too. But I vasn't quick enough to bait him about her. I should have ried to draw him out this afternoon. Maybe I can still—"

"Don't try anything like that!"

She gasped in irritation. "I can do—"

He shook her hard. "No. You conceded that you were out f this. Now stay out. I'm in contact with Prudence, and I'll andle this myself."

"All right," she bit back. "I guess I already have enough esponsibilities."

"Yes, like taking care of our children."

"As I've done all alone since the beginning," she shot ack tersely with the toss of her head.

"I know," he acquiesced on a quieter note. "But I want o be involved. You just have to let me inside your world." Ie pressed his mouth against her temple, inhaling her fra-rant hair. "I want to be here."

Valerie stiffened slightly, causing him to meet her eyes gain. "How can I know you aren't doing all this just to ave your children?"

"Excuse me?" he said.

"You don't have to play the lover," she croaked over the ump in her throat. "I'm more than willing to share them. t's only fair."

"I can't believe you said that!" he roared, releasing her vith a jolt that sent her stumbling back into a wrought-iron hair. "First, you thought I was tolerating the kids to get sex rom you, and now, you're worried that I'm using you to get o the kids!"

It was true. But he'd given her just cause for both lines of uspicion.

"Maybe you're feeling a niggle of conscience over your ehavior," she suggested.

"I don't have one!" On that last bitter note, he spun on his heel and reentered the kitchen.

Valerie watched him through the back window, hugging the children goodbye. They weren't throwing a fit, so he must have promised to return at some point.

Anguished doubt flooded her system. It was amazing how fast pain carried from one vessel to another. So many duels had been fought today. And there seemed to be no victories. Except, perhaps, for the twins. There was a determination in Michael's voice. He'd be back, for their sake.

Perhaps they would still have, in him, the father they'd always dreamed of. But was he a dream father? Or would he eventually let them down as Neal had?

Suddenly, she wondered how long Neal had known the truth. If it was a long time, it would explain his distance, perhaps even some of the strain that led to their divorce. In any case, her dealings with Neal were officially over. He had absolutely no business under her roof anymore.

Could Valerie still love Michael after what he'd done? She decided that she would take a leaf out of his book and opt for some space. It was crucial that she not make a mistake at this crossroads. Their whole life as a family depended upon her wisdom.

But, oh, how she yearned to tell her babies that Neal was not their father, after all.

She bit her lip in fervent prayer. *Oh, Michael, you've got to make them a better offer.*

MICHAEL WASN'T EXPECTING any visitors that following Friday night. He'd continued on leave, despite his rift with Valerie. No matter what had happened with her, he still was confused about his goals, distrustful of his inner circle.

Until he identified Prudence's blackmailer, he could not move a step forward. But it would all be over soon. Tonight was the night. The trap was set and he was playing the waiting game.

So who the hell was ringing his doorbell at eleven o'clock at night?

Kim Krenz.

Michael growled under his breath as he worked the locks.

"So, you are home!" The blond amazon breezed inside his apartment without invitation. He knew something was up from her body movements. Her long body was snaky beneath her navy knit outfit. Her blond mane was wild, and her eyes were even wilder.

"Been to see Valerie?" he inquired silkily, stroking his stubbled jawline.

"Yes! Naturally I expected to find you hanging around over there."

"Isn't this something we could've discussed on the telephone?" he complained, running a hand over his corded neck.

She surveyed his dark jeans and dark T-shirt. "You going out?" she asked sharply.

"Maybe I have a date," he returned snidely.

"You don't." She gloated knowingly. "You've got so many players in your life right now, you'd probably duck out of the mailman's way, to avoid a hello."

"I don't want to hear this right now," he growled in caution, waving his hands.

"Tough!" she snapped back. "You've got two beautiful babies and a loving woman across the border, and you're holed up here like a grumpy toad."

"I wanted to be there," he assured her tersely.

She squealed in disgust. "You didn't try hard enough!"

"I could've forced myself on her," he assured her, with a wicked glint in his eyes. "Moved all my gear in there and told those kids I would love to live with them. How could she have refused? The twins would've resented her. But I'd have been the bad guy again, don't you see? And Valerie, the anguished victim. It..." He turned away with a waving hand. "It never would've taken hold."

"Imbecile," she charged, causing him to reel back in fierce surprise. "You've got it all wrong. This isn't an issue of force. You'd be in over there right now, if you'd just said the right thing the other night. Given her the assurances she so desperately needs."

"Assurances of what?" he demanded.

Kim rolled her eyes with a sigh. "Look, it was human of you to suspect that she was keeping the paternity of those children from you—"

"Thank you for that much!" he said with real gratitude.

"It was crude and insensitive, but you aren't one to trust easily."

His thanks held a sarcastic edge this time.

"Well, the same could be said of me, of course," Kim appeased. "Anyway, when all the dust settled at the end, Valerie was bound to wonder if you truly wanted her as a woman, apart from her position as mother of your children."

"I stayed away all those years because Neal left the impression that he was still in her life. I told her that."

"I'm telling you, Hawkes," she said with a poke to the center of his chest. "You made only one fatal mistake. You didn't stake your claim clearly, make her feel desirable."

Michael heaved an exasperated sigh. "Why do you care, Kim? You're not the mushy, cupid type."

She shrugged fluidly, running her hands along her hips. "You're useless to everyone in your current state. You're in no condition to love or to parent. And you'd be a real pain in the field. Face it, you can't hide here forever. You have to do something!"

"Okay, okay, I'll swing by Valerie's tomorrow. Have another shot at it."

"Good man!" Kim gave him a hearty slap on the back, then headed for the kitchen. "Let's have a beer."

Michael attempted to protest, as she gave the swinging door leading to the kitchen a shove. "I don't want a—"

Michael moved after her swiftly, just in time to see her barrel in on Prudence Manders and Andy Freeman, seated at his small drop-leaf table.

"What the hell is this, Hawkes?" Kim gasped in surprise. She took a step back, toward Michael's refrigerator, adding Michael to the picture. Her eyes never left any of them as she openly calculated the development, clutching her shoulder bag, which was bound to be holding her pistol. "You in trouble here?"

"No," Michael hastened to explain. "Prudence is in trouble. I'm helping her, as a personal favor."

Kim eyed them keenly, sizing up the situation. "So Valerie must have been lying about Prudence's reasons for bugging her house. Right?"

"Yes," Michael admitted.

"Someone is blackmailing me, Kim," Prudence admitted, with a defiant flash in her huge violet eyes. "Took photographs of me on the island and is trying to sell me the negatives for three million. Unfortunately, the photos could prove humiliating. They could completely shatter the stable image I'm trying to give my Chapel Renew."

"And even more unfortunate," Andy Freeman added with a squeeze to his charge's hand, "is the fact that Prudence doesn't have that kind of cash right now."

"Well, you shouldn't have even considered paying, anyway!" Michael cut in with outrage. "You may as well know the rest, Kim," he relented. "We're attempting to trap this blackmailer tonight. I directed Prudence to set up a meet at the Crystal Dome discotheque right here in the city."

"Did you think I was involved in this extortion plot?" Kim asked Hawkes defensively.

"No. I never would've answered the door, if I thought you were a danger to Prudence."

"Then, why didn't you ask for my help?"

"I didn't want to pressure you, force your silence and loyalties."

Her jaw dropped in wonder. "Against whom?"

Hawkes sighed with a half smile. "Kim, honey, I've put in a lot of time on this. Our blackmailer is either Manuel or Neal. Or Alexander." He watched her absorb the last name on the list. "Alexander is your controller, too. I didn't want you to be put in a precarious position with him."

"Well, you should've just asked me about all this at the beginning," she flared. "I would've told you that Neal took pictures with the prop camera hanging around his neck."

"He what?" Michael demanded harshly.

"You remember, when he and I were playing the tourists, staking out the hut. We had the cameras for cover but were banned from snapping photos. The producers didn't want to risk any leak—"

"I remember, dammit! Why didn't you tell me at the time?"

"Why, I thought you ordered the pictures yourself, despite Alexander's wishes. Remember, when we were all sitting at the open-air bar after the rescue, when you were griping about how pictures of the layout would've helped us with our plan! I thought you and Neal had cooked something up on your own."

"He cooked something up on his own," Michael stated with new certainty. "But I searched his apartment. Very thoroughly."

"Aren't there a hundred places he could store those negatives?" Prudence asked.

Michael and Kim exchanged a thoughtful look.

"Not really," he replied slowly. "Neal obviously realized that his apartment was too risky. Places like safe-deposit boxes and storage units.... Well, they all keep records."

Kim nodded. "The best place is an untraceable place. Secure, temperature controlled."

"Where would you store them?" Prudence asked Kim. "I mean from an agent's point of view?"

Kim frowned. "That's tough. Because we move around lot in our work, we have very short roots. But I would look or a spot where they could remain undetected for an indefnite period of time. Where they would not be moved. I'd elect a suitable, unchangeable place. Like my mother's ouse, in her photograph box, perhaps. It's unlikely that nyone would disturb them, and they could be picked up on hort notice. Of course, Neal has no close relatives—we now that," she said, with an apologetic smile.

"But knowing it is him should help you a great deal, on't it?" Freeman challenged, drumming his fingers on the abletop. "Hawkes? Isn't that right?"

"Well cared for..." Michael waved off Freeman's prodings as he replayed Kim's reasoning. It suddenly clicked in is mind. The roots, the safe environment, all the games e'd played with Valerie. He snapped his fingers in trimph. "I've got him!"

"Tell us," Kim coaxed.

"It's been centered around Valerie all along," he erupted, oving toward the counter for his wallet and car keys. "The egatives are at her house!"

A frisson of fear traveled Kim's spine, as she gazed into he dark mirror of his eyes. "Are you sure?"

He nodded gravely. "Positive. I'd bet anything they're in ne of those showcase dolls the twins have in their bed-oom. The dolls from Neal. The dolls they aren't supposed touch because they're so valuable. Well, at least one of em is more valuable than any of us ever guessed."

"Yes, of course!" Kim agreed, momentarily ignoring rudence and her man. "Neal must have put the fear of od into the poor mites. They wouldn't even let me touch em during my baby-sitting stint."

"I'd have seen it sooner, if I'd known he'd snapped those hotos. But I just kept hoping that there was some un-nown solution, kept telling myself that Valerie was out of is because I wanted her out of it."

"I'll go with you," Kim promptly declared. She pause¢ to dig her gun out of her purse and check the magazine fo ammunition.

"Sit tight," Michael told his guests, making his ever) move count. "I'll call when I know something."

"What if you're wrong?" Prudence sounded half her ag« in the face of abandonment.

"Then, we'll revert to the original plan," he snapped bacl impatiently. "But I'm not wrong."

The pair raced down to the apartment's underground ga rage and scrambled into Michael's low-slung Firebird. A soon as they were up on street level, he directed Kim to cal Valerie's house.

"What's the number?"

He spared her a brief look. "Just press redial."

"So you have been calling her," she murmured in ap proval.

"Yeah. Just haven't managed to get past the twins yet."

"Well, I can't get past the busy signal now."

"Who would she be talking to at this time of night?"

"Probably Stephanie chatting with her girlfriends."

"Well, keep trying." Hawkes turned the wheel sharply careening onto the freeway ramp in the direction of Balti more. Grim realities swirled through his mind, tormentin; him without mercy. There were so many innocent people ii that house. People who believed they were safe behind th confines of a state-of-the-art security system. They didn' even know they had an enemy, much less that he was th designer of their blasted system.

Michael pressed harder on the gas pedal, urging the Fire bird into the eighty-miles-per-hour range. They just had t make it in time. He'd let Valerie down so completely si years ago, let Neal have her then. It just couldn't be hap pening all over again, all because he'd repeated the sam mistakes. But that's exactly what he'd done. Yes, he'd com terms with the truth: his bullheaded arrogance was to ame then, just as it was now.

If he could just have his family back intact, he would ove his pride into a deep, dark hole, once and for all. He uld take this opportunity to rebuild his life, give a stable e-style the chance it deserved.

In short, he would stop running away from the two peo- e who affected him the most, frightened him the most— lerie and himself.

"To think I forced that maniac back into that house my- lf," he ground out. "Thought I was so smart, setting that ap for him at the nightclub."

"Hawkes, he would've gone after that film whether you ited him or not," she consoled reasonably. "He decided was time to cash in. That's that."

"But if I'd only figured this out sooner. Even a couple of urs ago!"

"Quit beating yourself over the head." She hit the re- al, only to find it still busy. A lusty stream of expletives upted from her sweetly shaped mouth.

"Call the operator," he ordered. "Break into that line."

Kim did so. Apparently a receiver in the Warner house- ld was off the hook.

Chapter Fourteen

Valerie didn't really believe that Michael would call after eleven o'clock, but in anticipation of a long, peaceful bath she took the receiver off the hook of her bedroom phone anyway. It would be his chance to bypass her three message screeners—if he had any desire to speak to her, that is. The twins were fast asleep and Stephanie was overnight at a friend's house. Since Valerie had returned from Mexico, she had barely seen her sister. Stephanie had plunged headlong into her social life.

The warning bleat of a dislodged phone started as Valerie began to strip off her oversize purple pajama jersey. It stopped just as she was sinking into a nice hot tub of bubbles in the master bath.

Michael had called once this morning, then hadn't tried again all day.

He'd spent a solid half hour chatting with the children. She'd gone out to her garden behind the patio to do some weeding, listening to the chirping voices through the open window, shaking her trowel and her head when they asked if she wanted to talk to Michael before he hung up. She always found a believable excuse whenever the calls came, distancing herself from the telephone with laundry of ironing or cooking. The twins were so excited about Micha

at she didn't want to put a damper on their spirits by re-
aling her irritation to them.

To top off the day, Kim had shown up clear out of the
ue, and she'd been compelled to relate the entire pater-
ty mess to her in detail. They'd commiserated over the
llheadedness of the male population in general, consum-
g a bottle of Chablis in the process. It had felt good to
eak to a contemporary who knew and understood Mi-
ael and knew the stress and strain an operative faced day
ter day. By mutual agreement, they decided to renew their
d friendship.

If only her relationship with Michael could be so easily
juvenated.

Valerie drew a long, slender arm out of the water to tug
e curtain closed and envelop herself in a hot, steamy co-
on. Tipping back her head, she luxuriated in the warm,
apy suds, allowing her entire body to relax.

She was still in this dreamy state when she felt a presence
the bathroom, beyond the curtain.

The possibility of another human being creeping in on her
nt a shiver zigzagging down her spine, chilling her to the
ne in the heated water. But it had to be a friend, right?
fter all, the house was safe, with one the tightest security
stems around. Maybe Stephanie had come home early.
aybe it was Michael himself, hungry for another round.

This process of deduction was a lightning flash in her
ind. Only seconds passed between her awareness and the
ale hand on the curtain, tearing it aside.

"Neal!" Her voice was a squeak of a scream, as she
entified the husky intruder in indigo denim. Her hands
iftly rose to her bubble-covered breasts. The instinctive
action brought a chuckle to her ex-husband's mouth.

"I remember a time when you arched to greet me," he
id in mocking disappointment, resting his foot on the edge
the tub. "You were in the first stages of pregnancy, ripe,
ollen, delectable...."

Valerie could not suppress her gasp of fear and indignation as Neal leaned closer, running his hand over the layer
of bubbles on her chest. She recoiled in the water, slapping
his fingers away.

And he slapped her back, hard across the cheek.

She cried in pain and surprise, raising her arm to shield
her face from a second blow. But behind her shield she
could see his eyes. Dark brown pools of glittering rage. He
expected to dominate. And what a setup for it. He had her
trapped in her tub. With no way of summoning help. With
her precious children just down the hallway.

And they weren't just her children. They were Michael's
too. The secret was out for all to share.

Was that what this visit was all about? To exact some revenge? The situation of paternity wasn't her fault. It was a
stroke of fate. But the gleam in his eyes reflected a burning
madness beyond logic.

She had to try some line of reasoning, however. Get him
to talk. And hopefully, get him out of here. She slowly lowered her arm away from her face, leveling him with a flat
confrontational stare.

"Neal, if you've come to survey the damage done by your
ploy with Jerry Hawkes, I can tell you, you scored big. I
kicked Michael out and I'm back to single-parent life. I want
nothing to do with Cornerstone or its people ever again!"

"Funny, that last line was going to be mine."

"What do you mean?"

"I'm master of the moment, darling." He dipped his
fingers into the water, flicking up suds. "I'll ask the questions."

She inched back in the tub, in an effort to evade his touch.
"Stop it!"

"Feeling a little awkward? A little put out?"

"Yes," she said between gritted teeth. Anger and embarrassment surged inside her.

"I've felt those things myself," he lashed back in pain. Supporting those brats. Pretending they were mine."

"Why—why did you do that, Neal?"

"Because I had to win, that's why!" He was obviously illing to answer certain questions. "I had to get one up on lawkes. I should've been the team leader, you know," he id in a far-off voice. "At least part of the time. Alexan-r always dangled things like that in my vision, goaded me best his best man. Well, I finally did it. I got you. I knew lawkes was really smitten. All those months of teasing, dmiring your ways. You were the ultimate prize between s, my sweet. To win you, I knew I'd have to offer some-ing that he wouldn't, believed he couldn't."

"Marriage . . ."

"Yes. You can't imagine my agony when I discovered my ophy wife to be with child. Quite a blow to a sterile man."

"Sterile?" She shifted slightly in the water, clenching her sts beneath the bubbles. "You knew all along that the vins were his?"

He nodded. "Oh, yes. . . ."

"I thought maybe you'd come to realize later on that they sembled Jerry."

"I knew from the get-go," he lashed back. "What I asn't sure of was whether you knew. Michael was very in-rested in solving that little riddle, too. Did he tell you out our little meeting in Cancún?"

Valerie shook her head slowly. So Hawkes hadn't been lping out Manuel, after all. He'd been meeting with Neal, ying to find out if Valerie knew the paternity of her chil-en. The sham irritated her, but it also touched her. Mi-ael had been a desperate father trapped in a maze, trying figure out her intentions in advance. It was obviously a lf-protecting gesture.

"No, I didn't think he'd confess that move to you." Neal nirked. "I had figured it out myself at divorce time. You're ethical to a most sickening degree. Never would've allow me to pay all that child support under false pretenses."

"Why did you pay it?" she demanded, her face pale a perplexed.

"Couldn't have you going back to Michael, now could Couldn't let him win so easily. I figured one day he wou stumble onto the truth, just as he did. But I could see reason for hastening the discovery. What if he decided to t fatherhood, try you? Succeed where I so rottenly ha failed?"

"He's gained little," she lied, hoping to appease him.

But Neal appeared madder by the minute. On the bri of snapping. And there was a gun resting in a shoulder ho ster beneath his gaping jacket. She wasn't going to leave th tub alive if he didn't want her to.

"You know what's so ironic about it all?" He leaned ov her, his breath hot on her face as he waited for a reply.

She steeled herself, as not to show her revulsion. "N Neal, I don't."

"I inadvertently lit the fuse to this whole thing myself. sent him barreling over here with my clumsy extortio plan."

Valerie's brain ticked in calculation. "*You* are blac mailing Prudence, then?"

"Oh, yes," he assured matter-of-factly. "I foolishly fi ured she'd just pay up. I didn't think she'd start nosi around here, didn't expect you to reconnect with Alexa der. Of course what I should've done at that point was mo back in here to guard you myself." His mouth tightene "But I just couldn't face those blasted kids all over again. couldn't pretend to be their daddy when I hated them with an inch of their lives!"

Valerie gasped at the extent of his hatred. How could feel this way about the twins? "I . . . can't believe it," sh stammered. "Those gifts . . ."

"That's why I'm in here for this little hot-tub reunion, sweetie." He traced a finger over her collarbone. "I want one of those dolls back."

"Take them all!"

"I only want one. The little Dutch boy. It's missing from the children's shelf—"

"You were in their room?" Mortification swiftly surpassed all modesty and feelings of self-preservation. She rocketed up out of the water. "If you laid a hand on them, Neal—"

"I didn't," he impatiently cut in. "They slept through my search." He gripped a handful of her flame-colored hair to cease her protests. "Give me the doll and I'm out of your life forever."

Suddenly everything became clear. "The negatives are in the doll...."

"Still smart as a whip."

So that was what he meant when he said that he was through with Cornerstone. He was planning to take the money and run. Surely Michael was still in cahoots with Prudence and would be waiting for him at a drop site.

The wisest thing to do would be to give him the doll. Send him into the trap.

"Well..." With a firm grip on her arm and her hair, he yanked her from the tub. Pain shot through her body, but she bit back the scream climbing up her throat. She didn't want to awaken the children.

"Let me put on my nightshirt," she demanded, gesturing to the garment, pooled on the floor near the sink.

He released her with a shove. She fell to the cool white tiles, quickly pulling the shirt over her soaked skin.

"It's down in the family room by the sewing machine," she explained, rising to her feet and never once breaking eye contact. "Stephanie is making new outfits for some of the dolls and is using the Dutch boy for measurements."

"Lead the way."

"But you know the house—"

"Let's just say I want a kiss goodbye at the door. Just like old times."

Moonlight streamed through some of the windows, giving the house some shadowed light. Together they tiptoed down the staircase, step by step. Valerie's hand was firmly on the rail. His hand was firmly on her arm.

Gazing down over the railing, she thought she saw a fleeting glimpse of light. Or was it blond hair? Yes, there pressed against the hallway wall below was Kim. She moved just enough to allow Valerie to see her. Relief washed over Valerie, bringing tears to her eyes. But it wasn't over, not until Neal was subdued. And he was unpredictably dangerous right now.

She had to get away from him. Give Kim access to him. Keeping one hand on the rail for leverage, Valerie used her body as a ram, shoving herself into Neal, elbowing him sharply under the ribs to loosen his hold on her. The maneuver worked. He was caught completely off guard. He lost his balance and began to tumble down the stairs.

Michael leapt from the shadows on the opposite side near the closet, waiting to welcome his rival with open arms. Neal fell at his feet, making a flailing, but unsuccessful effort to rise.

"He's got a gun!" Valerie called through her tears. "Shoulder holster!"

"Aw, Neal, you must know by now that Val doesn't like weapons in the house," Michael seethed, roughly digging a knee into his rival's back as he cuffed his hands behind his back. "And coming back for your dolly in the middle of the night.... Not a nice way to play."

Valerie crumbled on the stairs. Resting her head on a newel post she wept quietly. She could hear Kim on the living-room telephone briefing Alexander, and she could hear Michael rolling Neal over on the entryway tiles, extracting his gun with a satisfied grunt.

"The cavalry's on the way," Kim reported succinctly. "I can handle him...."

Michael launched himself up the steps. He shielded Valerie from the scene below like a comforting blanket, patiently peeling her fingers off the post. "C'mon, baby, it's all right." Hauling her into his lap he cradled her close, kissing every inch of her face. "You're soaking wet," he gasped in surprise.

"Is that all you can say?" She sobbed, burrowing her face into the hollow of his chest.

"Guess I say the wrong thing a lot. How about, I love you? How about, I've been scared out of my wits all the way over here?"

"That's a pretty good start." She wound her arms around his neck.

"I know now that being frightened of caring doesn't stop a man from caring." He stroked her hair. "And I care for you, baby, so deeply that it hurts. You've got to give me a chance to make everything up to you."

Michael, anxious to read her face as they talked, reached down and cupped her chin in his hand. He lifted it to his for inspection, finding not only the tearstained smile he'd hoped for, but vivid red stripes across her cheek. A fierce, animalistic rage boiled inside him as he pieced together what must have happened upstairs. "Valerie," he said on a low, dangerous note, "did Neal really hurt you...?"

Valerie shivered slightly as she watched his eyes darken to a dangerous inky blue. "No, not that way," she hastily assured, moving her hands over his chest in a smoothing motion. "Let Alexander sort this out tonight. Please. I need you all to myself."

Michael held her close, infusing her with comfort and body heat. He would let Alexander call the shots tonight. But he would make it his business to make sure Neal got the punishment he deserved. And it would be his last official act for the group. This courting stuff was for the birds. There'd be no more testing, no more waiting. This family was his, and he would convince Valerie that he was ready to claim them.

"I have to check on the twins," she said with a heaving breath. "He said he didn't hurt them—"

Michael whirled to cast a lethal look down at the man sprawled out at the bottom of the staircase under Kim's stylish boot and gun barrel. "He wouldn't have dared."

"Go with her, Hawkes," Kim insisted. "This guy's going nowhere."

Amazingly, the twins had slept through it all. Val and Michael watched them for a long intimate moment in the glow of the cheery clown lamp, taking deeper, easier breaths.

"Everything's okay," Val whispered, tugging at his arm. Michael could only nod in reply.

The hour to follow was a busy one downstairs.

Michael then called Prudence with the news of the capture. She wanted her negatives back pronto, but Michael explained that they would be needed for the Cornerstone hearing. The company had a way of handling its own bad apples and would serve a dose of justice to Neal. Valerie, despite her distress, had a word with her also, assuring her that no publicity would ever stem from the incident, that Chapel Renew would go ahead without a hitch.

A Cornerstone sedan eventually arrived to collect the rogue agent.

Alexander was the first to burst through the door. He'd obviously been in bed. His clothing was haphazard.

"I'll be damned, I'll be damned," he kept repeating.

Michael strode over and grabbed the cuffed Neal up off the floor. He dragged him over to Alexander and spat out, "Here's to your sons. Which one of us has pleased you more, Father?"

Alexander aged before their eyes, his face crumpling.

"Do you have any idea what could have happened to Val and her kids tonight?" Hawkes raved. "All because this maniac flipped out. Because we were programmed by you to stick together in a cycle of cutthroat competition."

Alexander nodded slowly. "I'm sorry, Michael. I can see I did push things way too far. The rivalry, the Spartan guidance." He gestured for his two operatives to escort Neal outside.

The controller then shuffled across the entry tiles to Valerie, taking her hands in his. "Dear, sweet girl. Please try to find it in your heart to forgive me."

"I can, Alexander," she assured him softly. "If you let go of Michael. Professionally, I mean. He's torn between two worlds right now, but if he had your blessing—"

"Or the back of your boot," Kim put in bluntly.

Valerie smiled in thanks. "Yes. A combination would set him on the right course." She blinked back the tears. "You must see that we—the twins and I—need him more than you do."

Alexander paused, the disappointment deeply lined in his face. "All right. I have the feeling he's lost his edge anyway. What good would a sentimental father be out in the field? But I hope you'll not leave me out of things entirely." He took on a gentler note. "I'd hate to lose either one of you."

"You won't," Valerie exclaimed, giving him a short, fierce hug.

Michael stood by, his face sheeted in relief. He wouldn't have to persuade Valerie into his corner at all. She'd actually gone to bat for him all on her own.

Alexander took a deep breath. "Come along, Kim. Somebody has to give a full report."

"As team leader?" she inquired, gathering up her purse and the Dutch-boy doll containing the film.

"Maybe."

Michael locked up after the parade of operatives left, winding an arm around Valerie's slumping form. "You know what I want to do right now?"

Valerie nodded. "Yup. You want to go sit on that toy box and look at your kids."

"Right."

When they entered the bedroom this time, the twins stirred in their beds. Valerie swiftly soothed them, stroking each temple.

"Uncle Mike's here!" Timmy struggled to sit up. "See 'em, Tam?"

"Is it morning?" Tammy mumbled, rubbing her eyes.

"Not yet," Valerie told them in a hush. "But Michael has something he wants to tell you that can't wait."

The pair of groggy eyes opened wide.

Michael swallowed hard. "Now?"

"Yes, darling. Neither one of us is bound to get any rest until they know."

"Know what?" Timmy demanded.

Michael knelt in the narrow alley between their beds, setting a hand on each of them. "It seems that . . . Well . . . I'm your real dad."

Their cherub faces beamed with astonishment.

"I didn't realize it until just lately," he went on to clarify.

"How come it took you so long?" Tammy asked with a high-pitched gasp.

Michael let out a howl of laughter. "Are you guys five or twenty-five?"

"Hey, you already asked us that," Timmy scolded.

"Well, by the time you are really twenty-five, you'll understand everything."

"But for tonight," Valerie broke in gently, "all you need to know is that Michael didn't know. I didn't know. There was a mistake."

"A mistake that I am going to make up to you," he assured on a shaky note. "I'm proud and excited to be your father. I want to tell the whole world."

"And live here?" Tammy asked.

"And live here."

"It's about time we get a good daddy," Timmy declared with a sound nod. "Right, Tam?"

"Right."

The children scampered off the bed and dove into his arms, knocking him flat on his back.

Valerie slid to the floor to join fray. Tammy sat up with short, little breaths, looking from her father to her mother. "Oh, boy. I betcha we're gonna have a honeymoon now."

Michael eyes grew wide as he propped himself up on his elbows to meet Valerie's tender gaze. "Oh, boy, Mama, I betcha we are!"

Epilogue

One Year Later

"This is your final warning, Hawkes. Shoot that thing again and you'll be pushing up daisies in my garden!"

Despite the very serious threat from his very pregnant wife, Michael stood firm in the center of the backyard, aiming the camcorder in the direction of the patio. "*Our* garden, Val," he corrected with pleasure. "Your garden has been my garden for eleven months, two weeks and three days now."

Valerie set down the refreshment tray she was carrying on the wrought-iron table with a thump, jiggling its lemonade pitcher and glasses. "Shut off that camera!"

"Ah, the fat lady sings...." Humor crinkled his features, features already considerably softened by his year in the family-man role. His amusement was eagerly shared by the twins. They began to giggle uncontrollably from their new enormous swimming pool.

Valerie gasped in indignation over the conspiracy, wagging a finger in the direction of the frolicking pair of turncoats. "Don't encourage him!"

"I just meant that your voice is sweet music to me," he called out with a halting hand as Valerie shuffled across the deck. With a hand pressed into the small of her back she launched herself out into the grass, her loose white eyelet housedress billowing like a sail in the hot wind.

"I'm gonna get you, mister!"

"Now, now, Professor Mom, it's not wise of you to get so steamed in your condition." He retreated a couple steps, his legs butting up to the bench of the picnic table. "You've really never been lovelier," he hastily added. And he meant it. Her body was ripe like a fresh peach—soft, curvy and the epitome of femininity. Her flame-colored hair was long once again, per his request. Today it was gathered up in a ponytail, in an effort to cool her down.

But in lieu of boiling temperatures and her equally hot temper, a chillout seemed unlikely.

"Take pictures of us, Daddy!" the twins chorused, shamelessly showing off with splashy antics.

"I have been," he assured them, turning the lens back at them.

Val was finally closing in on him, with the only weapons she had left, her fingers. With wild-eyed vengeance, she began to tickle his bare bronzed stomach, right down to the waistband of his tattered denim cutoffs. He tried to turn the camera in her face in a desperate gesture of self-defense, but she ultimately won out, forcing his chuckling surrender.

"You've been using that thing all day long!" she scolded in exasperation.

He set the camcorder on the redwood table behind him and drew her into his arms. "You know I'm just testing it out. It's my way, you know...to get a feel for something before I commit." He wedged his knee ever so gently between her thighs.

Valerie raised her eyes skyward. "Yeah, yeah, who knows better."

He tipped his temple to hers. "This new client, Mutual Casualty Insurance, might become a steady customer. Apparently fraud is running rampant in our society. Videotaping evidence is standard procedure."

"Mmm, so I've heard."

"Well, be glad. Without troubles like Mutual's, there would be no work for a private eye like me."

"Oh, I think you'd have no trouble tracking trouble, no matter how rare it became." She tsked sweetly. "And I think you'd have bought one of these new Minicams for yourself, no matter what. Just to torture me, in the years to come, with my elephant-size body!"

Amusement slanted his mouth. "Okay, I will admit that I would have a recorder of my own by now, even if I'd, say, chosen to drive a cab for living. But certainly you know that Type A's like me can't change their spots completely. I was determined, observant and thorough, when I didn't have a personal life. Now that I do have one, well, it's natural that those traits would carry over."

She set her hands on his chest again, causing him to yelp. "I'm not going to tickle you again. I just want you to understand how I feel. It's hell being nine months pregnant in this sweltering weather. I am overheated, cranky. I'm four days overdue and still growing! The last thing I need is Ferndale's answer to Sam Spade taping my icky, fat condition."

"You aren't fat," he crooned. "Just a little rounded here...." His hand stole down to her belly, deliberately grazing her heavy, ultrasensitive breast. His mouth dipped to her ear, nipping her lobe. "You, Professor Mom, are sexier than ever...."

"No, Hawkes, I'm just plain hot. Tubby and hot."

Michael stared over her shoulder at the swimmers for a long, pensive moment. "You know, I think I have just the cure for you."

Valerie arched her brows under his mischievous glint. "What do you have in mind?"

Without another word he scooped her up like a newborn babe.

"Hawkes!" she squealed, desperately grabbing his neck

He gave her a bounce in his arms, as though testing her weight. "See, this should prove that you're still light. It's just like lifting you before—with a twenty-pound-bag of flour on your belly."

"Make it a fifteen-pound bag of sugar. And put me down," she frantically ordered. "Nice and slowly. Nice and easy."

"Your wish is my command."

Valerie gasped in shock as he began to march in the direction of the pool. "You wouldn't! You mustn't!"

Claps and cries of approval erupted from the water.

"I'm dressed, you fool!" She clung to him with all she had. "You cannot toss me in there!"

He balked at the very idea. "I wouldn't do that! No way. We'll submerge together, like a big, ole submarine." With an exaggerated hoisting grunt, he lifted one foot, then the other over the two-foot wall of the pool. Ever so gently he eased her down into the tepid waters. "Happy now, baby?" he purred, pushing the folds of her dress down beneath the surface.

"Happy, Mama?" Tammy chirped, dragging Valerie's ponytail through her wet little fingers.

Timmy kissed her cheek. "She's happy," he declared blissfully.

Valerie gave in to the floaty feeling, taking in all of their bright loving faces. "That camera, Hawkes—"

"I don't think I'd better risk it in here," he interposed with an infuriating grin.

She squinted at him in the sunshine. "Don't try and squirm out of this one with a joke. You left it running over here on the table, didn't you?"

"Well, I may have," he admitted, dragging her over his lap. "You see, baby, I just don't want to miss another moment because of a blind spot. Not ever again."

COMING NEXT MONTH

HARLEQUIN®

A M E R I C A N ◆ R O M A N C E®

Four sexy hunks who vowed they'd never take "the vow" of marriage...

What happens to this Bachelor Club when, one by one, they find the right bachelorette?

Meet four of the most perfect men:

Steve: **THE MARRYING TYPE**
Judith Arnold
(October)

Tripp: **ONCE UPON A HONEYMOON**
Julie Kistler
(November)

Ukiah: **HE'S A REBEL**
Linda Randall Wisdom
(December)

Deke: **THE WORLD'S LAST BACHELOR**
Pamela Browning
(January)

STUDSG-R

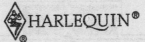

HARLEQUIN®

Don't miss these Harlequin favorites by some of our most distinguished authors!
And now you can receive a discount by ordering two or more titles!

HT#25483	BABYCAKES by Glenda Sanders	$2.99	☐
HT#25559	JUST ANOTHER PRETTY FACE by Candace Schuler	$2.99	☐
HP#11608	SUMMER STORMS by Emma Goldrick	$2.99	☐
HP#11632	THE SHINING OF LOVE by Emma Darcy	$2.99	☐
HR#03265	HERO ON THE LOOSE by Rebecca Winters	$2.89	☐
HR#03268	THE BAD PENNY by Susan Fox	$2.99	☐
HS#70532	TOUCH THE DAWN by Karen Young	$3.39	☐
HS#70576	ANGELS IN THE LIGHT by Margot Dalton	$3.50	☐
HI#22249	MUSIC OF THE MIST by Laura Pender	$2.99	☐
HI#22267	CUTTING EDGE by Caroline Burnes	$2.99	☐
HAR#16489	DADDY'S LITTLE DIVIDEND by Elda Minger	$3.50	☐
HAR#16525	CINDERMAN by Anne Stuart	$3.50	☐
HH#28801	PROVIDENCE by Miranda Jarrett	$3.99	☐
HH#28775	A WARRIOR'S QUEST by Margaret Moore	$3.99	☐

(limited quantities available on certain titles)

TOTAL AMOUNT	$
DEDUCT: 10% DISCOUNT FOR 2+ BOOKS	$
POSTAGE & HANDLING	$
($1.00 for one book, 50¢ for each additional)	
APPLICABLE TAXES*	$_____
TOTAL PAYABLE	$_____

(check or money order—please do not send cash)

To order, complete this form and send it, along with a check or money order for the total above, payable to Harlequin Books, to: **In the U.S.:** 3010 Walden Avenue, P.O. Box 9047, Buffalo, NY 14269-9047; **In Canada:** P.O. Box 613, Fort Erie, Ontario, L2A 5X3.

Name: _____

Address:_____City: _____

State/Prov.: _____ Zip/Postal Code: _____

*New York residents remit applicable sales taxes.
  Canadian residents remit applicable GST and provincial taxes.

HBACK-OD

"HOORAY FOR HOLLYWOOD" SWEEPSTAKES

HERE'S HOW THE SWEEPSTAKES WORKS

OFFICIAL RULES — NO PURCHASE NECESSARY

To enter, complete an Official Entry Form or hand print on a 3" x 5" card the words "HOORAY FOR HOLLYWOOD", your name and address and mail your entry in the pre-addressed envelope (if provided) or to: "Hooray for Hollywood" Sweepstakes, P.O. Box 9076, Buffalo, NY 14269-9076 or "Hooray for Hollywood" Sweepstakes, P.O. Box 637, Fort Erie, Ontario L2A 5X3. Entries must be sent via First Class Mail and be received no later than 12/31/94. No liability is assumed for lost, late or misdirected mail.

Winners will be selected in random drawings to be conducted no later than January 31, 1995 from all eligible entries received.

Grand Prize: A 7-day/6-night trip for 2 to Los Angeles, CA including round trip air transportation from commercial airport nearest winner's residence, accommodations at the Regent Beverly Wilshire Hotel, free rental car, and $1,000 spending money. (Approximate prize value which will vary dependent upon winner's residence: $5,400.00 U.S.); 500 Second Prizes: A pair of "Hollywood Star" sunglasses (prize value: $9.95 U.S. each). Winner selection is under the supervision of D.L. Blair, Inc., an independent judging organization, whose decisions are final. Grand Prize travelers must sign and return a release of liability prior to traveling. Trip must be taken by 2/1/96 and is subject to airline schedules and accommodations availability.

Sweepstakes offer is open to residents of the U.S. (except Puerto Rico) and Canada who are 18 years of age or older, except employees and immediate family members of Harlequin Enterprises, Ltd., its affiliates, subsidiaries, and all agencies, entities or persons connected with the use, marketing or conduct of this sweepstakes. All federal, state, provincial, municipal and local laws apply. Offer void wherever prohibited by law. Taxes and/or duties are the sole responsibility of the winners. Any litigation within the province of Quebec respecting the conduct and awarding of prizes may be submitted to the Regie des loteries et courses du Quebec. All prizes will be awarded; winners will be notified by mail. No substitution of prizes are permitted. Odds of winning are dependent upon the number of eligible entries received.

Potential grand prize winner must sign and return an Affidavit of Eligibility within 30 days of notification. In the event of non-compliance within this time period, prize may be awarded to an alternate winner. Prize notification returned as undeliverable may result in the awarding of prize to an alternate winner. By acceptance of their prize, winners consent to use of their names, photographs, or likenesses for purpose of advertising, trade and promotion on behalf of Harlequin Enterprises, Ltd., without further compensation unless prohibited by law. A Canadian winner must correctly answer an arithmetical skill-testing question in order to be awarded the prize.

For a list of winners (available after 2/28/95), send a separate stamped, self-addressed envelope to: Hooray for Hollywood Sweepstakes 3252 Winners, P.O. Box 4200, Blair, NE 68009.

CBSRLS

OFFICIAL ENTRY COUPON

"Hooray for Hollywood"
SWEEPSTAKES!

Yes, I'd love to win the Grand Prize — a vacation in Hollywood — or one of 500 pairs of "sunglasses of the stars"! Please enter me in the sweepstakes!

This entry must be received by December 31, 1994.
Winners will be notified by January 31, 1995.

Name _____

Address _____ Apt. _____

City _____

State/Prov. _____ Zip/Postal Code _____

Daytime phone number _____
(area code)

Account # _____

Return entries with invoice in envelope provided. Each book in this shipment has two entry coupons — and the more coupons you enter, the better your chances of winning!

DIRCBS

OFFICIAL ENTRY COUPON

"Hooray for Hollywood"
SWEEPSTAKES!

Yes, I'd love to win the Grand Prize — a vacation in Hollywood — or one of 500 pairs of "sunglasses of the stars"! Please enter me in the sweepstakes!

This entry must be received by December 31, 1994.
Winners will be notified by January 31, 1995.

Name _____

Address _____ Apt. _____

City _____

State/Prov. _____ Zip/Postal Code _____

Daytime phone number _____
(area code)

Account # _____

Return entries with invoice in envelope provided. Each book in this shipment has two entry coupons — and the more coupons you enter, the better your chances of winning!

DIRCBS